EPERTASE

"*Tamed* had me so eager to see what would happen next I couldn't turn the pages fast enough. *Tamed* is a whole new take on a werewolf story with humans being the true monsters. Douglas Brown has written a book so good, I read it in a single sitting and wanted to go back for more."
~Scott Poe, indiebookblogger.blogspot.com

TAMED

DOUGLAS R. BROWN

Epertase Publishing

TAMED

Published by Epertase Publishing
Copyright © 2012 Douglas R. Brown
Revised 2022

Copyright ©2012 by Douglas R. Brown
Revised 2022
ISBN   Paperback- 978-09899917-7-3
          eBook- 978-0-9899917-6-6
          AISN- B00AWF9QJE

Edited by Rebecca Brown
Cover art by Melissa Williams
Visit author Douglas R. Brown on the Web at
www.epertasepublishing.com

BOOKS BY THE
AUTHOR

THE LIGHT OF EPERTASE BOOK ONE
LEGENDS REBORN
THE LIGHT OF EPERTASE BOOK TWO
A KINGDOM'S FALL
THE LIGHT OF EPERTASE BOOK THREE
THE RISE OF CRIDON

DEATH OF THE GRINDERFISH

A FIREFIGHTER CHRISTMAS CAROL AND
OTHER STORIES

A WICKED LINE

ACKNOWLEDGEMENTS

In addition to being an author, I am also a firefighter/paramedic. I began writing several years ago as a cathartic way to cope with the single most devastating emergency call of my career. In the months after that call, I wrote about the little boy who died in front of me, along with every sad and emotional call I had been a part of during my seventeen years in the fire service. Though I didn't realize it at the time, writing about those tragedies sent me deep into a darker place than I had ever imagined. Only now, looking back, do I see what I descended into.

When I finished writing my fire department memoir, I wanted to continue telling stories, but I didn't like what I had been writing about. I gravitated toward genres I have always enjoyed. Fantasy and horror became my escape.

The reason I tell you this is because it directly relates to my acknowledgments for this book. I want to thank my family and friends for staying by my side and supporting me while I was in that dark place. My wife, Angie, and son, Aiden. My mother, Lillian. My friends Matt, Mick, Cory and Aimee, Bryan and Kara, Sean and Helena. My cousin, Greg. My sister, Amie, and brother, Brian. My father, Dale. My firefighter brothers at Station 22. You were there for me, and for that I thank you. I am an author now because of your strength.

Thank you, Breanne Rowe, for your friendship and for steering me in the right direction again and again.

Thank you, Bobbe Ecleberry, for teaching me so much and never getting tired of helping your pestering nephew. You are truly a talent.

Thank you, Jeff Stanforth, Amy Penrose, Sean Wooten, my mother, my wife, and my aunt, for reading *Tamed* in its infancy. What you now hold in your hands is a direct result of your unselfish help throughout the process.

Thank you, Steve Murphy, for everything you do. You're not just an artist, but a true friend.

Thank you, everyone on Columbus Fire, for your support.

Thank you, Lona Davis, for being such a wonderful and supportive grandmother.

Thank you, reviewers of *The Light of Epertase: Legends Reborn*. I appreciate all the kind words, and even the occasional not-so-kind ones.

Thank you, as always, Rhemalda, for being an incredible publisher while it lasted.

Thank you, Melissa Williams, for such an awesome cover. I love it.

Thank you, Becca Brown for your brilliance as an editor and the time you've dedicated to this story.

And thank you, everyone who reads this book.

Here's to many more years of entertainment.

To the love of my life, I dedicate *Tamed*.
For seventeen years you have been my world. I love
you, Angie. Now and forever.

TAMED

IN THE YEAR 10,000 B.C.E., THE DOG WAS
DOMESTICATED BY MAN.

12,000 YEARS LATER, THE WEREWOLVES
GET THEIR TURN.

FORTUNES BEGIN

1

The helicopter touched down on the beach of a remote, little-known island off the coast of Costa Rica. Fresh out of college with a business degree, Bernard Henderson had never headed up anything remotely like this mission, but after months of preparation he was confident he had everything he needed for success. His hands quivered at the immense opportunity.

Getting investors had been the easy part. He had always been a good salesman, dating back to elementary school when he'd made a couple bucks selling a completely fictitious answer key to a history quiz. The incident almost got him a beatdown by the bigger of the swindled kids, but an innate fast-talking ability saved his ass. Well, fast talking and half of his takings. But he was hooked from that moment. Freeing idiots from their money became his favorite pastime. He once told a friend in high school that he could sell underwear on a nudist beach, and he probably wasn't exaggerating. He was getting that good. His cunning became his best asset. He carried that skill into adulthood and his current multimillion-dollar endeavor.

Joining him on this trip was a team of eight hand-picked mercenaries, amped up and ready for action. He wondered how many of them would make it back. Not that it mattered. Everyone had their wills in order, their financials squared away, and their loved ones had been adequately lied to about where they were going. Standing on the desolate shore next to an immense jungle, Bernard and his men watched their helicopter lift away.

Bernard had seen the island of Sandalio thousands of times in his research, but never in person. His first look at the dense jungle made him second-guess his decision to tag along. But he was a go-getter, and even the most dangerous challenge wouldn't change that. A micromanager at heart, he was all in.

He followed his team through the previously unmolested jungle for nearly two days, sleeping beneath mosquito nets at night and fighting off softball-sized insects during the days. The hike was exhausting. Countless hours on the treadmill in preparation had helped, but he wasn't in the kind of fighting shape his elite soldiers were. By the second day he'd given up on swatting the insects, trusting his vaccinations and anti-malaria drugs to keep him safe. Despite the pain of insect bites, the relentlessness of the terrain, and the fear of what was yet to come, the money-making potential was there. And money was all that drove him.

His nervous excitement grew as they neared their destination in the predawn hours of the third day. He chewed a piece of jerky to quell his rumbling stomach and then drank from a canteen.

The hand-drawn maps created by his researchers led him and his team to the edge of an indigenous tribal village, mostly unknown to the rest of the world. The lead mercenary, Charles, was a talented ex-Navy SEAL. He led them upwind to the outer perimeter of the village where they hid within the overgrowth of weeds and thistles and some strange poison ivy. Thankfully he'd worn long sleeves. Bernard scooted forward with a set of binoculars pressed against his face.

The early morning sun peeking over the trees highlighted the small village ahead. Few civilized men had witnessed what Bernard now saw, and even fewer had lived to talk about it.

The mercenaries made their way to where they could see activity around a bonfire in the center of the village. It appeared to be a celebration, and all seventy known villagers were in attendance.

Bernard glanced over his shoulder as his team waited patiently. Their orange camouflage and proprietary orange face paint was crucial to the hunt. It was believed that their prey had trouble seeing orange.

Bernard smiled and whispered, "Stick to the plan, boys."

They didn't need the reminder.

Charles held up his hand.

Each mercenary took a final visual inventory of their weaponry before creeping from the brush in a staggered line. If Bernard's research was solid, which he had no reason to doubt, an early dawn attack was their best opportunity for success. The tribesmen should be sluggish from their frenzied night of hunting, feeding, and dancing.

Charles and his team crawled to the first hut and hid beside it. He silently counted to three with his fingers, and the men separated like a well-trained military force. They quietly circled the oblivious tribe while Bernard trailed them.

The men of the village, the hunters, danced around the magnificent bonfire with flames reaching higher than the tallest hut. Their bare chests were smeared with blood that they wore like a badge of honor. The women stood behind them, eagerly watching and waiting for their chance to feast. A closer look revealed the meat was from jaguar carcasses. Bernard couldn't believe his eyes.

Each tribesman took a turn leaping forward and ripping the flesh away with their teeth, not waiting for the meat to fully cook or the flames to dwindle. With blood and meat hanging from their jowls, they bounced back to rejoin their celebrating brethren, howling with delight.

Though the women shuffled anxiously from foot to foot, the tribesmen were in no hurry to share their bounty. A couple of younger women bravely inched closer, practically licking their lips. An older grey-haired man with a pointed bone pierced through his lower lip spun toward them, snarled like a beast, and lunged. They cowered and the older man returned to his dance.

Bernard locked eyes with Charles and Charles nodded. It was time. Bernard hoped Charles couldn't hear the patter of his heart because it was deafening to him. His hands trembled and he hid them near the assault rifle at his waist. Short of an occasional weekend paintball game, he had no real experience with firearms and no military training. Charles lifted his hand and closed his fist. The mercenary to his left took a deep breath and then squeezed off a burst of automatic gunfire. Despite being ready for it, the sharp, rapid blasts jolted Bernard to his core.

A tribeswoman fell to the cacophony of thunder first. The panicked tribesmen spun toward their attackers, bloody meat still hanging from some of their mouths. Complacent from generations of being the deadliest hunters in the forest, they were caught off guard.

Two more villagers fell before panic fully set in among the others. The men of the village scrambled. The women ducked and scurried toward the false safety of their huts. One hut had already met a mercenary's flare and smoke billowed from the entrance. More villagers absorbed gunfire and crumpled to the ground.

Several tribesmen fled toward the forest. They zigged and zagged as if they had caught the mercenaries' scent and knew how to avoid them.

Bernard charged, his head on a swivel. He knew as well as Charles that letting too many of them reach the forest to regroup would be devastating to the plan. They were too dangerous if given even a minute's peace. Their counterattack would be sudden and violent and possibly overwhelming.

One of the women bolted across Bernard's path. When their eyes met, she froze briefly and then released a beastly growl. The whites of her eyes darkened to a soulless black. Her fingernails extended into daggers and her jaw contorted with a bone-popping din. Bernard lifted his weapon, knowing she'd be harder to kill if she completed her change.

She tilted her head like a confused Rottweiler, thick fangs now protruding from her elongating snout.

An adrenaline rush unlike any he'd ever felt flowed into his finger and he squeezed the trigger. Her flesh ripped away and she howled. And then she dropped in a heap. Bernard stared blankly at her lifeless body. She was the first person he had ever killed, and he was surprised by his lack of guilt. He breathed short, excited breaths. As he dragged his eyes from her and looked around, he watched in awe as an entire tribe, one that had existed for thousands of years, if not longer, was annihilated within minutes. It might have been sad if it wasn't about to be so profitable.

Gunfire echoed around him. The natives had spears and primitive slingshots, but those weapons were worthless against Kevlar, automatic rifles, and modern warfare techniques. Bernard removed a flare from his utility belt, ignited it, and tossed it into the nearest hut. With flames swallowing the straw, he jogged back to the village center where the bonfire, so full of life only moments before, had become a beacon of death. His men chased and slaughtered every native they saw.

But the longer it took, the more time the tribesmen escaping into the woods had to regroup. Behind a hut nearby, a bear-like roar preceded the brief, agonized scream of a mercenary. Bernard knew what the sudden end of that scream meant. He took a cautious step toward the hut but stopped short. A shadow darkened the ground around him. His stomach dropped. A low, throaty snarl lifted from behind. Bernard swallowed hard. His finger inched toward the trigger of his weapon as he slowly turned his head. A seven-foot-tall beast stood behind him. Bloody drool leaked from its mouth and matted its coarse black fur to its face. Its eyes were enough to give the devil pause.

"Easy now, big fella," Bernard whispered, surprised he was still alive. He cautiously lifted his weapon. The beast leaped forward. Bernard stumbled back. He fired two panicked shots. They went wide.

The beast lunged. Before its deadly teeth could reach Bernard's throat, its head snapped sideways and blood and brain matter splattered the dirt. The beast dropped in a heap next to Bernard.

A glance left revealed Charlie standing with his gun barrel still trickling smoke. He gave a knowing nod and said, "Head shots once they change, sir. That's the quickest kill."

Bernard nodded, annoyed. It wasn't that he didn't know where to aim.

Charlie grinned before sprinting off toward his next prey. Soon, the gunfire throughout the village slowed to more sporadic bursts.

At the edge of the village, the flashlight beams of two mercenaries followed another fleeing tribesman into the shadowy tree line. The tribesman, still clinging to his human form, was strong and fit. He'd make the perfect prize and Bernard hoped his men wouldn't kill him. He decided to give chase.

He was already deep into the jungle before he realized he had lost them. With his hands on his knees and his lungs desperate for air, he realized he was completely alone. He pulled his rifle close to his chest and waited for some sign to guide him back to the village. Distant howls seemed to come from all directions.

Out of all the mistakes he'd made in his life, running headlong and alone into the most dangerous jungle in the world ranked among the worst. "Don't panic," he whispered, and backed against a tree to get his bearings. He stood motionless except for the quiver of his assault rifle. A branch snapped behind him. His every muscle flinched. "Charlie?" he whispered. He slid his finger alongside the trigger guard, closed his eyes, and took a deep breath. But a harsh snort told him it wasn't Charlie. The idea of capturing such a healthy specimen alive quickly faded into ensuring his own survival. Getting the drop on the beast was Bernard's only chance.

With his weapon clenched tight, Bernard dove and spun. Something darted from the undergrowth. Bernard closed his eyes, squeezed the trigger, and strafed wildly. He opened his eyes in time to see a wild boar race past, completely unharmed by the barrage of bullets. After a dozen or more rounds, Bernard had been lucky to hit one tree in a jungle full of them. He sighed and pushed back to his feet. He felt like an idiot.

Before he could regroup, another creature, this one as big as a grizzly and as fast as a cheetah, bolted from behind another tree and charged. Bernard fumbled with his weapon and squeezed off a single shot. A chunk of flesh tore from the beast's shoulder. The beast barely flinched. Silver only worked if the bullet didn't pass straight through, and even then it was a slow death. Charlie reminding him of the need for headshots flashed through his mind.

Bernard squeezed the trigger again with better aim. Only this time the rifle clicked. His eyes went wide as he fell into a bush. Thorns dragged at his skin.

The beast pounced and slammed a clawed hand against Bernard's chest with terrifying strength. Bernard sprawled to his back. The beast straddled him. Bernard winced and prepared for death. He pictured his pretty bride and wondered if she would ever find closure if his body was never found. It was the first moment he had had any doubt over what he was doing. Maybe it was wrong to tell her he was going to Italy on business. Or maybe kidnapping a fabled werewolf was a foolish dream in the first place. Money couldn't be everything, after all. But even as he was about to die, he wasn't convinced of that last part.

The creature rose to its full height, its true size one of nightmares. Bernard held his useless weapon in front of his face. The beast swatted it away. It lowered its teeth within inches of Bernard's face, as if savoring the kill. Bernard turned away, pressing his cheek against the ground. The creature sniffed him and then licked his other cheek as if tasting him.

When the beast tilted its head back and howled, Bernard flailed at its powerful chest. With one fluid swipe, the creature pinned Bernard's shoulder to the ground, its talon-like claws sinking into his flesh. He tried not to scream, but the pain caught him off guard. The beast grabbed Bernard's head and tilted it to expose his neck.

Bernard found defiance in his final seconds and hissed, "Do your worst, you bastard."

They locked equally cold and bloodthirsty eyes.

Then the beast yelped and released Bernard's head. The yellow fletching of a tranquilizer dart protruded from the side of its neck. A look of shock and confusion painted its face for only an instant before it pulled away and retreated into the dense undergrowth.

Bernard laid his eyes on good ol' reliable Charlie. He held a tranquilizer gun. Two other mercenaries stood beside him. He signaled them with a flick of his wrist and they gave chase. Charlie hurried to

Bernard's side and offered his hand. He even gave a slight chuckle.

Bernard winced and stood up.

Charlie pressed a cloth against Bernard's shoulder. "You gotta be more careful, sir. I'm not always gonna be there to get you out of a pinch."

Bernard brushed his hand away and held the makeshift bandage in place. "Thanks again, Charlie. That's two I owe you."

Charlie patted his back and answered, "Nothing a little bonus wouldn't fix."

Bernard nodded. "You'll definitely be getting a bonus."

A distant bang followed by the red glow of a flare above the trees gave them the direction back, though Charlie probably didn't need it. "Looks like we're wrapping things up. Let's head back."

When they reached the village, several of the mercenaries were standing around the bonfire where the killing had begun. One of them was eating a piece of the cooked jaguar. When Bernard approached, the mercenary offered him some. Bernard shook his head. He was too excited to eat.

Bernard looked around. Not counting the two mercenaries who were out tracking their tranquilized prize, his team was three men short. "Where are the others?" he asked.

"They didn't make it, sir."

Perhaps the loss of several of his men should have weighed heavier on him, but he felt no more than he had for the woman he'd killed. "What'd you do with their bodies?"

"Threw them in the fire with the rest of the kills, as per protocol, sir." He gestured to one of the flaming huts.

"Very good."

The sun had completely risen before the other two members of his team returned dragging an unconscious tribesman in a net. It was the same one he had hoped they would catch.

"You did well, boys," Bernard shouted. He reached through the netting and patted the tribesman's forehead. The yellow tranquilizer dart still protruded from the back of his neck. "We'll call this one The First." It wasn't a very clever name, he'd readily admit, but it would do. "Are there any females left?"

One of his men answered, "A few."

He pointed to three of the other soldiers. "You guys will stay here and keep watch. When we get back to the chopper I will send in the company. We will build an interim camp and keep the survivors here in case we ever need a new subject. Complete extinction, after all, wouldn't be very good for business."

They nodded.

He smiled. "If all goes as planned over the next few years, the '90s are going to be quite the prosperous decade for the WereHouse."

An out-of-the-way abandoned factory was the perfect spot for the night's festivities. The most nerve-racking part of Howard's trip was actually getting there. Though his driver had assured him everything checked out, he knew driving into the middle of nowhere at night in his flashy Cadillac limo was somewhat risky. He could easily be walking into an elaborate setup for a robbery or kidnapping for extortion. But the lure of seeing something few had ever seen was too enticing to pass up.

"Are we crazy coming out here, Joseph?" he asked his driver.

"Relax, sir. I told you I checked everything out. The promoter has the cops in his pocket. You have nothing to worry about. Just enjoy yourself and win some money."

Howard sank back into the plush seat of his limo. The two bourbons on the way helped his nerves. As did his first look at the parking lot. The stretched limos, Rolls Royces, and other expensive cars let him know he was in the right spot.

Joseph pulled up to the factory's front entrance. A doorman hurried to the car and opened Howard's door. He offered his hand and said, "Good evening, sir. Welcome to the Dog Park." There was a red carpet leading to the door.

Howard climbed out.

"Right this way, sir." The man led Howard through the door, along a long hallway, and into a wide-open room, bustling with activity. Long gone were factory machines and conveyor belts. The windowless walls were clean and freshly painted, which gave the musty factory an almost new-building feel.

Like the expensive cars outside, the crowd of tuxedo-clad men and gowned ladies made Howard feel right at home. He saw his friend and one-time mentor, Harley, across the way and hurried to greet him.

A row of voting-style booths and lines of people stretched into the crowd behind Harley. Next to the farthest right booth was a sign that read "Minimum Bet: $25,000." Howard smiled. Yes indeed, this was where he was supposed to be.

"Harley, you old fart," he shouted as the older man made his way over. "How the hell are you?"

Harley's hair had obviously been dyed brown, though his eyebrows were left grey and slightly overgrown. "You're cutting it close, Howard. You'd better place your bets. The fights start in five minutes."

"I don't know any of the dogs. Which one you got your money on?"

Harley looked around to make sure no one was listening and motioned Howard closer. "I put a hundred grand on a dog named Borg. He's won two previous tournaments. That makes him basically a lock in these kinds of fights."

"Borg, huh? What, is his handler a Trekkie or something?"

Harley shrugged his shoulders, probably clueless about Star Trek in general.

Howard clapped his hands together. "Borg it is. If you'll excuse me." He beelined to the betting line.

With a half million dollars spread between a few combatants, he shuffled his way back through the crowd to the front where three separate circular rings were enclosed in waist-high block walls. The concrete floor within each of the three rings had been jack-hammered down to the dirt and the painted white walls were stained with red.

"Why are there three rings?" Howard asked no one in particular. "I don't want to watch three fights at once."

The gentleman standing beside him leaned in and shouted over the crowd, "Pit bull fights take place here on most weekends. They use all three rings for those."

The crowd quieted as the promoter entered the center ring with a uniformed police officer at his side. Howard was relieved his driver had been right about cops being on the WereHouse payroll. The promoter held a microphone and wore a smile the size of the factory itself.

"Ladies and gentlemen, thank you for coming out tonight. We have a treat for you. My name is Bernard Henderson, and I welcome you all. Tonight's tournament will be unlike anything you have ever witnessed. I guarantee it. This night will be violent and, I must admit, quite bloody."

As he spoke, two bikini-clad models walked between the rings and into the crowd. They distributed clear plastic ponchos and face shields to everyone.

The announcer added, "Face shields are mandatory. Accidentally ingesting the blood of these creatures isn't the best idea."

Howard grabbed the gear from the model. He put on the face shield and joked, "This ain't no Gallagher concert."

She ignored him, continuing down the line. She'd probably heard that joke a thousand times.

He slipped the poncho over his shoulders and pulled the hood over his hair.

The ringmaster continued, "Without further ado, let's get on with our first fight."

Harley made his way through the crowd to Howard's side. He wore a similar poncho and had his face shield tilted up. He carried two glasses of champagne and handed one to Howard. He said, "Hurry and drink this before the start."

Howard downed it in one swig. Harley also finished his glass, dropped it on the floor, and tugged his shield over his face. "You ever seen one of these creatures in person before?" he asked.

Howard shook his head. "No, but I'm thinking about buying one for my boy."

Over the previous three weeks since Howard had learned he would be attending the fights, he'd felt like a kid approaching Christmas. As he waited, he realized he was shuffling from foot to foot in anticipation. Harley chuckled and patted his shoulder.

Six men wearing ugly orange army fatigues and carrying assault rifles filed from the far double doors and surrounded the center ring. Howard felt a touch more secure. The doors swung open again. A man tugging a long chain passed through. Attached to the end of the chain was a collar wrapped around the neck of the most magnificent creature Howard had ever seen. The creature walking on its hind legs was at least two heads taller than the handler, who was no small man himself.

Its ears were mangled stubs like a fighting pit bull champion, and scars replaced some of the fur around its face. It snarled with bared teeth from its exaggerated wolf-like snout. Its chest was thick and powerful, though its gut appeared emaciated like it was starving. Howard wondered if starvation was what made it so ferocious before a fight. Rage-filled spittle dripped from the creature's jowls, and Howard couldn't have been happier. The beast's roar echoed throughout the factory and ran chills up Howard's neck.

Another handler behind the creature zapped it with a cattle prod to push it toward the ring. The other handler fastened the chain to a hook mounted to the floor and climbed out of the ring.

"Oh. My. Lord," Howard mumbled.

"I know what you mean," Harley said with a playful elbow to his ribs.

Another handler led a different beast through the double doors and into the ring. The two creatures glared at each other with devilish black eyes.

Howard turned to Harley, unable to contain his excitement. "I thought these things were supposed to be docile," he shouted over the roaring crowd.

"They are," Harley answered. "The WereHouse sells some of the beasts that haven't been broken yet to the black market. But don't get too excited. If you want a champion, it'll cost you ten million, the way I hear it."

Howard balked at the price. "Why would anyone spend such money on a creature that could be slaughtered at its first fight?"

"The money from the bets, especially if yours manages to win once or twice, will more than cover your expenses. Now, shut up and watch. I think the grayish one with the scars around its snout is Borg."

Howard fixed his eyes on the ring—more specifically, on Borg. It was the finest creature that had ever existed, as far as he was concerned. Three of the six guards trained their weapons on Borg, while the remaining three aimed at Borg's opponent.

An announcement from the intercom echoed the words that would be forever burned into Howard's brain: "Unleash the werewolves."

The hooks in the ground released with a collective clank. As if the two creatures had heard that clank before, they launched at each other in an explosion of claws and teeth and blood. Their chains tangled around them as they rolled against the block wall in front of Howard. He wanted to touch one. Fear held him back.

They clawed and ripped at each other with unmatched ferocity. Their yelps and howls were unnerving and painful to Howard's senses, yet he wouldn't trade this experience for anything in the world. He shoved his hands over his ears. Harley nudged him with a chuckle and Howard noticed he wore earplugs.

Each rip of flesh and yelp of pain made Howard cringe, and though he wanted to close his eyes, he wanted to watch even more. Blood splattered across his poncho and speckled his face shield. He was in awe, unable or unwilling to wipe the crimson drops from the plastic protection.

As quickly as the battle began, it was over. One creature stood victorious over its foe. Howard's pick, Borg, gasped on the ground, defeated. Blood poured from a gaping wound in its neck and puddled on the floor. The victorious werewolf tilted its head back and gave a deafening roar. The crowd erupted.

What Howard had just witnessed was the single most exhilarating and amazing sight he had ever seen. His heart pumped almost through his ribcage. His hands shook and his lower lip quivered. He lowered his hands from his ears.

Harley leaned in. "Pretty incredible, huh?"

Howard couldn't answer, so he nodded instead. He had been to more dog fights and cock fights than he cared to remember, but nothing had prepared him for this.

Harley grinned and said, "Just think, we still have six more fights to go."

Howard could hardly contain his excitement. He whispered, "WereHouse, where have you been all of my life?" His lost twenty-five grand was as far from his thoughts as the moon was from Earth.

The handlers removed the victor along with the dead werewolf and dumped bleach over the pooled blood where the loser's carcass had been. After a few minutes of buzzing excitement, two more handlers entered with two more werewolves for the second match. Howard didn't care if he lost all his money as long as this night never ended.

3

Billy gave Christine all kinds of shit about missing his morning scrambled eggs and pepper jack cheese. No matter how hard she tried to convince him that the firehouse cook would save him a plate, he grumbled about how terrible reheated eggs tasted. Though he had a point, she would never admit it.

It wasn't Christine's fault the previous crew didn't do their job and now she and Billy had to pick up the slack. The morphine on hand had expired at midnight, and since morphine was part of a narcotic protocol, Christine and Billy had to replace it ASAP at the neighboring firehouse where their coordinator was stationed.

Billy grumbled, "Medicine is good for at least six months after its expiration. Six more minutes wouldn't make much difference."

"Liability, Billy."

"Yeah, yeah."

Today was Christine's day to drive the medic truck, which she preferred since she hated the tediousness of writing reports. She glanced at Billy, who sat slouched in his seat with one foot on the dashboard, his annoyance not lost on her.

He was twenty-two years old and unbelievably immature. He had a smug smile and arrogant swagger that were irritating at times, especially when he'd see an attractive woman and spit an unprofessional comment like "Look at that ass," or "I'd like to be her bicycle seat."

When Christine first met him, he had told her he was a cocksmith. When he followed that up with calling her a cougar to the other guys, she wanted to hold his head in a bucket of water. But instead, she had bitten her lip, taken a deep breath, and politely yet forcibly informed him she was only ten years older than him.

But Billy grew on her, and she now felt the same affection for him that she would for a little brother. She had learned to roll her eyes because inevitably five minutes after being a sexist pig he would be comforting an elderly lady who had woken up to find her husband not breathing. When it came down to the job, Billy shone.

He broke his hungry pouting silence in his own impersonal way. "Still dating Roger?"

"No."

"Why not?"

"He's a jerk and a cheater," she answered.

"Yeah, I know," he said.

"You know? You know? If you knew, why didn't you tell me?"

Billy shrugged his shoulders. "You're a smart girl. I knew you'd figure it out."

"Oh, well, thanks a lot. I've wasted six months and you've known all along? When did you get so smart?"

He shrugged again.

She tried to hide her annoyance in the same way she did at least three times every shift, but he had long since learned to read her body language. She stopped at a red traffic light next to a dog park that seemed unusually crowded for such a chilly afternoon. He leaned forward, trying to get her attention. "Hey now, Cougar, don't get upset with me."

"Put on your seatbelt," she snapped as she watched the traffic light, intentionally not looking at him. Though she tried to ignore him, she saw his huge grin out of the corner of her eye. "I told you not to call me that," she added.

"Did you watch the Buckeyes yesterday?" he asked. He always changed the subject when he knew she was getting too peeved.

She rolled her eyes. "Yeah, I saw it. I'm glad they won. Working in Columbus after they lose sucks."

He leaned past the center console until his face was between hers and the windshield.

She groaned. "Stop it, Billy." She leaned closer to the driver's side window, so she could see past him. Like an aggravating little brother, he followed her movements with his own head. Finally, she shoved his face away while fighting back a smile. "What are you, a sixth-grader? I'm trying to drive here. You know I hate when you do that."

"Come on, Chris. Is it that time of the month?"

Aaarrgghh! He'll never get it. "Grow up, Billy."

The light turned green and she pressed the gas pedal. Billy plopped back into his seat and leaned forward to retie his bootlace.

"You know, Chris, I'm going to give the other shift a piece of my mind about this morphine crap."

"Are you sure you can spare it?"

"Ha, ha. You're a funny gir—"

A loud collision rocked the truck sideways. Christine banged against the driver's door. She mashed the brake, bouncing Billy's forehead against the dash.

"What the hell was that?" he shouted and rubbed his head.

Christine's heart skipped. She'd never wrecked a medic truck before. What the hell did she hit? A skinny, blond cheerleader-type rushed across the park toward her. She had Botoxed lips and reengineered boobs. Just the kind of gal Billy would lose his mind over. The woman shouted something as she approached. Christine lowered her window to hear.

"I'm sorry, I'm sorry," the blonde shouted. The medic shook again, only this time not as violently. Christine glanced at the side mirror. She gasped.

"What is it?" Billy asked, still rubbing his forehead. He hadn't noticed the blonde.

Christine ignored him, her eyes locked on the two humongous dog-like creatures filling the mirror. They appeared to be fighting ... Or playing, maybe.

Christine stared, unable to take her eyes off them. They were more intimidating in person than they were on TV. She had never been so close to one of the WereHouse's creatures, let alone two, and it gave her serious creeps. She hated that the creatures were the latest fad, like Paris Hilton's Chihuahua matching her purse. Whenever one of the countless commercials came on during her nighttime sitcoms, or her favorite late-night talk show host regurgitated some hacky jokes about the creatures, she'd wonder why anyone would want something so dangerous and scary in their homes.

The blond woman shouted, "Rusty. Skeeter. Heel."

The two creatures ended their playful fight and tucked their pointed ears against their heads. Christine was stunned that such a petite woman could command such powerful beasts by simply raising her voice.

The woman held out her hand. "I'm Becky."

Christine reluctantly shook it. "Christine."

Then she heard Billy say, "Oh," indicating he'd just noticed Becky. He fixed his hair before leaning toward Christine's window with his hand outstretched. "Hi there. I'm Billy."

Becky shook his hand. Billy prolonged the shake and Becky smiled.

Then Billy saw the creatures in the mirror and nearly creamed his pants. He said, "Woah, what I wouldn't give to have one of those."

Christine wasn't sure if he meant the creatures or Becky. She pushed him back to his seat. "Down, boy," she said.

"What's wrong, Chris?" he asked when he noticed her rubbing her face. It was her tell when she was nervous. "You never wanted to pet a werewolf before?"

She ogled him like he was crazy. "Why would I wanna do that? They're filthy creatures. Besides, I don't trust them. I've seen *An American Werewolf in London*, and that's enough for me."

Billy snorted. "You believe everything you see in the movies? It's not like they're changing into people or anything. That was just a movie. This is real."

The two werewolves sulked while Becky scolded them for getting out of hand. Once she finished, they rose to their hind legs and sniffed the air, revealing their true height. One of them was bigger than the other, though they were both taller than any man Christine had ever been around. Their fur was jet-black and nearly identical as if they were brothers, except that the smaller one had two baseball-sized patches of missing hair on its back.

The smaller one's eyes drifted away from their master and the bigger one grabbed its arm to get its attention in the same way a person might. Christine was stunned at how similar their front paws were to hands. In fact, they basically were hands, only with elongated fingers and thick, claw-like nails. The smaller one snapped at its brother, threatening to start the tussle again.

Becky snapped their attention back with a stern shout. She looked back at Christine with a coy grin and said, "You've got to show them who's boss."

Once the creatures were sufficiently calmed, Becky invited Christine out to meet them.

Christine shook her head. There was no way she was getting out of the truck. Billy, on the other hand, slung open his door.

Christine's eyes widened. "Billy, what're you doing? Stay in here."

He scowled back. "Are you kidding me? I've never been this close to one of 'em." He leaped from his seat and raced around the front of the truck.

One of the werewolves lifted its ears as Billy approached. Becky snapped, "No." She wagged her finger at them.

The creatures drooped their heads forward with their long, pointy ears tucked back along the contours of their skulls.

Billy asked, "Ma'am? These are your wolves?"

She turned to him. "Yep. I'm terribly sorry about this. When they start playing, sometimes they get a little rambunctious."

Billy circled the beasts, cautious yet curious. The larger one glared at him and perked its ears again. Billy hesitated. Becky snapped the creature back in line with a shout. The creature lowered its ears and looked back to the ground.

"Can I pet them?" Billy asked.

"Of course. Just don't pet the back of their necks. They're sensitive there."

Billy reached out with his palm down like he would approach a strange dog. "What happened to this one's hair?" he asked as he petted the smaller one between the ears.

"Hotspots," she answered. "He's due for his cream."

While Billy petted the creature, Becky continued chastising them as if they understood her.

"What have I told you about going near the road? No! No! No! You stay in the park or we will not come back."

"Do they understand you?" Christine asked, her finger on the power window button in case they got too close.

"I don't know. Sometimes I think they look at me like they understand. Then other times I tell myself they're just dumb animals."

"Aren't you afraid they might … I don't know … snap or something?"

"Oh, heavens no. Since the WereHouse went into business, they've never reported any problems with aggression. Unless, of course, you pay for one to be a guard wolf, and even then it's 100% controllable by the owner."

Billy rubbed the creature's arm down to its sharp claws. He peered at Christine around the mound of fur. "Chris, come 'ere. He won't hurt you."

"Go ahead, honey," Becky said.

Christine shook her head again. "No, thank you. I'm fine in here."

"It's okay," Becky assured her.

Under Billy's and Becky's stares, Christine felt pressured to put on a tough act. She was oddly reminded of trying to fit in with the guys at the fire academy. She reluctantly lowered her window. "I'll pet him, but I'm not getting out."

Becky giggled and shot a knowing glance at Billy. Billy smiled back.

Christine sighed. *Oh great, a love connection.*

Becky reached for one creature's collar and jerked its head toward her waist. The creature dropped to all fours and inched forward with her tugs. Christine reached out. The creature leaned into her hand. She brushed between its ears once and then yanked her hand back.

The creature snorted and Christine flinched. Billy laughed again. "He's just breathin', Chris."

Becky smiled. "He's right, you know."

Billy asked, "So, is that what they're called? Werewolves?"

"That's what they look like, I suppose. Though they don't turn into humans or anything like that."

Billy glanced at Christine as if to say, "I told you so."

She rolled her eyes.

Becky continued, "The company calls them wergs. I think it's just an old name for werewolves."

Billy turned back to Becky. "Wergs, huh? I like it."

She smiled. "I've also heard Lycans."

Interrupting their budding romance, Billy's face twisted and he turned away. His nose twitched and his mouth distorted as he fought back a sneeze. Christine smiled, knowing what was coming. He covered his face with both hands and let loose a series of sneezes that didn't stop until he reached the seventh rapid-fire blast.

At first, Becky tried to bless him after each explosion, but gave up at number three.

Christine joked, "Stay back so he doesn't get anything on you."

Billy finished and excused himself.

Becky giggled. "I think it's cute."

Christine rolled her eyes. *Yeah, cute. Nothing says adorable like snot flying out of your nose.*

Billy gave Becky an awkward smile. She brushed her finger along his shoulder and said, "We have to be going now. Sorry about the accident." She dug into her baby blue purse and removed two diamond-studded leather leashes. The smaller creature lowered its head and she hooked the leash to a bright blue collar previously hidden beneath its fur. The collar conveniently matched her purse.

The perfect accessories, Christine thought.

After Becky fastened both leashes and started walking away, the smaller creature dropped to all fours next to its brother and followed her.

Billy watched, no doubt enamored with her tight-fitting yoga pants. Once he had broken his gaze, he turned back to the truck. That's when he groaned, "Oh, shit."

"What?" Christine asked.

"Look at the truck, Chris."

Christine climbed out. A huge dent in the shape of the larger creature's shoulder decorated the side of the truck. She turned back to find Becky, but Becky and her pets had disappeared. She smacked the side of the truck. "This is just great, Billy. You know, this is your fault."

"My fault?"

"Yeah. You were so concerned about three pieces of tail that you let her leave without checking the truck."

"I'm checking it now."

"Real great. She's *gone* now."

"Let's go find her. How hard could it be to find two of those creatures with a hot blond chick?" He hurried around to the passenger seat.

They circled the park, but Becky had pulled a David Copperfield. After a few minutes, it was obvious they had lost her. Christine was fuming. "You're explaining this to the lieutenant," she snapped.

Billy sat quietly. He knew as well as she that they were going to get written up for not getting Becky's information. It would be Christine's first write-up. Billy, on the other hand, had had a couple for being late for duty and one for inappropriate language during an elementary school presentation. In all fairness, he didn't know his mic was on and that the kids could hear him. Regardless, "Deez nuts," wasn't something a firefighter should ever say in a school.

The onboard computer chimed and the dispatcher interrupted their argument with an emergency call for a woman in labor.

Annoyed, Christine flipped on the emergency lights and siren. Billy gave her a dismissive wave and settled in for the ride. He read the notes on the computer screen.

"Oh great. It says her water broke, Chris. We might actually deliver a baby today."

"Don't act so surprised. That's what we get paid to do. You ever delivered one?"

"Not yet. You?"

"Yeah. Once."

As they pulled into the parking lot of an apartment complex, they noticed a crowd near the dispatched address. The whole crowd moved toward them in a wave. Christine noticed a pregnant woman grimacing and struggling to walk in their center.

Billy bounced out before Chris completely stopped the truck. He raced around to the back and pulled out the cot. He dragged it to Christine, who was already at the patient. Together, they lifted the pregnant woman onto the cot.

Billy motioned for the crowd to back up. "Give us some room."

"That's my wife," someone shouted.

Billy pointed to the front seat. "You can ride to the hospital with us, but you gotta get up there."

"But I wanna be with her."

"You will be. Just from the front. We need the room in the back." Billy and Christine slid the cot and the patient into the back and pulled the doors closed behind them. The crowd gathered at the rear.

"What's your name, ma'am?" Billy asked.

"Jada," the woman answered between moans. She was sweating.

"Do you know if you're having a boy or a girl?"

She bore down for nearly a minute before she answered, "A boy."

Christine positioned herself between Jada's legs. "She's crowning, Billy."

Billy grabbed the OB kit from the compartment and spread it out on the bench seat. He helped Christine put on a paper gown.

Christine smiled at Jada. "Okay, ma'am. It's time to push."

Jada groaned. Billy's eyes widened when the baby's head popped out. Christine carefully cradled the baby's head in her palm while giving Billy a nervous glance.

Billy squatted beside her. "What's wrong?" he whispered.

"The cord's around his neck."

Jada's face twisted. "What's that mean?" she said, panic rising in her face.

Billy answered in a soft voice, "The umbilical cord's around his neck. It means we have to get it off before we can keep going. You have to keep from pushing for a minute, okay?"

Jada nodded and collapsed back against the cot. Her husband watched nervously from the front seat.

"How tight is it, Chris?"

"Not too bad yet. I can still get my fingers beneath it."

The engine company pulled up and Billy shouted from the back door that they needed someone to drive. Willie climbed into the driver's seat. He leaned through the passageway between the front seats. "Ready to go?" he asked.

Billy nodded. "Get us there quick, Willie."

Willie introduced himself to the father and then sped out of the complex with the sirens blaring.

Christine guided Billy's gloved hand to the umbilical cord. "You have to slip it off while I direct his head through."

Billy nodded.

Jada cried, "I need to push."

"Not yet," Billy and Christine shouted in unison.

Willie weaved through traffic and almost threw Billy across Jada's belly.

"Easy, Willie," Christine shouted.

"Sorry 'bout that, homeslice," Willie shouted back.

Billy held the cord, careful not to tug. Christine slowly guided the baby's head beneath it. When the cord slipped free, Christine gave Jada a relieved smile. "Okay, Jada. You can push now."

Jada cried as she pushed, and Christine guided the baby's shoulder downward. And then a rush of fluids followed the baby into Christine's arms. Billy quickly suctioned the baby's mouth and nose with a bulb syringe and then dried him off with a towel.

The baby wailed with wonderful, healthy lungs. Christine passed him to Jada, who was openly sobbing.

Christine shouted to Willie, "You can slow down. We're good back here." Willie killed the sirens.

Billy shook the father's hand and congratulated him on a healthy baby boy. Then he recommended William for a name. Willie seconded the idea.

The father smiled and answered, "Sorry. We're naming him after her father. Terrence James."

"I guess that's a good name," Billy mumbled.

Willie pulled the medic truck into the hospital parking lot with one more patient than they had started with. After they transferred Jada and young Terrence to the nursing staff and Billy had cleaned the cot and truck, he met Christine in the report room. He had a smile that would last for days.

"Can you believe what we just did, Chris?"

She smiled back. "Pretty awesome, huh?"

"You did great."

"Thanks. Does that mean you'll write up the report for your girlfriend's dogs hitting the truck?"

He threw his hands up in fake surrender. "Woah, Chris. Slow down. You just delivered a baby. It's not like you cured cancer."

"Yeah, that's what I thought."

4

With the Becky incident a couple of weeks in the rearview mirror and the pile of paperwork for the damaged medic truck finished, Christine dredged through another shift at the firehouse.

It was 3:30 in the morning and she couldn't get back to sleep after another bogus "person down" call. Checking a sleeping homeless man who was taking cover from the pouring rain on a bus stop bench left her just damp enough to be uncomfortable, but not so drenched that she needed to change.

She flipped on her nightlight in her private bunk room. The biggest benefit of being a woman on the male-dominated fire department was that she didn't have to share the jockstrap-smelling bunk room with the other guys. It wasn't that she was prudish or afraid she might accidentally see one of her male coworkers in his drawers, but that they might see her. It was hard enough to be taken seriously on the fire department without the others seeing her in her skivvies.

Before the "person down" call, she had gotten enough sleep to not be exhausted, but not enough to be rested. Like with most nights after a 3AM run, she lay in her hard army-like cot and tossed and turned, unable to get back to sleep. Though her eyelids were heavy, her mind was too scattered. Her rumbling belly all but assured sleep would remain elusive. Maybe a peanut butter sandwich and a glass of milk would help.

After making her snack and taking it back to her room, she channel surfed from one loudmouthed salesman shouting about the latest must-have absorbent towel to another who told her about the best way to wash her car.

What I wouldn't do for a DVR.

The news channels all repeated the same garbage about the latest politician and his hooker scandal. One station actually had one of the alleged prostitute's previous johns on for an interview. It was unbelievable. People getting famous for paying for sex.

Christine stuffed the last piece of crust into her mouth and decided to flip the channel one final time before trying her luck at sleep again.

The TV landed on yet another werg commercial. They seemed to be everywhere nowadays. She even saw one during the last Super Bowl, which was a good indication the creatures were here to stay.

The handsome, dark-haired spokesman asked, "Tired of paying monthly fees for a security system that doesn't get the police to your house until after the crime has been committed? Afraid your Doberman

Pinscher may lick an intruder more than he scares him away?

"You've no doubt heard fables of werewolves and vampires and boogiemen."

The screen cut away from the spokesman's square jaw and gorgeous brown eyes to footage of a fenced-in corral surrounded by stables full of large cages.

The hunk's voice continued over the images. "How would you like to own your very own pureblood werepet? These magnificent cousins to the wolf are safe, tame, and 100% loyal. One of these werepets can be yours for the very reasonable price of $250,000 plus a yearly maintenance fee. But we'll get to that in a bit."

That was all she needed to hear. That price certainly put the creatures out of her budget, not that she would ever buy one anyway.

The picture closed in on the cages. The handsome spokesman walked into the shot, which kept Christine watching longer than she normally would have. He opened the closest cage. A snap of his fingers brought a set of green-tinted eyes from the darkness. The eyes were followed by a furry beast similar to the two she had met a couple of weeks before. The werewolf slunk from the cage with its ears back and its head tucked below its shoulders. It knelt and nudged its massive body against the spokesman's hip. Here was a creature that could devour this man in seconds, yet instead of mauling him, it cowered at his side and waited for the next command.

The spokesman continued his pitch. "These creatures are just like dogs, only smarter. Not to mention safer. With a dog, you may get a pit bull puppy that grows up to maul your nephew or the neighbor's kid. These wolves are 100% guaranteed to never show aggression, unless you want the premium security package, but we'll talk about that in the next segment." He paused with a smile that could sell her season football tickets despite her hatred of football. "Unlike dogs, these gentle giants are fully trained and completely safe prior to leaving the farm."

The camera switched to an aerial view of the property. At its center was a two-story barn attached to a building similar to a strip mall. Beside it was a second, larger, two-story office building. A long gravel drive led to the closed front gate while a hilly forest butted against the rear beyond a corral. What looked like a horse stable ran alongside the buildings. The view from the camera-mounted helicopter pulled back, revealing creatures wandering around the corral.

Once the handsome spokesman wrapped up his sales pitch and the credits filled the screen, her eyes felt heavy enough that she thought she might be able to get back to sleep. She made her way to her bunk, took off her boots, and curled up beneath her blanket. She sighed, looking forward to a few more hours of rest. The nightlight faded as her eyes drifted closed. She had just entered the dazed world between sleep and consciousness when the dreaded EMS tones blared over the PA system. She groaned, cursed beneath her breath, and slipped on her boots again. The dispatcher reported somebody's medical alarm had been activated.

She joined Billy at the truck and headed out.

The house sat at the bottom of a long and creepy gravel drive within a copse of trees. The nearest neighbor was at least a quarter-mile away. The rain had stopped, but the trees still dripped into puddles of mud.

The house was silent. The half-moon offered enough light that Christine could see the clearing around the house was empty, but that didn't ease her nerves.

She hated calls where little was known other than the address and the fact that someone had pushed an I've-fallen-and-I-can't-get-up alarm. But this house seemed creepier than the usual. She was careful not to let Billy see her rub her face. She said, "Maybe we should call for an Engine company or the police before we go inside." She kept her head on a swivel.

Billy looked over with surprise. "It's just a medical alarm, Chris. Some old bird probably rolled on her button while she was sleeping. Look, there aren't any lights on. What's up with you tonight?"

She rubbed the back of her neck and shook her head. "I don't know. Something just doesn't feel right."

Billy turned on a small flashlight and grabbed the medical kit from the side compartment. Christine joined him at the porch.

Billy leaned into her line of sight with the flashlight under his chin like they were telling ghost stories around a campfire. In the spookiest voice he could muster, he said, "Afraid of a little dark?" He followed it with a poor attempt at a creepy Vincent Price laugh.

Christine pushed him aside. "Don't be a jerk, Billy. Let's just get this over with."

She banged on the door, shouting, "Hello? Fire Department. Anyone home?" She rattled the handle, but it was locked.

Billy keyed his radio mic and said, "Medic 22 to Dispatch."

"Go ahead, 22," the distant voice of their dispatcher replied.

"We're at the residence and no one is coming to the door. Do you have a call-back number or any more information?"

"That's a negative. Came from the alarm company."

"All right. Notify PD that we're going to force entry."

"You're clear, Medic 22. Forcing entry. We'll let PD know. Just a heads up, they'll be awhile. They're pretty busy and backed up on calls."

Of course, they are, Christine groaned inwardly.

Billy hopped from the porch. Christine knew how much he enjoyed breaking down doors and smashing windows and figured there was no stopping him now. To her pleasant surprise, instead of retrieving an ax from the truck, he said, "I'll see if a window's unlocked first." His flashlight beam disappeared around the side of the house.

Christine peered through the frosted glass of the small dormer windows alongside the door. Sometimes on those types of calls, she'd see someone lying on the floor and that would tell them exactly what they had going on. But not this time. She couldn't see anyone. She rang the doorbell and pounded on the door again.

Billy seemed to be gone forever. Christine crept to the edge of the porch and leaned around the side of the house. "Billy?" she whispered. Her skin crawled with nerves. He wasn't there.

"Hey, Chris," Billy shouted from behind, nearly sending her through the porch roof. She shrieked and spun around. "Billy, you scared the hell outta me."

He smiled. "Sorry."

She clutched her chest and gathered herself. "Any luck?" she asked.

He shook his head. "We're gonna have to break in." He jogged to the medic, grabbed a flathead axe, and crowded past her to the door. He said, "You're kinda jumpy tonight. Relax. It's probably just some rich old bag who fell going to the pot and can't get up." With both hands clenched around the axe handle just below the head, he drew it back like a battering ram. He gave a coy smile and tilted his head curiously, like he always did before he blasted someone's front door from the hinges. "What do you think? One whack or two?"

She rolled her eyes. "Just get on with it."

Billy hit the door inches below the decorative handle. Then he smashed it again, but it still held. Embarrassed, he gave Christine a look.

"Probably reinforced steel," she lied to soothe his ego.

But Billy was no quitter. He drew back a third time and grunted as he slammed the axe head against the door again. The wood frame splintered, and the door sprang loose.

Christine dragged her fingers along the frame. "Hmph. I guess it wasn't steel after all." She knew that would tweak him. She pushed the door open. "Fire Department," she shouted.

Billy set the axe beside the door. "I didn't have very good footing," he said.

Christine nodded. "Yeah. That's kind of what I figured." Her grin gave her away.

Billy pushed past her into the dark living room. Christine felt the wall for the light switch and flipped it. Nothing happened. Billy pointed the flashlight at an end table with a lamp on it. He bobbed the beam toward it to get her attention.

She whispered, "Right. I got it."

She started across the room when Billy grabbed her shoulder, stopping her cold. "Chris, stop," he whispered. His voice quivered.

She froze. "What is it?"

His eyes were wide and fixed on something at the opposite side of a large living room. His mouth was hanging open and his breaths had quickened.

Slowly, she followed his gaze. An end table sat against the farthest wall beside a dark hallway. It was what she saw in the hallway that made her legs go weak. She backed up beside Billy. "Oh no," she whispered under her breath.

Two green eyes glowed in the blackness. A low growl told Christine everything she needed to know. "It's a werepet, Billy," she whispered.

Billy nodded. "Just back outside. Slowly." He guided her behind him as if *he* could protect her. He held up his hand and whispered, "Easy, boy." Then he directed his flashlight to the creature's face. Bloodstained teeth glistened in the light. Without taking his eyes away, Billy whispered, "Get me the axe."

Christine's stomach turned. She remembered he had left it on the porch beside the door and took a step toward it. The beast roared and dropped to all fours. She froze.

Billy whispered, "Run, Chris."

The creature pounced. Billy shoved Christine toward the door. The beast slammed into Billy and swatted him against the wall like he was a pesky fly. Inches from the porch and the axe, Christine felt a powerful hand grab her shirt collar from behind. She felt weightless for an instant before her cheek crashed against the hardwood floor in the center of the room. Her radio slid under the couch. Billy's flashlight had settled on the floor with its beam shining on the door. The werepet stepped into the light and closed the door.

Christine swallowed hard.

The beast sniffed the air.

Christine grabbed the flashlight and directed the beam at Billy. He was facedown and snoring. She knew that meant he had been knocked unconscious. But it also meant he was still alive.

The beast released another staccato growl and stalked side to side as if it wanted her to run. Before she got the chance, it pounced again. She scrambled inches from its path.

Underestimating the slipperiness of the hardwood floor, the creature slid past her and crashed against a set of French doors leading to a home office. Glass shattered. The beast yelped and shook its head. That gave Christine her best chance to escape. The front door was no good as she'd have to beat the creature to it. The hallway was her only choice. If she was quick, she could make it to one of the many doors. She bounced to her feet, grabbed the lamp on the end table beside the hall as she passed, and yanked the cord free of the outlet. She raced to the farthest door.

The creature's claws scraped the floor as it charged. She was almost at the door when she felt the beast's breath on her neck. She panicked. On instinct, she spun and swung the lamp with everything she had. It was the luckiest swing in history. The bulb shattered across the creature's snout, temporarily stunning it. Her momentum threw her to her ass and her back slammed against the door.

The creature righted itself and glared at her. There was only death behind its eyes. It scratched the floor with its front nails like a bull ready to charge. Christine fumbled for the handle above her head and turned it. The door swung open and she fell into the room. The beast charged. She yanked her legs from the doorway and slammed the door closed.

She twisted the lock just as the werepet grabbed the knob and shook it like he understood how it worked. It released a frustrated roar when the knob didn't turn. She wondered why it didn't simply break through. Remnants of its training, perhaps.

She turned from the door. She was in a bedroom with enough moonlight shining through the window to make out a grisly sight. Her heart sank. Two elderly people lay on a blood-soaked bed. She didn't have to be an expert to realize they had been mauled. The man was missing part of his arm and his neck had been filleted. The woman was equally mutilated with her stomach ripped open. Christine took a step toward them, her paramedic instincts telling her she should do something to help. But their injuries and the color of their skin told her there was nothing she could do.

She reached for her radio before remembering it had slid under the couch. The werg rattled the door handle again. She could hear it pacing the hall, which hopefully meant it had forgotten about Billy.

She had started for the window beside the bed when something clutched in the woman's hand caught her eye. It was a medical alert button. "I'm so sorry we couldn't help you," Christine whispered.

When Christine reached the locked window, the door exploded from its hinges. She spun toward the beast that filled the doorway. It panted in obvious frustration.

Christine whispered, "Please. It's okay. I won't hurt you. Just let me go."

The creature tilted its head as though it understood her, even sympathized with her. Seeing that speck of what had made it a pet in the first place gave her an idea. Maybe the same training that made the creature hesitate to break the door down would make it obey her, at least temporarily. She found the courage to snap, "Stop." She imagined herself correcting a dog that had gotten into the trash.

The beast tilted its head. Christine wagged her finger and then pointed aggressively at the ground like Becky the blond cheerleader had. "Get down."

The werg started to crouch but hesitated.

"Get down," she snapped again, only louder and more authoritatively.

The werg's eyes brightened slightly. It was working.

And then its eyes darkened again.

Oh no.

The creature leaped forward with murder in its savage eyes. Christine dove between the bed and the wall, just out of the creature's path. Its claws raked a gash in her thigh. Her skin felt like it was on fire before she hit the ground. The beast's head shattered the window. It yelped. When it pulled back, a bloody shard of glass protruded from the side of its neck. The creature's chest lifted and fell with deep, angry breaths.

Christine dragged herself to the wall near the head of the bed. The werg dropped to all fours and stalked closer, blood pouring around the glass shard. Effortlessly, it flung the bedframe against the far wall. Christine pulled her knees to her chest. Her leg wound bled freely. The werg lowered its snout close to her face. She closed her eyes and pressed her head against the wall. The creature sniffed her cheek. Its rank, hot breath pounded her face with each exhale.

The werg tilted its head back and howled victoriously. It shook blood from its neck like a dog shaking off bath water. Droplets splattered Christine's cheek. Her back slid down the wall until she was flat on the floor.

The beast's blood gushed onto her face. She turned away and screamed. At the moment she screamed, the creature shifted, and its blood poured into her mouth. She gagged on the salty goo, choking back vomit.

Her mind flashed to Billy lying on the floor in the other room and thoughts of what was going to happen to him when the beast had finished with her. It made her angry. That anger pushed away the fear. She found an inner resolve that she didn't know she had. If she was going to die, she was going to face it like every house fire she'd ever been in. Each puff of the werg's rotten breath struck her like the deepest insult.

She opened eyes filled with distain and whispered, "Go ahead, monster. Kill me. Get it over with."

But the creature stopped short and perked its ears seconds before a deafening pop exploded in the room. A blinding light engulfed everything. The werg backed off. Christine blinked away the spots until she could see again. The werg rubbed its eyes and rose to its rear legs. Confused, it turned toward the broken window. Someone stood outside with a gun trained on the beast. Two other men burst into the room from the doorway.

The creature roared and backed into the corner like a scared pup.

Christine used a clean section of the bedsheet to scrub the creature's blood from her face. She vomited, this time unable to hold it back.

One of the men by the doorway screamed, "Kill the bastard."

The creature snarled and bared its teeth.

The first gunshot sent a jolt through her soul. The creature recoiled and howled in pain. Another shot rang out, followed by a third. Blood splattered the wall behind the beast with each blast. Stunned but not helpless, the werg charged its attackers. They unleashed a hail of bullets as they retreated into the hall. Flesh ripped from the beast as it chased them.

Christine pushed to her feet with her hands pressed against her bleeding thigh. More gunshots rang out from the front room. She thought of Billy again. She limped to the window where a stranger wearing SWAT-style gear and carrying an assault rifle met her.

"You're safe now," he said. Over his shoulder, a spotlight mounted to the top of a black van with blacked-out windows highlighted the werg running from the porch toward the trees. He shouted, "Release the Savages."

The back doors of the van swung open. Two werewolves rocketed from the back and disappeared into the trees behind their prey.

The stranger turned back to Christine. For some reason, maybe woman's intuition, she didn't trust him. There was something in the way he looked at her.

"Everything's all right now," he said. His voice was soothing. Calm. Fake.

Mentally and physically exhausted, she turned away and sank to the floor beneath the sill with her back against the wall. The stranger reached in and touched her shoulder, sending a nervous chill through her.

"You're safe now," he said. She didn't believe him. "Sit tight. I'm going to come in through the front. Wait here and I'll explain everything." Then his hand lifted.

After a minute, he appeared at the bedroom door. Before entering, he examined the splintered doorframe and picked at a piece of the wood. He glanced over his shoulder and said to someone in the hall, "Replace this frame." Then he entered the room and righted a floor lamp that had been knocked over.

His pants were baggy and lined with bulging pockets. His belt held a holstered gun. He looked like a cop. The assault rifle he'd been holding outside was now strapped to his back. He reached out as he approached. "You are one lucky lady tonight. Come with me. We'll get that nasty cut looked at."

She hesitated.

He smiled and waved his hand. "Come on. I won't hurt you." He retrieved a long, narrow strip of fabric from one of his many pants pockets and squatted beside her. "You didn't get bitten, did you?" he asked as he wrapped the fabric around her bleeding thigh.

She answered with a shaky voice, "No. I don't think so."

"What about this wound? Not a bite?"

"His claws," she answered.

He smiled again. "Ahhh. That's good to hear. My name's Greg. I'm a hunter of sorts." He held out his hand again.

This time she let him help her up. She was trembling. He motioned to someone standing outside the window and the person passed a blanket through. He wrapped it around her shoulders. He said, "You've been through a lot. This area is crawling with rabid coyotes, and you have unfortunately come across a pack of them."

She leaned back, shaking her head. *No, no, not coyotes*. What was he talking about? "I ... I thought ..."

He tilted his head. "You thought what?"

"It's just ... it wasn't coyotes. It was a—"

He didn't let her finish. "Sure, it was coyotes. My team is tracking them as we speak. This isn't the first time this has happened out here. We've been trying to eliminate the threat for quite some time now."

Christine pushed away. His eyes burned through her soul. "I-I-I gotta get back to the station. I ..." She limped toward the hall.

Another man dressed like the first cut her off at the doorway. Greg nodded to him and then to her. "You're hysterical. It's okay. We have something that'll help you."

Christine shook her head as she backed away. "St-stay away from me," she stammered.

The second stranger approached. "It's going to be all right," he said, and reached for her wrist.

"You both keep saying that," she snapped, and yanked her hand away. A third stranger entered from the doorway and joined them. Greg reached for her. She slapped his chest and he grabbed her wrist, his fake politeness completely gone. She struggled in his grip, but he was too strong. The other stranger grabbed her legs and they lowered her to the floor. No matter how hard she fought, she couldn't break free.

Greg held her with one hand and removed a syringe-full of clear fluid from his breast pocket with the other. He pulled the cap from the syringe with his teeth.

She screamed, "Wait. Why are you doing this?"

He leaned in. "I'm saving your life."

"But the werewo—I mean the coyotes are gone."

"Not from the coyotes."

One of the other two men extended her left arm from her chest and held it still. Greg jammed the needle into her arm.

After injecting her with whatever drug was in the syringe, he stood up. The other man freed her legs and they all backed away.

Christine pushed to her feet, glaring hatefully at her assailants. She had never been drugged before and she didn't like it. The room spun. She stumbled toward the hall and they moved from her path. Her stomach turned. She lost her balance and her shoulder slammed against the doorframe. She staggered to the front room where more men stood with flashlights and guns.

"Help me," she whispered.

They stood and watched as she staggered across the spinning floor. When she was almost to the front door, her legs gave out and she fell to the hardwood. She looked toward the spot where Billy had been knocked unconscious, but he was gone. In his place were two coyote carcasses. None of it made any sense.

Greg knelt beside her again. He whispered, "We're gonna get you to the hospital. It seems you've been drugged. Just lie still and relax. You'll be fine."

She tried to ask about Billy but couldn't form the words. The world faded around her. Greg stood up and said, "Get her out of here."

NEVETS
PART 1

5

It was just another day in this shithole of a world for Steven. He rubbed his throbbing temples and sat up to orient himself to his third park bench of the week. If there was any benefit to living on the streets of Columbus, Ohio, it was the number of park benches.

His mouth tasted like an ashtray. He rubbed his beard, quickly finding a stubborn ingrown hair he'd been battling with. It was probably infected by now. He spent a few seconds digging at it, but since the area was raw and painful, he decided to let it be. His stomach cramped, reminding him of his need for a morning drink. When he stretched, he remembered how stiff his back had gotten.

A woman walked past with her young daughter, maybe seven. When she realized her daughter was staring, she gave her hand a tug.

"Don't look at him," she whispered, but Steven heard her.

Seeing the little girl reminded him of his own daughter who he hadn't seen since she was twelve. That was twenty years ago. When he returned home from the first Persian Gulf War, he just couldn't face her. He had been in the Battle of Khafji where his friend died in his arms. The big wigs called it friendly fire, but the battle was so chaotic, how could they know? They ultimately ruled the bullet had come from his gun, but they had to be wrong. Whether they were wrong or not, he could never know for sure, and it was a devastating burden to bear.

As the years passed, it had become harder and harder for him to contact his daughter because he had allowed too much time to pass already. Ultimately, he decided he'd waited too long and turned to the bottle to drown the pain.

The park had become overcrowded with the homeless in recent years, and their numbers seemed to grow each day. The shelters were no good either. They didn't let him drink and he didn't particularly like the other bums who stayed there.

Steven didn't like who he'd become. Most people who passed him probably thought he was little more than another drunk mooching off society. And they were mostly right. But they didn't understand what he'd seen. When his friend died, it did something to his brain. Before going to the Gulf War, he'd never drunk more than an occasional beer, but since coming back he couldn't stay away from the hard whiskey.

Some people might have ended it all after seeing their friend's head split open, especially after the brass ruled it friendly fire, but as hard as the world treated him when he'd returned, he had two reasons keeping him from lying down on the railroad tracks. First and most important, he had dreams of patching things up with his daughter one day. And second, even after all he had been through, he didn't hate the world for how it had treated him. He blamed himself as much as anyone else, and part of him believed he might yet find a life that he could be proud of one day.

However, this wasn't that day. He needed a drink. And a piss.

He heaved himself off the bench and tugged his many shirts, coats, and gloves into place. His multilayered, mismatched, vomit-stained outfit wasn't much to look at, but it kept him warm in the chilly Columbus weather. He pulled his outermost coat tighter across his chest.

"Hey, Nevets," a familiar voice shouted from across the park.

Great. It was Smells-Like-He's-Dead Fred. Steven ignored him. He hated Fred.

Fred shouted, "What's wrong, Nevets? Wake up on the wrong side of the bench again?" He chuckled as he gathered his things and put them in his stolen shopping cart from Kroger.

Steven grunted. *Same stupid joke every day.* He flew his middle finger, hoping Fred would get the blow-off and move on. Once Fred started talking, he usually wouldn't shut up. When they'd first met years ago, Steven had liked him, or at least tolerated him. But then he'd caught Fred trying to steal his shoes while he slept one night.

"See ya later, Nevets," Fred shouted.

And then there was the name Nevets. He hated Fred for that, too. *What an asshole.*

Steven grabbed his handwritten "Spare a Dollar" sign and headed to the nearest alley for his morning piss. Fred, on the other hand, splattered urine all over the sidewalk in plain sight. An early morning jogger called him an asshole while avoiding the puddle.

Steven ducked deeper into the alley for a little more discretion. As he finished, a jet-black van with heavily tinted windows rolled to a stop and blocked one end of the alley.

Steven cocked his head. *Now what?* He stood motionless and stared. The van's dark windows stared back. Steven turned toward the opposite end of the alley, but two men dressed in all-black SWAT uniforms and holding assault rifles blocked the only other way out. This wasn't good. Steven decided to put his head down and march past the van, ignoring whoever was in it, and hope they were just trying to scare him. And that's what he started to do. As he got closer, he picked up his stride and headed around the back bumper.

That's when the side door slid open, and three men climbed out. They too were dressed in black, only they also wore ski masks. Steven picked up his pace.

"Wait a minute, buddy," one of them shouted.

They surrounded him in a flash. Steven lifted his hands in surrender. "Hey, guys, just leave me alone, okay? I don't want any trouble."

Even from the park, Fred recognized something was wrong. He yelled, "Nevets, you okay over there?"

Steven shouted, "Fred, go find a cop."

One of the men grabbed Steven's arm. He was strong and big, like a professional wrestler. He shoved a towel over Steven's face.

When Steven grabbed for it, a deep, stinging pain jolted his lower back. His muscles stiffened and then gave way and he collapsed to the pavement.

The man said, "Don't fight us or you'll get another blast."

It felt like a mule kick. Steven had never felt anything like it. He lay on the ground, the towel still covering his face.

The big man lifted his arms, and one of the other men grabbed his legs. Together, they tossed him into the van. He heard the door slide shut. This was among his worst nightmares. He'd heard of college frat boys giving homeless guys a beating once in a while, but this was something much different. Inside, they zip tied his wrists behind his back so tightly that the plastic dug into his flesh. The van's muffler roared through the floorboards and the vehicle launched forward. Steven slid along the metal floor until he struck the inside wall.

He shook the towel from his face. The big man sat on a stool while the other two men sat on a maroon bench seat along the side wall. They took off their ski masks.

One of them zapped a stun gun in front of his face. Then he lowered it onto his lap and asked in a voice so scratchy Steven wondered if he had swallowed glass, "Hey, buddy. Why'd that guy call you Nevets?" He smiled, revealing a chipped front tooth.

"Because he's a jerk," Steven answered reluctantly.

"No. I mean, where did he come up with that name? Your name's Steven, right?"

"Yeah. Nevets is my name backwards."

"Oh …" His face twisted. "I don't get it."

Steven took an annoyed breath. He considered not answering but didn't want another zap. His back was still throbbing from the first one. He swallowed what little pride he had. "We were drunk one night, and I told him I was dyslexic. He started calling me Nevets after that."

All three men started laughing. The stun gun wielding bastard said, "You dirt balls are a real riot."

"Where are you taking me?" Steven asked.

Still laughing, the big man said, "On the adventure of a lifetime. Now, you might as well take a nap. It's a long drive." He nodded, and one of the other men leaned toward Steven and stuffed his head back under the towel. They were crazy to think Steven might sleep.

The van drove for at least an hour with none of the men talking. When they stopped once for fuel, Steven quietly panicked, recalling stories of homeless people being burned alive. They filled the van and started again.

The smooth highway eventually turned rough with rocks peppering the undercarriage. Steven couldn't imagine a more suitable road to get to someplace where you could set a man on fire without anyone bothering you. He decided if he were about to die, nothing they could do would make him beg.

When the van eventually stopped and the side door was yanked open, the men pulled him to the dirt. The big man cut his restraints. Steven waited for his eyes to adjust. He was in front of what looked like an old, vacant factory with boards covering the broken windows. He looked around. They were surrounded by a forest. A coyote howled somewhere in the distance.

"Let's go," the big man said, and helped him to his feet. They led him around the side of the building to a pair of doors that sat at a forty-five-degree angle, like the kind that led to a basement or cellar. The big man unlocked a padlock and gave the doors a tug. They swung out and cocked open. He smiled. Then he held his hand out in invitation.

The man holding Steven's arm gave him a shove. Steven crept forward until he could see inside. A wooden staircase led into darkness. He paused at the top. The big man gave him a nudge.

"What are you going to do to me down there?" Steven asked. He'd rather be shot in the back of the head than go inside.

"Just get down there," the big man answered. He gave Steven a harder shove toward the steps.

Steven swallowed hard. He gingerly stepped onto the first creaky stair.

"Keep going," the big man growled.

Steven took another step, ducking his head beneath the top of the doorframe. The big man followed. The stairs ended at a concrete floor. It smelled of musty air, sour milk, and urine. Steven covered his nose with the crook of his elbow.

The big man flipped on a flashlight as his two partners pulled the doors closed and then joined him at the bottom of the stairs. They peeled off Steven's coats and shirts until he was down to one ragged undershirt.

Steven dug into the right front pocket of his jeans to make sure the only possession he really cared about was still there. His finger touched the irreplaceable silver locket and he sighed. The locket held the only picture he still had of his daughter, and it meant the world to him. Hell, he'd almost killed Smells-Like-He's-Dead-Fred for trying to swipe it a few years back. He wrapped his fingers around the locket and pulled it to his mouth. "I love you," he whispered into his fist.

One of the men pulled a chair from the back wall, the metal feet making a horrible screeching sound on the concrete. He shoved it against the back of Steven's knees. The big man pressed down on Steven's shoulders.

Steven looked over his shoulder at the big man. "Now will you tell me why I'm here?"

The big man held a finger to his lips. "Shhhhh. This is my favorite part." He lifted his eyes to the darkness ahead. The room fell silent, except for Steven's panicked breaths. At least he didn't smell gasoline. Though he expected someone to slit his throat at any moment, he didn't beg.

A low, guttural growl rose from the darkness. Steven dragged his sleeve across his sweaty forehead. Were they feeding him to a lion? His life flashed past his eyes. He remembered how strong he once was and wished he could find that strength again. He wondered how he could have let his world collapse so badly that his imminent death wouldn't be grieved by anyone. He pictured his daughter's face in the locket, and for the first time in years he wanted to change, but now it was too late.

A chain rattled in the dark as the growling creature moved. The big man shut off his flashlight and pulled a string that was dangling from an exposed bulb above Steven's head. The dim light left the farthest recesses in darkness.

Steven suddenly needed to piss again. "Are you going to feed me to a lion or something?" he asked.

"Shut up," the big man answered. He leaned close to Steven's ear and pointed. He whispered, "Just watch. It'll all be over soon."

The chains rattled again and the shadowed outline of what must have been a grizzly rose out of the darkness. Steven's eyes went wide. Maybe begging wasn't such a bad idea.

And then the most dangerous creature known to man stepped into the light. Steven suddenly wished it *was* a bear. The beast was nearly seven feet tall with a thick barrel chest and emaciated gut. Patchy black fur covered him from pointy ears to flesh-tearing nails on his feet. His elongated snout sniffed the air. Drool dripped from his chin. All that held him back was a collar around his neck hooked to a chain that stretched into the dark. The beast drew in a breath and then roared like the champion he was. It was deafening.

Steven's bladder let loose. He was ashamed to be so weak. He looked over his shoulder to his abductors as they stood stoically behind. One of them smiled slightly.

A PA system crackled from an unseen speaker. A man's voice followed the static. "Steven," the man said.

The beast roared at the speaker.

Unfazed, the voice continued, "Welcome to the WereHouse. My name is Mr. Henderson. We are excited to have you here. You, my friend, are about to make us a lot of money, and for that I thank you."

The beast snorted and licked his jowls.

"Do not fear death," Mr. Henderson continued, "for my pet will not kill you today. But rest assured, the next couple of weeks will not be pleasant by any stretch of the imagination. Well, not for you, anyway. Steven, your shitty life is about to change. Though I'd like to say for the better, I really don't think that would be entirely true."

The werewolf locked soulless black eyes on Steven.

Mr. Henderson added, "I know a lot about you, Stevie. I know how you were once a soldier and that you lost a close friend on the battlefield. I know how they blamed you for his death. It must have been an awful time for you, wondering if it was indeed your errant shot that took his life. I also know how you turned to drinking after you returned home. If it's any consolation, when the boys came to me with your file, I considered passing you by simply because of your military service. As a company, we love our vets, after all. But ultimately, I had to reconsider. You understand, don't you? If I left all the bums—I'm sorry, I mean home-challenged people. If I left all of you alone because of your past military service, well I wouldn't have much of a business, now, would I?"

In that instant, Steven realized why he was there. He hadn't been so far removed from the world that he didn't know what the WereHouse was about. They were in the business of selling werepets, and Steven knew all too well he was a man who wouldn't be missed.

"So, your creatures *are* human?" he croaked. There had always been whispers among conspiracy theorists.

The PA was quiet for a few seconds before Mr. Henderson answered, "You sure are a bright boy, Stevie." After another brief pause, Mr. Henderson added, "Okay, boys. Do your thing. I'll be watching."

That's when Steven saw the tiny red light of a camera near the ceiling in one corner. Defiant, he lifted his middle finger just as the big man grabbed his arm.

The other man clamped a strange metal sleeve around Steven's neck and fastened it in the front.

"Can't have our friend ripping out your jugular, now, can we?" he said.

The beast lunged forward, the chain stopping him inches from Steven's face. Steven recoiled against the back of the chair, tipping it over and throwing him to the hard floor. The guards laughed as they grabbed his flailing arms and jerked him up. The big man grabbed Steven's hair.

Steven forgot about his vow not to beg and screamed, "Please, don't let it eat me alive."

The guard pulled him close and whispered, "He's not going to eat you." And then he shoved Steven away. Steven grabbed for his shirt but only caught air. He fell backward in what felt like slow motion. Terror swallowed him.

The beast buried his claws in Steven's calf and dragged him thrashing into the dark. In his panic, the locket fell from his fist.

The beast grabbed Steven's shoulders and lifted him from the ground. Steven squirmed but the beast was too strong. He squeezed his eyes closed and silently begged for a fast ending. The creature's hot breath washed over his shoulder before sharp fangs sank into flesh. White-hot pain exploded up Steven's neck. The beast was in a rage. He tore a chunk of flesh away. Steven wailed.

The PA crackled. Mr. Henderson shouted, "Okay, okay, okay. That's enough."

One of the guards fired a pistol. The beast yelped and recoiled.

Steven dropped to his knees, blood pouring down his back and chest. His left hand went numb. The light of the dim bulb blurred as his blood spilled to the concrete. He lifted his weary eyes to the guards who frantically waved him toward them.

The big one shouted, "Come on. Crawl over here. You're bleeding to death."

Steven was too weak to crawl anywhere. The beast might not have been supposed to kill him, but that's exactly what it may have done. Steven leaned forward to crawl, but instead his chin met the floor.

"Go get him," Mr. Henderson screamed over the PA.

The big guard stammered, "B-b-but The First isn't down yet. The tranq hasn't had long enough to work." Then he frantically waved at Steven again. "Come on, Steve. You can do it."

Steven envisioned himself crawling out of danger, but his arms wouldn't work. The beast snarled behind him. He sounded pissed.

"Get him now," Mr. Henderson shouted.

"The First will kill us."

"Then shoot it with another dart. Do not let Steven die or you two will take his place."

They fired a second dart into the beast, and he wailed.

Steven's eyes drifted down. Something small sparkled beneath the light. He smiled, seeing his locked had popped open in the fall and his daughter stared back at him. She gave him the strength he needed to face death like a man.

The chains rattled again as a heavy clawed foot landed beside Steven. He fought to lift his eyes to the beast now standing over him. This was it. But the beast didn't attack. Instead, he staggered to the side wall, two feathered darts lodged in his neck. He wobbled and tried to hold on to the wall as he slid down. He could only watch as the guards approached him, weapons outstretched. As the big guard raced to Steven's side, his boot landed on Steven's last treasured possession. The loud crunch was worse than anything the werewolf had done.

The big guard grabbed Steven under his arms and dragged him out of the beast's reach as the creature slumped to his side.

Steven closed his eyes.

6

A TV hung in a strange room where two stale white walls met. A pair of local news anchors read a story about the latest homicide in the city. Christine watched the screen, disoriented but having enough sense to recognize she was in a hospital bed. The camera closed in on the female anchor who read the intro to the next story.

"We have an update on last night's report involving two deaths in connection with a suspected wild animal attack. We're going live now to the scene with our investigative reporter. Here's Mindy with a special report on this story."

The screen switched to a reporter standing next to a middle-aged man dressed in a dark blue Giorgio Armani suit with pinstripes. Their backdrop was a house within a copse of trees with yellow crime scene tape across the front door.

Christine remembered responding to an alarm at that house, but anything about what had happened there was fuzzy.

"Thank you, Andrea. This story continues to develop. As we previously reported, two local paramedics whose names are being withheld responded here at 128 Skelwaller Lane late last night for what they thought was a routine medical call. What they discovered when they arrived was anything but. The homeowners had been mauled to death, and the wild animals responsible were still on the premises. The two paramedics were themselves attacked. We're told one of them is in stable condition at an area hospital, but as of tonight the other is still missing."

Christine covered her mouth. *Oh no. Billy.*

The reporter went on. "The official police report claims that rabid coyotes were the culprits, but there are rumors that a werepet may have been responsible. Here to comment on this theory is Senator Wooten, who is here as part of his committee's separate investigation. Thank you for joining us out here this late in the evening, Senator. I know you're busy."

"Thank you, Mindy." The senator's voice was deep and authoritative. It was the kind of voice that even when he whispered everyone could hear him. "As you know, I founded and head the WOC and—"

Mindy pulled the microphone away from him. "Pardon me, for our viewers who aren't familiar with the WOC, you are speaking of the Werewolf Oversight Committee." She shoved the microphone back toward the senator.

"That's right, Mindy. Though the WereHouse insists their products are safe, my constituents, along with all Americans, must be protected. The best way to accomplish that is with a tight leash on the werepet industry, pardon the pun. I have spoken with the mayor about my concerns, and he has assured me the police will further investigate just to make sure this unfortunate couple's family pet didn't have anything to do with this attack."

"So it's true the victims owned a werepet?" Mindy asked.

"That's correct."

"And where is the werepet now?"

"A WereHouse spokesperson says it was returned by the couple a few days ago."

Mindy dug deeper. "Why was it returned?"

"My team is still looking into that. Probably due for its regular maintenance."

"Do you have any reason to doubt the initial investigation reports of a coyote attack?"

"Well, Mindy, it isn't that I question the police, as they are doing a fine job, but we have to remain vigilant."

"As I'm sure you are aware, there are those who question your motives. They say you are using your public opposition to the werepet trend to further a future presidential bid."

Senator Wooten chuckled. "Well, I didn't see much of a boost in the polls back when I started the WOC, and I doubt I'll see much improvement now, either." He smiled. "Regardless, I have no plans at present to run for president."

She smiled back. "It's no secret that you have aspirations."

He shook his head. "We're not going to make any news here tonight on that front."

"So, what's the WOC doing to keep werepets safe?"

"As you know, we have already fined the WereHouse tens of thousands of dollars, and I plan to keep fining them as long as they commit violations."

Mindy pulled the microphone back. "PETA says you're not doing enough."

"Well, if we went by what PETA wanted, no one would be allowed to own goldfish. The fines appear to be a good deterrent for now."

"Let's talk about those fines for a moment. If I'm not mistaken, to date they have been for relatively mundane infractions, most of which involve working conditions at the farm and not werewolf regulation. Why should we believe you aren't wasting taxpayers' money on—"

The TV screen went blank and the power indicator light turned red. A stranger stood near the door, holding the TV remote. He said, "That damn WOC." He wore a black suit with dark sunglasses and a three-quarter-length leather coat.

"Who are you?" Christine asked.

He strolled to the foot of the bed, ignoring her question. "How are you feeling, Ms. Alt?"

She pulled her sheets up to her chest. "Why are you here?"

The man lifted her medical chart from the foot of the bed, though he didn't open it. "Tell me, Christine. Did you get bitten by the coyotes last night?"

Christine hesitated before answering, "I'm sure it says in the folder you're holding. Why don't you look and see?"

"Oh, I wouldn't want to invade your medical privacy. You know, with HIPAA laws and all. If you want to tell me, I'll believe you."

Christine scowled.

"Come on, Christine. Tell me what I need to know, and I'll be out of your hair. Did you get bitten?"

She hesitated before shaking her head.

"It is very important that I know for sure." He removed his sunglasses, revealing gorgeous hazel eyes. His glare sent a chill along her spine.

"It didn't bite me. Will you tell me who you are now?"

He set her file back on the bed and strolled toward the door. Before leaving, he turned and said, "Just think of me as animal control. Don't be concerned, we've taken care of the coyotes." With that, he opened the door.

Christine's fire lieutenant, Alex, passed him as he left. "Hi, Chris. How're you feeling?"

Still wondering who the stranger was, she didn't answer.

"Christine?" Alex said again, breaking her daze.

"Oh. Alex. How's it going?"

"I'm fine. The question is how are you?"

"I'm okay, I guess. Tired."

"Who was that just in here? Family?"

She shook her head. "I'm not sure." She paused, considering whether she should tell Alex what the man had said or not. Thinking better of it, she changed the subject. "Any word on Billy?"

He shook his head. "But the guys at the station have been out searching the woods since it happened. We're not going to rest until we find him. That's the only reason they're not here with you right now. I told them I'd let 'em know how you're doing when I get back to the search." Alex pulled up a chair. "Do you need anything?"

She smiled. "No. Thank you, Lieu."

The two talked for the next few hours, and the stranger in the sunglasses slipped from her mind.

AIDEN'S FIRST DOG

7

Aiden Talik reclined in the passenger seat of his Dodge truck while his teammate drove. He pulled his ballcap over his face and said, "Let me know when we're close. I'm gonna get some rest."

His partner, Greg, shook his head. "I don't know how you can sleep right before a job."

Aiden turned to his side, facing the passenger window. "I haven't slept for three days. It shouldn't be a problem."

"Well, sweet dreams. Pass me a beer before you're—"

That was the last Aiden heard before he drifted into dreams.

He was twelve years old again, riding with his dad in the company limo. Typical jet-black with tinted windows and highly-polished chrome accents. The fresh wax job glistened in the blinding sun on the bright but cold Ohio fall day. The driver slowed to a stop in front of an old rehabbed three-story brick building with windows tinted as black as the limousine's that blended in with the dark façade. The front door was tinted glass as well and a red "Welcome" sign hung from a hook on the outside. Between the second and third floor windows were large red letters that spelled WEREHOUSE. The letters were not lit, nor did they sparkle with any type of fancy paint. They were simply red—blood red.

The car rocked slightly as the sweaty, overweight chauffeur climbed from his seat behind the wheel. He dabbed moisture from his forehead with a handkerchief, waddled to the back door, and complained about the broken AC in the front. Aiden bounced from the back seat almost before the chauffeur could completely open the door.

"Come on, Dad," he shouted to his backseat companion. He was more excited than on Christmas Eve.

His father's snakeskin boot poked from the vehicle as he climbed out, grunting with the effort.

The chauffeur said, "I'll circle the block and find somewhere to park. Take your time, sir. Your next appointment isn't for a few hours."

Aiden grabbed his father's hand and dragged him toward the store. A little bell above the door jingled when they entered. The lobby was magnificent— plush carpet, reclining leather chairs, and a projection TV that was at least a sixty-inch model in the corner. A soap opera was playing.

At the far end of the lobby was a glass desk with a brown-haired beauty sitting behind it. She was everything a model would want to be, with collagen-puffy lips and actress-caliber makeup hiding any blemishes she might have. Aiden didn't get girl crazy yet, but he had been around his father enough to understand that Daddy sure did.

Aiden caught his father ogling the secretary's long legs extending from beneath the hem of her red leather miniskirt.

"How may I help you today, sir?" she asked.

His father lifted his eyes and smiled. "With Christmas coming soon, I need a special gift for the boy. I was sent here by Harley Jacobs."

"Oh, Mr. Jacobs. Of course. Your son is going to love what we have to offer." She glanced at her notebook. "Ah, yes. Our two o'clock. You must be Howard?"

Howard nodded. "I am."

"Very well. Have a seat and Mr. Henderson will be with you right away."

The white-faced clock behind her read a quarter till and Aiden couldn't wait.

Howard leaned on the desk. "I'd rather stand here and talk with you, if you don't mind."

She grinned shyly but didn't rebuff him.

Howard adopted the same swagger he got whenever he talked to pretty girls. "So, what's your name?"

Aiden rolled his eyes. He'd seen this game before.

The secretary's blue eyes moved down his father's arm to his left hand, zeroing in on the white gold wedding band on his ring finger.

"Let's not worry about that," his father said. Aiden glanced to the clock again, the second-hand creeping along like a glacier. He hated when his dad talked to pretty women, especially knowing Mom was at home.

The secretary reached over the desk and brushed her finger across his hand. "I wasn't." Her cleavage seemed about to burst from her white V-neck blouse and part of her lacy bra peeked out.

Howard asked, "You wanna get something to eat later?"

Though she shook her head, she didn't really look like she was saying no.

The door opened behind her, interrupting the game. Another woman at least as pretty as the secretary stood in the doorway. Her dark hair was pulled into a ponytail. She peered over her black-rimmed glasses and said, "Howard?" His father nodded with the same grin he'd given the secretary moments before. "Mr. Henderson is ready to see you, now."

"Come on, boy." Aiden smiled at the secretary, who appeared less than pleased with his father's roving eyes. Howard caught her glare and asked, "See you later?"

"Not likely."

"Was it that obvious?" Howard asked.

"Maybe you should wipe your drool," she said, and turned back to her computer. Aiden glanced at Howard's chin to see if he actually had drooled. He hadn't.

Howard lifted his hands and shrugged his shoulders, as if to say, "Oh well." Then he nudged Aiden toward the door with a tap on the back of his head.

They were immediately met by a large man with the physique of a retired football player. He wore a tacky beige suit and a mustache more fitting for a car salesman than an employee of a multi-million-dollar corporation.

The man offered his thick left hand. He said, "I'm Bernard Henderson. You must be Howard Talik. It's nice to meet you." The two men shook hands. Bernard scowled slightly and tilted his head. "You look familiar. Have we met before?"

"I attended one of the dog fights you hosted. We met briefly after the event."

"Ah, yes." He looked down at Aiden. "And what's your name, little man?"

"Aiden, sir."

The office was as large as the front lobby with a single oak desk smack dab in the center. The pretty brunette sat in a chair next to Bernard's desk with a notepad and a pen.

Mr. Henderson settled in behind the desk in a worn-out leather chair that creaked when he sat. Aiden and Howard took the only other seats. Aiden sat on the edge of his. There was another door at the farthest end of the room. It didn't look like a regular door in that it was metal with three steel bolt locks along one side and thick metal hinges down the other. It looked like a vault.

Mr. Henderson started the conversation. "Well, I know you're a busy man, so let's get right to business." He leafed through a folder full of papers until he found what he needed. "Ah, I see Harley Jacobs recommended you. How is old Harley?"

"He's well," Howard answered.

Aiden sat quietly like his father had instructed before they arrived. He had said, "When grownups talk business, young 'uns keep their yaps shut."

His father leaned forward like he always did before things got serious and began talking money. "Let's get to it. I want your product, but a quarter of a million is a lot of cash for something so ... how should I put it ... perishable. What kind of longevity will I get from it? Ten ... fifteen years of use?"

"No, no, no," Bernard said with a slight chuckle. "You should get at least forty years of enjoyment from a single purchase."

"Forty years, huh?"

Bernard nodded.

Howard rubbed his chin. "Harley said there is considerable upkeep. What are we talking in terms of maintenance?"

Bernard's demeanor switched from jovial to all business in an instant. "Fifty grand a year."

Howard winced. "That's pretty steep."

"I'll give you that. But honestly, isn't it the bang for the buck that's important?"

"Go on."

"On top of all medical issues that are completely covered as long as you take the product to a WereHouse licensed facility, you receive twenty-four-seven access to our help desk. And more importantly, you'll speak to a live human and not some automated machine. Also, and this is where your money really goes, because we know this is a lifetime investment and not some one-off, spur-of-the-moment purchase, we retrieve the product once a month and keep it for a weekend. Kind of like the National Guard does with their rank and file." He chuckled. "Seriously, though, you do nothing except make sure we have access, and we do the rest."

"And what do you do over those two days?"

Bernard grinned. "Several things. We evaluate and tune it up. We make sure there are no behavior glitches, and if we find one, which we rarely do, we reeducate the product and return it as good as new."

"What happens if I opt to not enroll in the maintenance program?"

Bernard took a deep breath and sighed. "Unfortunately, the maintenance program is mandatory. It is part of the contract you'll sign with us upon purchase. It is for liability reasons as much as to ensure you to have a good life-long experience with your purchase. Plus, there is an unbeatable warranty."

Howard's ears perked. "Oh. What kind of warranty?"

"Ten years, no questions asked. If there are any defects, we'll replace your purchase free of charge."

Aiden's father nibbled on his lower lip. He looked to Aiden, and Aiden gave his best pleading eyes. Howard clapped his hands together. "All right, let's see it."

Bernard grinned like he had just won the lottery. He rose from his chair and started for the vault.

The brunette stood as well. She nodded. "Right this way, sir." She led Howard and Aiden across the room.

Bernard glanced back as he unbolted the third bolt. "You will not be disappointed. Trust me." He pulled the door open.

The brunette tapped Howard's shoulder and said, "I know the price is steep, but we are the only company in the world with such a product."

Bernard bobbed his head. "She's right. As of today, we are quite small, but that'll change with our pending government approval and aggressive marketing." He rolled his eyes and added, "The hoops we must jump through with the government are …

well, you know … ridiculous. That's part of the reason for the monthly maintenance. Our product has to be perfect, and that's the only way we can make sure it stays that way."

Howard shrugged. "I get it. The maintenance fee isn't a deal-killer."

Bernard bobbed his head. "That's great to hear." As he led Howard and Aiden into a long hallway, he added, "You're getting in at the right time if you decide to purchase. You will be on the cutting edge of the greatest advancement in household pets since man domesticated the wolf. We expect this business to blow up as soon as we get government approval. If all goes well, we will have advertising during the Super Bowl next year. At least, that's the plan."

Even at twelve years old, Aiden could tell Bernard was a talented salesman. The way he keyed in on his father's competitive penchant for buying the latest and greatest was very skillful.

Mr. Henderson changed the subject as they continued down the hall. "By the way, has old Harley decided whether he's going to take the plunge yet? He's been on the fence for a while now."

Howard answered, "You know Harley. He takes two hours just to decide on breakfast. But he sounds pretty interested."

"Hm. Maybe I should send him a little reminder and a slight nudge."

"Probably a good idea. Though, if *we* buy one, he'll see it next time he's over for dinner."

"Yeah, I suppose so. Heh, imagine if you buy one today. You'll beat Harley to the punch."

Bernard *was* good.

Howard grinned. "Enough with the sales pitch. Let's just see it."

The hallway ended at a second vault-like metal door. Bernard opened it into a dark gray room with unpainted concrete walls and a sterile tile floor sloped slightly to a drain in the center. It stank like the time Aiden left his Golden Retriever in the laundry room for too long after being out in the rain. The back half of the room was behind iron bars and hidden in darkness.

Bernard whistled once and walked to the bars. Aiden looked past him into the darkness. Two glowing green orbs stared back.

"Lights please, Tonya."

A clunk and a hum preceded an overhead light flickering to life.

Aiden's eyes flew wide and he took a step backward. Howard grabbed his shoulder and pulled him close again.

Bernard glanced back from the bars. He waggled his eyebrows and smiled. "Pretty cool, huh?"

Standing hunched over in the back of the cell was what must be the most incredible creature to ever walk the earth. Its dagger-like nails and deadly fangs screamed predator, while its scared greenish eyes begged for mercy. Its dark gray fur flowed like a well-groomed mane. It sniffed the air with a wolf-like snout and then rose to its intimidating height. Aiden forgot how to breathe.

Bernard snapped his fingers through the bars. "Get over here," he hissed.

The creature's long, pointy ears tucked tight against its bowed head like a dog caught digging in the trash. Its eyes filled with a sorrowful blend of humility and shame. Though Aiden should have been the one who was afraid, something deep down pulled him closer to the bars. Maybe it was curiosity. Or maybe sympathy.

As he watched the creature in awe, his eyes wandered downward. The beast's waist was thin, but its chest was thick and muscular. Aiden's gaze traveled lower and he realized that *it* was in fact a *he*.

When Bernard noticed Aiden's embarrassment, he said, "When you leave today, we'll give you a catalog of orderable accessories, some of which will hide such unsightly things. Also, you should know that all of our werepets are neutered before going to their forever homes."

Aiden couldn't take his eyes from the creature's deadly claws. He wondered if they were bigger than a polar bear's. The creature sniffed the bars and then snorted.

"Can I pet him?" Aiden whispered, surprising his father.

Bernard nudged him from behind. "Of course. He's as safe as your cat or puppy or whatever you have."

Aiden stepped forward cautiously and reached for the bars. His father and Bernard continued talking behind him, but he didn't hear anything they said. The creature seemed sad.

Aiden whispered, "It's okay. I won't hurt you."

The creature dropped to all fours with his head still below his shoulders. Aiden reached through the cell bars. The creature sniffed the air above his hand and then snorted again, this time startling him. Undeterred, Aiden rubbed between the werewolf's ears. His fur was rough and his skin feverish. The creature shied away from Aiden's gaze as if afraid of looking him in the eyes.

"That's a sign of respect," Mr. Henderson said. "A good werg, like a good dog, should never stare down a human."

"And if he did?" Howard asked.

Mr. Henderson chuckled. "Well, it's never happened, but if it did you would call us immediately and we'd take him back for reeducation."

The creature flicked his tongue just below Aiden's wrist. Aiden held the top of his hand up to the werg's snout. Its tongue was rough like wet sandpaper but gentle.

Aiden turned back to his father, excited and impatient. "Dad, can I have him? Can I have a … a werg?" He looked to Bernard. "What's a werg, anyway?"

Bernard smiled. "My dear boy, we just call them wergs. The average uneducated person would call them werewolves like what you've seen on TV and in scary movies. Werg is another word for werewolf."

"A werewolf?" his father asked.

Bernard chuckled again. "Yeah. But don't worry, sir. They aren't werewolves in the same sense as the werewolves in the movies. We only call them that because of their similarities to the mythical creature. Think of it as a marketing ploy."

"I'd say it's more than a ploy. Hell, he looks like all the werewolves I've ever seen in the movies."

"Hence the name. But rest assured, he's no more dangerous than a Shih Tzu." Bernard laughed louder. He smacked Howard's shoulder and added, "And he's not going to turn into a human after the next full moon, either."

Howard laughed in return. "Yeah, I don't suppose I much buy into fairy tales and mythical creatures."

"Actual movie werewolves are about as real as unicorns or ... or ... living gargoyles, even."

"Yeah, I suppose that makes sense. So, what's he eat?"

"His dietary needs are similar to a dog's. In fact, our scientists have determined that werewolves, like dogs, are actually descended from wolves. He'll eat dog food or raw meat like beef or chicken. It's all in his manual and video guide, which you'll get as part of the package. It is very important that you feed him every day and don't forget."

Howard's eyes widened. "What happens if I forget?"

Bernard chuckled again. "Oh, it isn't anything to worry about. If you do forget, they have been known to snatch a wayward squirrel or even the occasional cat." He paused. "And you wouldn't want to piss off any of your neighbors when their pets start disappearing, would ya?"

"I don't suppose so. He must eat a lot, though. Look at his size."

"That's also one of the features with the maintenance program that I forgot to mention. One of the reasons we retrieve the creature every month is to take him to a preserve owned by the company and let him hunt larger game. It gives them an opportunity to supplement their diets, along with a chance to be with others of their kind. Think of it as a doggie vacation at the most fun dog park ever."

Aiden secretly wished his father would shut up so he could take his new friend home, but Howard seemed full of questions.

"Have you ever had problems with an aggressive one?"

"Oh no, no, no. Never. Really, do you think the government would even consider letting us sell these things if they weren't safe?"

"No, I don't suppose they would."

"So, when can I get one delivered to ya?"

Aiden blurted, "You mean I can't take this one now?"

Bernard shook his head. "I'm afraid not, young man. This is a display model. You'll get a brand new one."

"Like a puppy?" Howard asked.

"No. It'll be fully grown. Puppies are too difficult to train and take a lot of time. I just mean new as in not owned by anyone else."

Howard squinted, deep in thought. Then he said, "I'll take one."

Aiden thought he might explode with excitement. "How soon can we get him?" he asked, getting a side-eye from his dad. *Business. Right.*

"It's quite all right, sir. He has every reason to be excited. He's about to have the coolest present in the neighborhood. You won't be sorry."

Aiden stared at the werg. "I'm going to name mine Rufus," he muttered.

"What's that, son?"

"Rufus. His name is Rufus."

"I think Rufus is a great name," Bernard said.

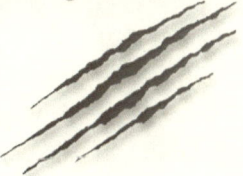

"Hey, Aiden, wake up. We're almost there."

Aiden rubbed his eyes and tugged a lever on the side of his seat, raising the back for a better look through the windshield. "How many times do I have to tell you, Greg? When we're hunting, call me Talik or Mr. Talik or whatever, but don't use my first name. Got it?"

Greg rolled his eyes. "You're such a squirrel. The only thing that'll hear me call you by your first name out here isn't going to be around long enough to remember it."

"Just the same."

"Yeah, yeah. I got it … Talik."

The headlights of approaching traffic blurred through the heavy rain beating against the windshield. "How long have I been asleep?"

"Four hours, man. You must have been dreaming some wild shit because your eyelids were fluttering like mad. We had a hell of a laugh, didn't we, Jeffrey?"

The man in the back seat agreed. "You looked like a clown, man."

Talik ignored him.

"So, what were you dreaming about," Greg asked.

"A friend I had when I was a kid. His name was Rufus."

"Rufus? What, was he a dog or something?"

"Yeah, something like that."

"Well, you'd better get your head on straight, 'cause we're about to be in the shit."

8

Greg pulled to the side of the road, parked, and turned on the truck's flashers. He removed a pistol from his waistband and jammed the slide backward with a clunk. "Go silver or go home, eh, Talik?"

Jeffrey passed Talik an AK-47, fully loaded and ready for battle.

Greg smirked at Talik's weapon of choice, as he did before every hunt. "When are you going to trade that sloppy AK for something with better aim?"

"When they make something as reliable in the rain and mud." When it came to hunting game as dangerous as wergs, Talik couldn't risk his weapon not working. He had shot his AK once when it was covered in mud, and he wouldn't be here today if it had failed.

He pointed over the embankment at the forest. "The reports say he's livin' down there by a creek that flows under that bridge up ahead." He pointed to a one-lane, graffiti-covered bridge at the end of a rutted dirt road. "This one's gone completely rogue. He'll kill you as soon as run from you, so be careful."

"Good," Greg said with a grin. "I get tired of picking them off while they stare at me like I'm bringing them meat."

Talik grunted and swung his door open. "Let's go." He pulled on his raincoat and used it to cover his rifle before climbing out of the truck. Greg and Jeffrey joined him as he descended the muddy embankment.

The rain was cold and biting, striking his face with stinging velocity. His footing was precarious at best. He stopped at the creek's edge. The small bridge hid its underbelly in shadow, creating the perfect temporary shelter for any creature, human or otherwise. As wild as the rogue wergs could be, he had never met one that enjoyed being out in the rain. He signaled with a flicked of his hand and Greg stalked to his left.

With Greg moving into position, Talik and Jeffrey stepped into the ankle-high creek. Talik knelt and opened his raincoat to expose his weapon. His partner moved a couple of feet to his right. Talik lifted a flashlight with his left hand and pressed it flush against the underside of the AK's barrel with the beam still off. He put the butt of the gun against his right shoulder and his finger alongside the trigger guard. And then he waited.

Greg continued around the bridge, giving it a wide enough berth that he could flush the hiding creature toward the others.

Aiden's knee ached against the rocky creek bed. He had injured it in a chase six months earlier and it refused to completely heal. Maybe if he took some time off it might get better, but hunting rogues for the

WereHouse was a time-consuming job. His calf muscle cramped from the uneven terrain. The frigid bite of the water made him reconsider his choice of profession. But he didn't waver. He was a good hunter.

The clouds parted, briefly revealing a half-moon, and then hid it again. The rain was relentless. Talik shivered.

As he waited, his heart raced, as it always did when a fight was approaching. He had hunted enough rogues with his crew to have a sense of their timing. He shifted his weight from his aching knee, his weapon still trained on the distant bridge. Most rogues wouldn't make the first move unless they were starving. If this one was indeed waiting in the shadows, it was following suit.

And then a flare rocketed toward the bridge from the trees on the opposite side. The flare struck the stone like a missile and exploded into white sparks that fell on the water.

"Here we go," Talik whispered.

The rogue werg bounded from its hideout, heading straight for Aiden. Aiden flicked on his flashlight and squeezed the trigger of his weapon. Jeffrey did the same.

The werg flailed under the hail of bullets, appearing to dance as chunks of flesh ripped from his body. He howled in pain, dropped to all fours, and charged. Talik's weapon clicked. He dropped his flashlight and grabbed a fresh magazine from his belt. The werg closed in, its flesh rippling and tearing away with each accurate shot from Jeffrey until he too needed to reload.

The werg was within twenty feet and coming fast. Talik slammed the new magazine into his weapon.

Fifteen feet.

Jeffrey tossed his assault rifle into the creek and drew a pistol.

Ten feet.

Talik yanked the AK's slide back.

Five feet.

Jeffrey squeezed off his first shot from the pistol.

The werg dove at him. Talik fell to the side, his weapon trained. He couldn't fire for risk of hitting his partner and had to trust in his friend's skill. Jeffrey scrambled from the werg's path.

The wounded and bloody creature slammed its open hand against Jeffrey's chest, sending the hunter to the creek bed. Talik opened fire again as the quick werg disappeared past the tree line.

"Jeff, are you solid?" Aiden shouted.

"Yeah. Just need to catch my breath."

"All right. Wait for Greg. Tell him to pick up our trail."

"You're going without us?"

Aiden glared back. "What do you think? We can't let it get too far."

Jeffrey grunted as he tried to stand. "Hold up. I'm coming."

Aiden was already in a full sprint in pursuit of his prey.

In his haste to escape, the werg left a path of broken branches along the way. Aiden was a skilled hunter and the werg was wounded enough that he could track the creature in a monsoon. It was just like hunting deer. When the creature's adrenaline wore off, his wounds would slow him, and the effects of the silver would take hold. And that's when Talik would find him.

The trail of broken branches led to a small clearing. The werewolf staggered to a tree at the edge of the clearing and sat against it. He licked his many wounds. When Aiden approached, the werg's ears perked and the creature struggled to his feet.

Aiden aimed his weapon. Silver to the heart was the best way to kill them. He cracked his neck before settling his eye on the site. "Come on, you beast," he whispered. When they charged, they were most exposed. But instead of charging, the creature lifted his eyes. What could only be described as sadness seemed to fill them. Aiden felt a tug in his gut.

And then the werg came at him. Aiden steadied his aim. The werg closed in. Aiden waited for his shot, and when the werg's chest was exposed, he squeezed the trigger. The silver round slammed square into the werg's chest. The creature wailed and kept coming. Aiden aimed again, but the werg was upon him and swatted the weapon away. Aiden pulled out a silver-bladed knife. It was about to get messy.

The werg lunged for his throat with its deadly fangs. Aiden pulled back and jammed the blade upward below the werg's sternum, beneath his ribs, and hopefully into his heart. The werewolf froze with fatal realization as the two slammed the ground.

Aiden scrambled from beneath the limp beast and retrieved his weapon. He stood over his prey and welcomed the cold, cleansing rain, hoping it would wash away the nastiness he had just committed. He must have watched the dying beast for five minutes or more before Greg and Jeffrey caught up to him.

"Aiden, you okay?" Jeffrey asked.

Aiden grunted. "Do what you need to do." Without looking at them, he headed back to the truck. Once there, he stripped down to his boxers and tossed his drenched clothing into the truck bed. Inside the cab, he pulled a towel and a fresh set of clothes from his duffle bag. As he dried off, he noticed blood still on his wrist. It wasn't his. He eyed at it for several minutes. The thrill of the hunt had left him some time ago and now he felt sick to his stomach. Killing creatures in cold blood was no way to live.

He grabbed his towel and scrubbed his forearm raw. No matter how hard he scrubbed, he couldn't shake the sick feeling. His days of killing were numbered.

He slipped into his dry clothes and watched the falling rain through the windshield. He was alone like he had always been, and he suddenly felt like crying. Though his lower lip trembled, he held back tears, knowing how his team would respond to them.

Soon, his men emerged from the forest dragging the werg carcass. Aiden gathered his composure and joined them outside. So much for dry clothes. Together, they heaved the dead werg into the truck bed and covered it with a tarp.

"Good job, Talik," Greg said as he hopped into the driver's seat.

Aiden settled into the passenger seat and glowered through the windshield. "Just another day's work," he said.

He was starting to hate his life.

NEVETS
PART 2

9

Steven woke with a jolt. His ears rang relentlessly. He sat up and looked around, momentarily forgetting what had happened to him. That was until he moved and felt tearing pain in his shoulder. He winced.

He looked around. He was in a horse stall of some sort with dirt floors and a saddle hanging on one of the walls. A pile of hay sat in the far corner. He reached for the wall to pull himself to his feet, but his shoulder and chest screamed for him to stop.

He was wearing cut-off sweatpants that weren't his and an equally unfamiliar sweatshirt. The front was covered in dried blood. Something crawled on his injured shoulder. He pulled the sweatshirt away enough to see maggots wriggling across bloody sutures.

His head throbbed and he longed for a shot of whiskey. His stomach twisted with the same idea. He shivered. His breath misted in the air. He tried to move. Thousands of needles poked and prodded beneath his skin from his head to his toes, as if his whole body had fallen asleep. A terrible itch grew along the left side of his chest, and then another one on his neck. He dug incessantly, unable to battle the urge. His skin grew red and raw beneath his nails. As he scratched, the fingernail of his middle finger peeled back and ripped away. He stopped scratching and examined the oozing, throbbing nailbed. His pinky swelled before his eyes and that nail fell off as well.

His eyes were blurry and rapidly getting worse. He tried closing them, taking a deep breath, and praying he was dreaming. Any chances of that went away with the next wave of crushing pain in his chest. What was happening to him? When he opened his eyes again, the world looked different. The color was gone, leaving only black and white with a greenish tint. It was like looking through night-vision goggles.

He tried to stand again, but his ribcage tightened and squeezed his chest like someone had sat on him. He backed against the stable wall.

The smell of a skunk caught his attention, and it was stronger than any skunk he had ever smelled. Holding his chest, he fell to the ground. He couldn't breathe without excruciating pain. Was he having a heart attack? He tried to scream but howled like a dog instead.

What is happening to me?

Pain shot from his chest into his teeth, through his eyes, and deep into his brain. He rolled to his side. Something came loose and his chest popped and ripped beneath his flesh. It felt like something foreign grew where his heart should have been. In agony, he clawed at the ground with impotent, nail-less fingers until blobs of blood speckled the dirt. His gut hurt like he had swallowed lava. He curled into a ball. *Please, God, stop the pain.*

As he lay dying on some cold stable floor, he thought back to how he had gotten there and couldn't find the memory. He writhed on the ground with another brutal seize of his chest. His heart let loose with one final jolt of indescribable pain before the black and white and green world faded again. He was glad to sink into darkness.

Christine's doctor had requested she take a few more shifts off work until she could get in to have the stitches in her thigh removed. She was going stir crazy sitting around her condo. A morning jog felt like it might do her some good.

Before she dressed for the day, she sat on the edge of the bathtub and peeled the dressing from her leg for a peek at the progress. The wound was due for a cleaning anyway. To her surprise, her laceration was closed, a bulging purple scar under the stitches. But that was impossible. It had only been a few days. She retrieved a pair of scissors from a drawer and started picking and cutting at the stitches. Once they were out, she traced the scar from one end to the other with her finger. It felt solid and tight. It didn't make any sense. She gazed at it for an eternity.

Despite the wound's mostly healed appearance, she covered it with Neosporin and a fresh dressing. Then she put on some sweatpants and a sweatshirt. After slipping on a pair of running shoes, she went to the front porch for a stretch. With her tight hamstrings loosened, she started for the road, quickly picking up her pace.

Three miles in and she was hardly winded. It was shocking because she hadn't done three miles in a few years and never as fast as she had just done. She felt like a twenty-year-old again, ready for another five miles. But she didn't want to push it. She returned to her porch.

Her stomach grumbled, reminding her she hadn't eaten since the night before. Though she seldom ate meat, she had the strangest craving for a fast-food hamburger, the greasier the better. She imagined hamburger grease running down her chin, which would have normally made her gag. Nothing short of McDonalds would suffice.

Without a shower or even a change of clothes, she grabbed her keys from inside, hopped in her car, and sped to the closest McDonalds. After downing two double cheeseburgers on the ride home, she felt slightly ashamed at herself for craving a third. It had been a long time since she had eaten even a single fast-food burger, let alone two at one sitting. She wondered if she could be having pregnancy cravings, but a quick assessment of the state of her love life assured her that was impossible.

She was getting out of her car when a twinge in her chest doubled her over. She pressed one hand to her sternum and the other against the pavement. Her first thought was a heart attack, but she dismissed it right away. Though the junk she had just scarfed down was artery-clogging crap, it didn't happen that quickly. Maybe a couple of Tums was all she needed.

She straightened and started for the porch. She was halfway there when a second, more crippling, pain grabbed her chest and dropped her to her knees again. Whereas the first twinge of pain had come and gone in a moment, this second one hit her with wave after paralyzing wave.

This was more than indigestion. She'd helped enough people having heart attacks to know she could be in serious trouble. She ran through her medic training. Crushing chest pains? Check. Shortness of breath? Check. Following intense exercise? Check, check, and check.

She pictured her cell phone sitting on the center console of her car and realized she was in too much pain to get to it.

And then, as suddenly as the pain had begun, it ceased. Stunned, she sat up and looked around.

Her neighbor from two doors down stepped onto his porch. When he noticed her on her knees, he shouted, "Christine? You all right?"

"I'm fine. Just a little fall." She got up, still rubbing her chest. *Where were you five minutes ago?* She gave a polite wave as she hurried into her condo.

NEVETS
PART 3

11

The maggots were still crawling over his shoulder when Steven woke up again. It was funny how the strangest thoughts went through a person's mind when all hope had been lost. Steven's thoughts drifted to a show he'd once watched about maggots being good for open wounds, and it was that unexpected memory that helped him push away the queasiness.

Lying on his dirt bed, he looked away from his maggot-infested shoulder to orient himself. The dew on the stable fence said it was morning. A slight breeze pushed a chill along his spine. He saw his breath. The pain that had gripped his chest on the day before was now gone. He sat up.

Other than a bird singing somewhere outside, the morning was quiet and almost peaceful, like waking up in an out-of-the-way cabin on a weekend getaway. But this was anything but a vacation. He wondered if he was in purgatory on the verge of heaven, and for a split second he was hopeful his wife might be there. But then the familiar stench of manure brought him back to reality. He wasn't in heaven. Maybe he was in hell, the victim of sick torture. He imagined the evil men who had brought him there were watching through some closed-circuit video camera and laughing as he realized how beautiful the world could be right before they fed him to their pet once again. He extended his middle finger toward whatever invisible puppet master might be watching. Maybe it was that Mr. Henderson prick.

As they had each day since his abduction, two guards soon entered and gave him a shot in his arm. This time Steven had enough strength to ask, "What are you giving me?"

The man on his left answered, "Just something to stunt your growth a bit." The fluid from the syringe burned in his veins and continued to burn for at least an hour after they left. He thought about his wife again. Though he had thought of her hundreds of times, maybe thousands, over the years, he was saddened that it was getting more difficult to picture her face. While he could still see a trace of it in his mind's eye, it was fleeting, and he tried desperately to recapture it. He feared he would soon lose it altogether. That thought was worse than any physical pain his captors could inflict.

Then he heard something terrifying over the relentless ringing in his ears. It was the howl of a wolf, only he knew it was no ordinary wolf.

As he sat on the dirt floor searching for some sign of hope, a low, staticky buzz filled his head. His thoughts grew fuzzy.

His lips stung like they had split and his mouth felt as dry as if he'd sucked on cotton. Then he noticed a horse trough less than ten feet away. Self-doubt told him the trough would be empty. Or full of piss. But he had to try to reach it or else he'd die of dehydration.

He crawled weakly toward it. His body felt like he'd been through a meat grinder. Every inch forward was a victory and he convinced himself the trough was his salvation. Eventually, he touched the base. Then he grasped the rim with one hand. Using all his strength, he pulled himself up. By some undeserved miracle, the trough was full. Though a thin green film coated the water, he didn't care. He shoved his head in and gulped the water into his desert of a mouth. It was warm and stale and wonderful.

With his thirst momentarily quenched, he flopped to his rear with his back against the trough.

That's when the padlocked gate on the other side of the stall jingled and then flew open. It was the first time he had been visited twice in the same day and it couldn't be good.

Two men wearing flak jackets over old-fashioned, Viet Nam era army fatigues, gloves, and helmets dragged some kind of limp carcass into his stable.

One of the men shouted, "Eat up," before they both backed out.

Flies swarmed what appeared to be the hindquarters of a cow. It was raw and bloody. *Do they think I'm an animal?* Steven wondered. *I'll starve before I'll eat a piece of that.*

Christine's stomach twisted with the same jitters as her very first day on the job. Yesterday's pain in her chest was still fresh in her mind and she worried she should have gone to the hospital. As a medic, she would have told a patient with similar complaints that they should go to the hospital, but she hadn't heeded her own advice. Knowing time is muscle when it comes to the heart, she hoped it hadn't been a mistake.

As she pulled into the parking lot of Station 22, her concerns over her chest pain faded to worries of how she would be accepted by her crew. She had never been injured on the job and didn't know how the others would react. Being a woman on a male-dominated fire department meant it was especially important to not show any weaknesses. At least, that's how she had always attacked the job, and she didn't plan to let up anytime soon.

Though the doctor had given her two more duty shifts off, she wanted to get this moment over with and return to some sort of normalcy.

Pulling into the parking lot was the first step. She sat in her car for another fifteen minutes before finding the courage to continue into the building. As with every other challenge in her life, she found that courage, took a deep breath, and strolled into the open truck bay as if nothing had happened. She put on a confident front even as her insides were a tangled mess.

A few of the guys from the off-going unit stood around the station truck, jabbering about their busy night. She walked past them as if it was just another workday, hoping to avoid their attention. One of the guys, Brett, made eye contact and nodded before rejoining his conversation. The bay where the medic truck usually sat was empty, meaning it was out on a call.

Christine went to the small office where Willie, Jed, and Mick were gathered.

Willie was the first to see her coming. He smiled. "What's up, corndog?" he said in his usual Willie way.

She nodded. Though she had called Alex every day since the accident and she already knew the answer to her next question, she asked anyway. "Any word on Billy?"

They bowed their heads.

Mick answered solemnly, "Not yet."

To break the ominous silence, Jed changed the subject. "Why you back already?" he asked.

"Doc says I'm healing faster than expected." She didn't want to talk about herself.

Jed nodded. "Like Supergirl, huh?"

She shrugged. "I guess."

He squeezed by to get ready for roll call. "It's good to see you again, Chris. I'm glad you're all right."

Alex walked over from the kitchen. "Christine, I didn't know you were coming back today."

"I know, Lieu. I just couldn't sit around my place for another day."

"You look tired."

She scowled. "'You look tired' is a polite way of saying I look like shit, right? I am tired, but I'll be fine."

"You been sleeping?"

"Sure," she lied. "I just need a hot shower, a good breakfast, and for everything to get back to the way it was."

"Well, good luck with that—the breakfast part, I mean. Willie's cooking today."

Willie rolled his eyes.

She smiled. "You guys are too hard on poor Willie. He's a fine cook."

"So, what the hell happened that night?" Mick asked.

"Honestly, I don't remember much. I remember going to the house with Billy, but that's about it. The next thing I remember, I was in the hospital."

"People are saying it was a werepet attack. Was it?"

"I honestly can't remember. The whole incident is one big blur. They say I was attacked by coyotes, and I guess that's as possible as anything else."

Alex patted her shoulder. "Well, we're just glad to have you back."

"Thanks, Lieu."

Working while knowing Billy was still missing was tough. She understood she had to work, that people still needed fires put out and heart attacks dealt with, but part of her believed the fire department should stop functioning until he was found. He was part of their family, after all.

Chuck, the firefighter sent as Billy's temporary replacement, was someone she had worked with a few times over the years. He was an older guy who had been on the job probably longer than Billy had been alive. It wasn't that working with Chuck was a problem, other than writing reports slower than a root canal, but he just wasn't Billy.

It didn't take long to get their first call of the morning. It was to a gated community within the suburb of Bexley. Christine's first indication the call wasn't going to go her way was a "Werepets Within" sign on the wrought-iron gate. Whether it was coyotes that attacked her or not, she had definitely had her fill of the whole werewolf movement.

From the moment they drove through the gate, her head was on a swivel. She locked her eyes on a distant werepet hunched over next to a garage. A woman wearing headphones power walked past as if there wasn't a giant beast lurking a few feet away.

Christine drove the medic forward at a snail's pace past several long driveways. Chuck focused on addresses, calling out each one as the numbers climbed closer to the dispatched address. At the correct one, she stopped.

Something caught her eye out the side window, and she jerked her head around. Her breaths doubled at the sight of a werepet walking toward the rig on his hind legs. Once he got close, he sniffed the door handle.

"Will you look at that?" Chuck said, noticing the creature.

Christine nervously rubbed her face and then jerked her hand away, hoping Chuck didn't notice.

"What's wrong, Chris?" he asked.

Damn. He noticed. "Just a little jumpy, I guess."

The creature paced outside her door.

"I think he likes you." Chuck reached for his door handle.

Christine grabbed his arm. "Maybe we should wait for its owner to come it before we get out."

Chuck cocked his head. "Nonsense. These things are harmless." Then he studied her face briefly before adding, "How 'bout you just stay out here? I'll go inside and see what's going on and let you know if I need anything." He winked.

She appreciated the gesture. "Are you sure?"

"These things aren't for everyone." As he said it, a second werepet appeared on his side of the truck.

She thanked him for understanding. He climbed out with his report tablet in hand, immediately meeting the werepet. Christine cringed. Chuck removed the first-aid kit from the back as the werepet watched him. Christine locked the doors.

The werepet dropped to all fours, arched its back, and stretched as though it had just awakened. It lowered its head next to Chuck's hip like a docile puppy. Chuck scratched behind its ears before heading into the house.

The werg beside her door howled, scaring the shit out of her. The other werg crossed the road in front of the truck. Another creature walked around a house up ahead and made his way toward her.

My God, how many are there?

The third creature approached the passenger side and sniffed the handle like the first one had. Then it gave the truck a nudge. The entire medic truck rocked.

Now, all three of them were pacing around the truck as if drawn to her. Christine wondered if it was the emergency lights, so she turned them off. It didn't do any good. A fourth creature headed toward her from another house. If she'd been nervous before, she was borderline having an anxiety attack now. Her eyes kept darting to the house Chuck had gone into, and she nearly rubbed her cheek raw.

"Come on, Chuck," she whispered. The wergs circled the medic. Another one had come from somewhere and now she counted five. *What do they want?*

One of the creatures, a brownish beast, lifted his leg and pissed on the truck's grill. Another more aggressive werg crowded him, lifted his own leg, and claimed the medic as his own. That caused the brownish one to bare his teeth. The two wergs circled each other as if ready to fight. She thought they weren't supposed to be aggressive. She grabbed the radio mic, debating whether she should call for help or if she was overreacting.

Then she lowered the mic and bit her lip. *Come on, Chuck.*

A werg rounded the side of the truck and moved to her door. He stood up tall and grabbed the door handle, wriggling it in the same way a human would.

That was the last straw. Christine blared the air horn, immediately scattering the creatures like roaches when the lights came on.

Chuck raced from the house, report pad in hand. "Christine? Are you all right?" he shouted.

With nearly the entire neighborhood now on their porches and the wergs gone, Christine lowered the passenger window. "Do you need anything?" she shouted.

He shook his head. "Almost finished. We're not going to the hospital, so let me get a few signatures and I'll be right out."

She gave him a thumbs up. He went back into the house. Someone knocked on her window and she almost went through the roof.

"Ma'am?" the stranger outside called. Seeing how he had startled her, he added, "I'm sorry. I didn't mean to scare you."

She lowered her window and smiled, relieved that he was a human. "That's all right. I've been a little jumpy lately."

He said, "I wanted to apologize if Boone was bothering you. I saw all the wergs surrounding your truck for some reason. By the time I got my shoes on to come and get him, you'd honked your horn."

"That's okay," she lied. "Do they always act like that?"

"No, actually. It's strange. Boone has never acted like that before. In fact, I've never seen any wergs act so aggressively, especially none of the neighborhood ones. Hell, Boone is still acting funny in the house. I had to put him away because he kept trying to come back out. He isn't listening very well, all of a sudden."

"What do you mean, put him away? He opens doors, doesn't he?"

"Yeah. We had a room built without knobs on the inside so we could keep him in while we were out. Mostly, the neighborhood wergs have free rein inside the gates, though."

"Well, you really should keep them away from strangers. Not everyone likes them like you do."

"Point taken, ma'am. My apologies." He bowed his head, wished her well, and headed back to his house.

Chuck returned a few minutes later. "What happened out here?" he asked as he climbed in.

"It was nothing. I was just getting impatient."

As the neighborhood filled her rearview mirror, she hoped to never have a call there again.

A rush of cold water woke Steven with a start. "Wake up, animal," one of his captors shouted.

The radio static in Steven's head was more intense than before. He blinked and shook his head until the world, though still black and white and green, came into focus.

"Are you awake?" the guard asked.

Steven nodded but didn't look up.

The guard slammed a baton against Steven's mid-back, and Steven yelped. "Look at me when I speak to you."

Steven's fingers went numb as needles ran down his arm. He squeezed his fist to get the blood flowing again.

The guard snapped, "Down on your belly, dog."

What the hell?

The man hit him with his weapon again. Steven's ribs cried out in pain.

"Down," the man shouted again.

This time, Steven dropped to his belly.

"Good boy," the man said.

Steven looked up, locking eyes with his tormentor. That drew another blow, this one to his lower back.

The guard shouted, "Don't look me in the eye, dog." As Steven writhed on the ground, the guard continued shouting. "You aren't a man anymore. You're nothing more than a filthy dog, and we are your masters."

As if on cue, another man entered stable. Steven didn't want another beating. He directed his eyes to the ground as ordered. But not before he was able to catch a peek at the approaching guard.

The man held a long pole and wore a blue handkerchief across his mouth and nose like a bandit. "Is he ready?" he asked.

The first guard answered, "He's ready."

"Walk," the man with the long pole ordered.

Steven slowly pushed to his feet. The man shoved the pole against Steven's right flank, and an ungodly jolt shot through his entire body. Steven hit the dirt with a thud.

The man shouted, "That's not how you walk, dog. On your hands and knees." He leaned over to the other guard and whispered, "I thought you said he was ready."

The guard answered, "Sorry, sir," and then kicked Steven in the ribs. While Steven tried to catch his breath, the guard hooked a leather strap to the chain collar around Steven's neck.

Steven's blood boiled. The soldier in him had had enough and couldn't hold his tongue. "What the f—"

Before he finished, the chain around his neck jerked tight, yanking his head to the side. He grabbed at the collar as he fell to the dirt again. Before he could recover, the bastard tugged upward, sending a second rush of stabbing pain through Steven's body. Steven pushed to his hands and knees.

The guard snapped, "Heel," and started marching toward the gate. Fearing another pummeling, Steven stayed next to him, the rough ground torture on his old knees. Once outside, the guard led Steven in sharp figure eights while Steven tried desperately to keep up.

Their "training" continued for several painful hours. By the time they were finished, Steven's knees and palms were bloody and raw. The chain around his neck had dug into his flesh. He lay on his side inside his stable pen, exhausted and licking his wounds until he fell asleep.

14

Steven's stomach groaned, waking him to another sunrise. Though there was frost on the ground, it didn't feel as cold as it had been. He hadn't eaten in several days and the trough water had given him the shits before they changed it out. At least his "trainers," as they called themselves, had shoveled out his stall that evening. His thoughts were fuzzier this morning and he struggled to remember why he was there.

His stomach repeatedly sent his eyes to the decaying cow carcass on the opposite side of his prison stall. Though it stank something fierce, he desperately craved a bite. He knew better, but for some reason it was harder to resist this morning.

Today was the first day he wasn't met with a shot from his trainers when he woke up. A glance down showed him his hands were swollen with coarse, dark-gray fur covering his skin. Black, razor-sharp nails had poked from his fingertips sometime during the two hours he was able to sleep.

Despite not getting his shot, he knew from the previous three days that sunrise meant his trainers would soon arrive. When they did, he was determined to pay better attention to what they ordered. The tiny reminder burns from their cattle prods guaranteed as much.

His eyes went to the decaying carcass again and he seriously considered tasting it. He caught himself licking his lips. *Maybe just a little,* he thought. But before he could do something his stomach would surely regret, he heard approaching footsteps and the stable gate swung open. He caught the familiar scent of his trainers and scurried to his hands and knees as he had been trained.

"Come 'ere," the trainer with a cattle prod snapped. Though the previous days were running together in his increasingly fuzzy brain, something told him this trainer was the meaner of the two. Steven crawled to him.

The trainer smiled and said to his partner, "See, Cliff? He's ready." Cliff smelled like Axe Body Spray.

"I don't know, Ray. There's something about his eyes that are different than the others."

"Pffff." Ray rolled his eyes. "You're too soft." He latched a leash to Steven's collar and led him in tight figure eights around the pen before stopping. Steven immediately sat at Ray's hip, unsure how he knew that was what he was supposed to do but unable to fight the urge.

Ray gave Cliff a look. "See? I told ya. He's ready. He'll be fine."

Cliff scratched behind Steven's ear. Steven would be embarrassed to admit that it felt amazing.

"Hey buddy," Cliff said. "You have a big day today."

Ray winced. "I'm afraid it's not gonna be a good one."

"Why do you do that?" Cliff asked.

"What?"

"Be mean to them?"

"They don't know any better. You know they don't have any conscious thought left by this point."

But what he said didn't make sense because Steven understood him. Though he couldn't find the thoughts that allowed him to argue or even move without their orders, he knew something was wrong with how they treated him. He sensed he needed to do something different than what he was doing, but for some reason there was a wall in his brain preventing him from doing so.

Cliff stopped scratching behind Steven's ear and answered, "Well, it helps me sleep at night. What if they do have some conscious thought left?"

"Impossible."

"Even so, if there's even the smallest chance, shouldn't we take it easy on him today? You know, with what they're about to do and all?"

"I couldn't care less about him. Better him than me. You keep that hippy attitude and you might find yourself heeling right next to him." Ray was smiling like he enjoyed being a prick. He snapped the leash and barked, "Heel."

Steven and Cliff followed him from the stall to a building behind the stables. They entered and continued down a long hallway toward a single steel door.

As they approached, the door opened and two other trainers escorted a werg out. The werg was upright on his hind legs with his head bowed below his shoulders and his ears pinned back. He didn't look up when Steven passed, though he sniffed the air slightly. Steven wanted to watch him leave, but knew enough to keep his eyes forward.

Once the other werg passed, Steven's trainers led Steven into the room. The door slammed shut behind them. Steven looked around. The block walls were cold and pale. Three stainless steel tables sat spaced apart in the center of the room. Several men dressed like janitors and wearing respirators, aprons, and oversized rubber gloves cleaned blood from one of them. The pungent stench of bleach nearly gagged Steven.

"Stay," Ray ordered. He dropped the leash and walked to a man holding an assault rifle.

While they had a discussion, Steven watched the janitors finish scrubbing the table. Once they were done, the table glistened in the overhead florescent lighting. One of the lights flickered and buzzed. The janitors began mopping the concrete floor, swooshing the dirty water into a drain. Steven caught a whiff of blood over the bleach.

Ray returned. "Take him to the center one," he said to Cliff. Cliff retrieved Steven's leash and tugged him forward. A stainless steel tray beside the table held medical instruments like forceps, syringes, scalpels, and clamps.

"Up," Cliff snapped with a slight upward tug of the leash. Steven leaped onto the table with surprising ease. Then Cliff whispered, "Be strong, boy," and stepped back.

Ray marched over and grabbed the leash. He rolled his eyes at Cliff as he passed. "Down," he ordered as he jerked the leash toward the tabletop. Steven lowered his chest, which had just started aching again, to the metal surface. He considered using his new sharp nails on Ray, but thought better of it.

Ray and Cliff fed leather straps through holes along the edges of the table and loosely wrapped them around Steven's wrists and ankles. Steven easily wiggled one of his hands free.

Ray jammed him in the side with the blunt end of the cattle prod. "No," he snapped. Then he guided Steven's hand back into the restraint.

Cliff cocked his head and paused. "Hey, Ray. I can't believe he just did that. They don't usually pull their hands out. You think he's not rea—"

"Shut up. Of course he's ready."

The door swung open, and a new scent entered. Steven turned his head toward it, pressing his opposite cheek against the table. A man wearing surgeon scrubs and a surgical mask entered.

"Is he ready?" the man asked.

Ray and Cliff circled the table to meet him. Ray answered, "His brain is as docile and primitive as a dog's, Doctor Sanchez."

Cliff side-eyed him.

The doctor stretched medical gloves over his hands and continued to Steven's side. "Good. Let's proceed." Ray and Cliff followed.

The ache in Steven's chest grew worse and he squirmed slightly.

Ray jerked his collar. "Be still, dog."

Doctor Sanchez looked over the rim of his glasses.

Ray gave a nervous smile. "He's ready, Doc. Trust me."

Steven concentrated on not moving despite the pain.

Doctor Sanchez lifted a syringe from the tray. He jammed the needle into Steven's arm and ice-cold fluid raced through Steven's veins. Steven shivered. Within seconds of the shot, the skin of his face tightened and a sudden ache rushed deep into his brain. He moaned.

Doctor Sanchez leaned in with a scalpel.

Steven's eyes went wide.

"Turn his head," Doctor Sanchez ordered.

Ray grabbed both sides of Steven's head and forcibly turned it until Steven's face rested in a hole in the table. Terrified, he stared at the floor.

Ray draped a leather strap across the back of Steven's head and cinched it down.

The first slice to the back of Steven's neck was excruciating. He tried to squirm, but the strap held firm. The next slice made him roar like an animal.

Doctor Sanchez cut and prodded and tore at Steven's neck. Then he stuffed something foreign into the hole he had created. He strained as he worked the wound. The agony seemed never-ending until Doctor Sanchez removed his hands. He was breathing heavily and Steven smelled sweat. Doctor Sanchez retrieved another tool and stapled the wound closed with seven painful clicks.

He leaned in and whispered, "It's time. Change for me, dog. Release your inner beast."

Steven strained against the leather strap and turned his head so he could see the doctor again. When their eyes met, he growled, "Nooo."

Doctor Sanchez's eyes widened. Steven strained harder against the strap.

Ray grabbed it with both hands and yanked his head back to the table.

"You said he was ready," Doctor Sanchez shouted.

"I-I-I thought he was," Ray answered. "He obeyed everything. Hell, he even had the paw-like feet when he woke up this morning. They're always ready by that point. Tell 'em, Cliff."

Cliff didn't answer.

A red haze crept into Steven's vision. His face went numb. He fought the urge to howl in pain, but he couldn't stop himself. Something in his nose broke loose with a bone-cracking snap. Blood splattered the table. He pushed against the strap and this time Ray couldn't hold his head down.

Ray backed away.

Steven's nose and mouth stretched outward from his face.

More guards carrying assault rifles poured into the room.

"What should we do?" Ray screamed as he backed away.

Doctor Sanchez stepped back. "There's nothing we can do now, you fool." Then he faced Steven as Steven turned to his side, the loose straps around his wrists and ankles tightening as his muscles swelled. "Gooood. Change for me, dog."

Steven tried to fight it, but he could only roar as the change took hold. The guards surrounded the table.

"Should we kill him, sir?" one of them asked.

"No," Doctor Sanchez screamed. "We need him to change and that's what he's doing."

Steven's bones cracked and shifted. The fuzz in his head pushed out any rational thought he had left. He roared again.

Ray yanked Steven's leash, snapping his attention away from the guns trained on him. Cliff rushed in with Ray's cattle prod and sent fire up Steven's back.

Steven swatted him away, knocking him hard to the floor. Then he strained and pushed against the table, lifting his deforming chest from the steel. Steven wanted blood. Instead, he tasted more lightning from another prod.

Doctor Sanchez shouted, "He's magnificent. He will make a fine pet, but you'll have to break him again."

One of the guards asked, "Are you ready to tranq him, sir?"

Steven strained against his restraints. His fur-covered chest jutted outward.

"Not until his change is complete. The chip won't work if you do it too soon."

The guards watched nervously as Steven thrashed and his body twisted and popped. The change took a toll until his straining against the straps weakened and the desire to fight waned. The doctor crowed in pleasure as Steven slowly relaxed on the table. He panted relentlessly.

Doctor Sanchez moved closer with a wide grin. "Very good." He gently touched Steven's shoulder, and Steven no longer wanted to bite off his hand. Doctor Sanchez scanned Steven's neck with some sort of handheld electronic device. Then he turned to Ray. "The chip is activated. You can put him to sleep now." He walked away. Then he turned back and pulled his surgical mask from his face, wadded it into a ball, and discarded it into a biohazard container. "Oh yeah. Take those staples out after you re-tame him. You'll be hearing from Mr. Henderson about your failure here today." He stormed from the room.

A tranquilized dart slammed into Steven's neck. As his eyes grew heavy, Cliff approached carrying a canine surgical cone. He whispered, "This is to remind you not to scratch your surgical site."

Behind him, Ray snapped the cattle prod in the air. "And this is to remind you not to remove the cone."

One of the guards wheeled in a gurney. That was the last Steven saw.

When he woke up again, he was back in his stall. The rotting cow carcass was still there, and he was still painfully hungry. He crawled over and devoured it to the bone while navigating around his surgical cone. When he finished, he curled into a ball. The back of his neck ached, but he couldn't remember why. With his stomach full for the first time in days, he fell asleep again.

CHANGES

15

It had been a slow second shift back at the firehouse for Christine, and she was starting to feel like she was getting back on track. Though she thought about Billy every time she saw his gear sitting on the rack or passed his bunk, this was the first day she was able to put him out of her mind long enough during emergency calls to be halfway proficient.

The other guys recognized her lack of focus, but nobody mentioned it. They quietly picked up her slack.

After dinner, Alex joined her in the watch booth and closed the door.

"What's up, Lieu?" she asked.

"How are you doing?"

He had always been a good lieutenant. Christine considered confiding in him how hard it was with Billy missing. Or how she'd been having chest pains, which had happened twice more since her first episode. She even wanted to tell him how some of her toenails had fallen off and how unquenchable her hunger had been since her attack. He'd be shocked to hear she'd been eating meat, let alone how many steaks she'd devoured since her hospital stay. As she opened her mouth to say something, she decided not to burden him with her problems. They were all worried about Billy and he didn't need her stating the obvious. She nodded and said, "It's been good being back."

"I'm glad to hear it. If you need any more time off or anything, let me know. We'll work something out."

"Sure, Lieu. I'll be fine. I think I'm going to get a shower and turn in early tonight."

"Sounds good. Hopefully, we'll have a quiet night and you can get some rest."

"You can say that again."

Christine excused herself from the watch booth and went to her locker. She gathered her towels, shampoo, and a fresh uniform before heading to the women's shower on the opposite side of the station. It was little more than an old closet converted into a bathroom way back when women started joining the fire department and the city realized they needed their own areas. As such, it wasn't the ideal setup. Just getting the temperature of the water right was tricky. The hot water knob was cracked and had a leak at the handle which spewed scalding water over it, making it nearly impossible to adjust. She had to turn it and hope she got it right. That wasn't as dangerous as turning it off, though. That was a game of roulette to keep from getting burned.

She showered fast, the threat of an emergency call never far from her thoughts. While lathering her hair, she glanced at the tile floor. As the water ran down her face and poured from her chin, the white suds of her shampoo mixed with a hint of red. She paused, her hands still buried in her lathered hair. It was blood. She messaged her head and felt something sharp in her hair. She pulled it free. It was a fingernail. She turned her hand over to find her nailbeds were bloody and missing the nails.

She dropped the nail and staggered. A fresh wave of pain seized her chest. Her back slid along the tile until she nearly tumbled through the opening. She slipped and caught the curtain, slowing her fall until the metal hooks ripped free and her hip struck the floor.

As she lay naked and cold, her right hand jerked sideways and then twisted and deformed before her eyes. Black, pointed claws slid out of her nailbeds. A patch of coarse black hair sprouted from the top of her hand. The muscles in her face twitched and ached.

She pushed to her feet, wrapped herself in a towel, and staggered to the door. She cracked it open and looked into the bay. No one was there, probably in the TV room or the kitchen. "Guys?" she shouted weakly.

Next to the women's bathroom was a weight room where there was a phone she could use to call Alex on the PA and get help. Her shoulder blades jerked and popped, throwing her to her knees. She crawled to the exercise room and practically fell through the door before it swung closed behind her. She used the bench press machine to pull herself to her feet.

She grabbed the phone and saw her left hand. It was also covered in fur and strangely elongated with sharp black nails fully extended. Using her knuckle, she pressed the intercom button and then collapsed to her rear with the receiver dangling beside her.

"Alex," she shouted over the PA. "I need to call off." The word "off" came out as a growl.

Then she released an uncontrollable howl that echoed through the firehouse.

She heard Alex shout for her from the bay.

A low snarl lifted from her gut. She muffled it with her hands and fell to her side.

Christine?" Alex shouted, this time just outside the door.

Christine's leg jutted and twisted and then snapped at the femur. The pain was ungodly. Though she had wanted Alex's help a few seconds before, she didn't want him to see her now. She crawled to the dangling receiver, concentrated, and said, "I'm fine, guys. I just need to go home."

The door started to open. She shoved it closed with her foot.

"Chris?" Willie shouted from the bay. "You in there?"

Hair grew over her legs as her foot elongated and dagger-like nails popped her remaining toenails off. She smelled Alex's shaving cream on the other side of the door.

"Chris? Are you in he—"

She cried, "Don't come in, Alex. I'm not dressed."

The pressure eased from the other side of the door. "Are you all right?" he asked.

"Yes," she growled in a strange, deep voice.

"You don't sound all right. Willie, go get a towel."

Christine snapped, "No. You don't understand."

Just then, the overhead loudspeaker blared a fire tone. She had never been so relieved to hear a fire run. *Oh, thank God.*

Alex shouted, "Chris? I gotta take this run, but I can't leave you if you need help."

It took everything she had to answer, "Just go."

"Are you sure?"

"Yes."

The fire engine rumbled to life and then revved as it left the station. Within seconds, the firehouse was empty.

Christine lay in agony as her bones cracked and popped and contorted before her eyes. Her jaw snapped painfully and shifted before pulling away from her face. As she lay on the cold, lonely floor, writhing in pain, the color drained from the world.

And then, as quickly as the torture had begun, the pain subsided. She lay motionless, waiting for the next shoe to drop. But it never did.

Christine gingerly stood up and looked around. She wobbled on what felt like new legs. Everything was black and white and green. When she turned, she bumped her head on the top of the squat rack, which was odd because of how tall it was. She grabbed it to steady herself. Her next breath was a snort.

She suddenly felt strong and stood to her full height, looking down at the tops of the weight machines. An unfamiliar urge filled her. She tilted her head back and released an ear-piercing howl that caused the neighborhood dogs to join in. A mix of rage and power washed over her unlike anything she had ever experienced. She turned to the bench-press machine, grabbed it, and hurled it across the room like it was a toy. It felt weightless.

The distinct distant rumble of Engine 22 broke her out of her rage as they returned from a likely false alarm. She started for the door and caught her reflection in the window. The face of a wolf stared back. She reached up and felt her snout. *No, no, no. How could this be?* She tried to speak but only a growl escaped. As she gazed slack-jawed at her reflection, she saw the engine approaching. She needed to get away before they saw what she had become.

She exploded through the door and into the empty bay as the rear overhead door started to rise. With nowhere else to go, she returned to the weight room. The engine pulled through the bay and squeaked to a stop.

"Christine?" Alex shouted as he bounced out.

There was nowhere else to go. She could hear his footsteps approaching. She glanced at the door as it started to swing open. She had no other choice. She lowered her head, closed her eyes, and blasted through the window, sending glass everywhere.

Alex shouted her name. She never looked back.

After a full day of training, Ray told Cliff, "This time I'm positive he's ready."

Cliff didn't look so sure.

Ray ordered Steven to lower his head and Steven did as commanded. He took off the cone and used pliers to remove the staples from Steven's neck. "Now, that healed up nicely." He rubbed Steven's head. "Today's your day, big fella." He led Steven from the pen toward the entrance of the stables where a six-foot-tall crate stood with one side opened. It was surrounded by guards and a man in a suit. Once they reached the crate, Ray said, "Sit," and Steven sat.

The man in the suit examined Steven from head to toe as he circled him. He smelled of expensive cologne. He lifted one of Steven's hands and studied it, turning it palm up and really giving the claws a once-over. "He sure is a big one, ain't he?"

Ray answered, "Yeah, he's been a real pain in my ass, Mr. Henderson."

Steven's ears perked at the name, though he didn't know why.

Ray continued, "This bastard didn't listen worth shit for a while." He patted Steven's shoulder like they were old friends. "But you figured it out, didn't ya, boy? You be good where you're going."

Mr. Henderson lowered Steven's hand and stepped backward. "Go ahead and get him in there."

Ray tugged Steven toward the crate. Steven lowered his head and stepped inside. It was a tight fit. Ray unhooked the leash from his collar and stepped aside.

Everything went black as the others lifted the lid of the crate and sealed it with nails.

A forklift revved to life and slid the forks beneath the crate. The crate wobbled as the forklift lifted it into the back of a running pickup truck. Steven smelled diesel. Ray climbed up beside the crate and pounded on the roof of the truck. The truck eased forward.

"I'll be glad to get rid of you," he said over the truck's exhaust.

The crate bounced and bobbed for several hours before it reached its destination. Ray climbed down and met a strange man behind the truck.

The stranger, who smelled of cigar smoke and sweat, said, "Well, let's see 'em. I've been waiting weeks for this." The end of a crowbar wiggled through the top corner of the crate and pried the nails away.

The sun hurt Steven's eyes and he cowered against the back of the crate. The smell of raw meat wafted past his snout.

A little girl whispered, "Come 'ere, boy. It's okay. I won't hurt you."

Steven's eyes adjusted to the brightness. He was on a farm. Though he wanted to stay in the crate, the irresistible aroma of fresh meat drew him gingerly out. He was very hungry. As he peered cautiously from the opening, he caught five distinct scents besides the meat. Two were Ray and the driver. Another was a lavender scent that probably belonged to the little girl holding the meat. She appeared to be eight or nine. The last two scents belonged to her parents, who stood hand in hand. The overweight man held a cigar between his teeth.

Ray led him from the truck bed and stood between him and the family.

Steven rose to his hind legs to stand a head taller than either of the men. The little girl backed up behind her father's leg and peeked around it. Ray reached up and grabbed a handful of Steven's fur at the side of his neck. He yanked Steven down to all fours.

He glanced at the man and woman. "I'm terribly sorry, sir. This one must be a little excited. He'll be fine once he gets settled in. You just need to take charge exactly the way you learned during your pre-ownership classes."

The father stepped forward with his chest puffed out. Steven considered destroying the man's false confidence with a roar, but he resisted the urge. Instead, he sniffed the man's extended hand. He didn't realize he had released a low, guttural growl until Ray crowded between them. Steven sensed his anger.

Then Ray turned to the father with a smile. "I am so sorry, sir."

Steven hunched his shoulders and tucked his ears back.

Ray attempted to smooth things over. "I'll tell you, sir. This is completely unacceptable."

The father answered, "Well, I should think so. Maybe this wasn't such a good purchase after all."

"Oh, sir. Please don't say that. There's no need for that. I'll tell you what. We will get you a brand-new werepet within the week and I am authorized to give you one year of free upkeep for your trouble."

The man turned to his wife and then back to Ray. He dabbed his sweaty forehead with a handkerchief. "Well ... I suppose."

"Very good, sir. This one has been acting a little unusual lately. We will take care of him and get a new model to you ASAP." As Ray once again apologized for Steven's defects with his best positive spin and repeated his promise to send a better replacement within days, the driver grabbed Steven's collar and nudged him backward.

The back of Steven's leg met the open tailgate. "Get in there," the driver snarled. Then he whispered, "You're going to the fighting pits."

Steven stepped back into the bed with little effort. The driver climbed up beside him and directed Steven back into the crate. Then he pushed the lid in place, returning Steven to the darkness.

Ray said to the family, "We'll just grab our hammer and nail up the crate again and be on our way. Trust me, you cannot go wrong with a werepet purchase. This one was just a rare fluke."

The strangest thought filled Steven while he stood in his dark crate listening to Ray's confusing words. He didn't understand the feeling he was having or how to handle it, but it was strong. And it told him to run. He decided to listen.

Steven burst from crate, splintering the wood. The little girl shrieked and retreated toward the house. Her mother followed close behind. Steven looked around, panting with a combination of anger and excitement.

Ray shouted into a handheld radio, "We've got a rogue. Send the experts." He shoved the father behind him and reached for his gun.

Steven leaped from the truck and swatted Ray's chest. Blood sprayed into the air as Ray crumpled to the ground. It was a deep wound. Steven had felt bone. The driver sprinted for the glovebox. The father stumbled backward and lost his footing. He landed on his back, his cigar sending red embers into the air when it struck the ground. Steven pounced and straddled him. The man cried out.

Steven snarled within inches of the man's face. He tilted his head back and howled victoriously. He smelled fresh urine on the man's pants. He felt the urge to kill all of them, but the same nagging voice that had told him to run a minute earlier now told him to let the man flee. He hesitated a second too long.

He heard a pop. A sharp pain exploded in the side of his neck. He tumbled over. The truck driver pointed a pistol at him.

Steven swatted at the new pain in his neck and knocked a small, feathered dart away. The black-and-white-and-green world blurred and swayed. He snorted and lunged at his attacker.

The man shoved the gun between his legs to load a fresh dart. Before he could finish, Steven flung him violently into the bushes lining the driveway. Steven dropped to all fours, staggered, and then galloped toward a distant line of trees.

He was in the forest before anyone could give chase. The last thing he did before the dart's effects completely took hold was find some thick brush to hide within.

17

Steven woke up still in the brush. It was nighttime. He was hungry and scared. He started to reach for a throbbing spot in the back of his neck, but yanked his hand back for fear of another beating. He remembered running from someone, but as he sniffed the air he didn't smell any familiar scents.

He crawled from the brush and stood tall and quiet to listen. First, he only heard a squirrel climbing a tree. And then an owl. He wanted to find the squirrel and relieve the pain in his empty gut, but a loud muffler in the distance grabbed his attention. A wolf howled from the same direction. Steven didn't know if the muffler was coming for him, but he knew he'd be better off putting distance between them.

He dropped to all fours and ran in the opposite direction. The forest soon opened into a parking lot next to a factory of some type. The stink of garbage led him to a Dumpster under a light at the other end of the lot. Maybe he could find something to eat there.

He approached a concrete enclosure with two wooden doors concealing the Dumpster. He pawed at the latch, unsure of how it worked. It seemed so easy, yet his brain couldn't figure it out. He looked around for another way in and settled on climbing over. With an effortless leap, he landed on the top of the wall.

As he started to drop behind the wall, the rear door of the factory opened. Steven hid beside the Dumpster as two men exited the building. He watched between the wooden slats. The men approached, carrying trash bags.

Steven squatted in wait. He should have run when he had the chance. The men reached the wooden doors, complaining and joking and laughing. Something about their "pain-in-the-ass supervisor" forcing them to work overtime.

Steven had the urge to kill them before they could hurt him like all the other men he could remember. They swung the doors open and lifted the flap covering the Dumpster. Steven didn't budge.

After they tossed the last bag in, one of them stepped around to the side to close the flap. He froze, his eyes suddenly like giant orbs. He slowly backed up and held his hands up in front of him. "Eeeeasy, big fella," he said.

Steven rose to his full height and the man's wide eyes followed.

"What's up, Jere—" the other man also froze and his mouth dropped open when he saw Steven.

Steven had no choice now—he'd have to kill them. He couldn't risk being caught and sent back to his angry master. He was preparing to pounce when the nagging voice from before told him to wait.

Jeremy whispered, "Hey there, boy. It's okay. Come on out. We won't hurt you." He made kissing sounds with his lips. Steven considered killing him just for that. Maybe it was the voice in Steven's head, or maybe it was because the two seemed benign in their approach, but Steven had more of an urge to obey them than to maul them.

Jeremy glanced to his friend and said, "You ever seen one that big, Ryan?"

Ryan shook his head. "I ain't never seen one, period. Not in person, anyways."

Jeremy reached into his inside coat pocket and pulled something out. It smelled like beef jerky. He inched forward, hand outstretched.

Steven hesitated and then snatched the jerky and shoved it into his mouth.

Ryan said, "Well, look at you, Jeremy. You're like a regular werg whisperer."

Jeremy shushed him and continued creeping forward.

Instinct told Steven to fight or flee, but the inner voice told him to wait again. He pulled away from Jeremy's touch.

"It's okay, boy. I won't hurt you."

Jeremy turned to Ryan. "Go get my lunch. He's hungry."

Ryan raced to the building and disappeared inside. After a minute or so, he returned with a brown paper bag and a warning. "Sullivan's looking for you," he said.

"Did you tell him where I was?"

"Nah, man. But it's not our lunch break yet."

Jeremy shook his head and looked back to Steven. "I hate nightshift." He opened the bag and removed a plastic baggy that smelled like ham. He took out the sandwich and extended it.

Steven devoured it in one bite.

Jeremy set the lunch bag on the ground. "Was that good, boy?" Steven dropped to all fours and ripped through the bag, scarfing everything inside. While he ate, Jeremy reached over and scratched behind his ears.

Steven didn't react to his touch.

When Jeremy's hand moved over a sore lump on the back of Steven's neck, Steven flinched and growled.

Jeremy yanked his hand back. "What's wrong, boy?" he asked. He reached for the back of Steven's neck again.

Ryan cried, "Are you crazy? What are you doing?"

Jeremy scowled at him. "Shh." He gently touched the lump again. "Are you injured, boy?"

Steven reached back to where Jeremy touched. Though it stung, he picked at it slightly. There was something stuck in his neck.

"What is it, boy?" Jeremy asked and looked closer. "It looks like you had surgery or something."

I brief flash of a doctor cutting him raced through Steven's mind. He pawed at the lump again.

Jeremy said, "We should get you to a vet or something. Hey, Ryan? Who works on these creatures?"

Ryan shrugged.

Steven pushed the lump against Jeremy's hand and picked at it again. Whatever was there didn't belong. Maybe Jeremy could get it out.

"He wants me to help him, Ryan."

"Help him? How?"

"I don't know."

Steven pressed the back of his neck against Jeremy's hand again. Then he picked the lump raw with his nails.

Jeremy looked back. "He's got something stuck in there. It's a lump or something. I think he wants me to dig it out."

Ryan stared at him. "Dig it out? Are you crazy?"

"I don't know. Maybe." He retrieved a pocketknife from his pants pocket.

Ryan gasped. "You're not really going to do this … Are you?"

Jeremy shrugged. "Why not?"

"As soon as you touch him with that knife, he's going to kill you."

"Pfft. If he wanted to kill me, I'd already be dead. Besides, he wants me to."

"You have no idea what he wants."

Jeremy brushed him off with a wave. "There's something back there. Think of it as a splinter. You'd help your dog get rid of a splinter, wouldn't you?"

"That's more than a splinter."

"Relax." Jeremy grinned.

"Maybe it's supposed to be there. You know, like a bone?"

"It's not a bone. Look. He's already exposed it a little. It's black. I don't think it's supposed to be there. Just chill." He opened the knife. "You want me to get this out, boy?"

Though Steven didn't know why or what he wanted out, that nagging voice told him he did. He bowed his head lower.

"See. I'm just going to help him a little."

Ryan gave a nervous half-laugh as though he didn't know how else to react. "You're sick, man. I'm telling you. The second that knife touches his neck, he's gonna rip you to pieces. And don't look for me to help. I'll be too busy running."

Jeremy pressed his lips together and shook his head. "Wuss."

Steven didn't move as Jeremy's blade touched his neck. At first the knife merely stung, but as Jeremy grew more confident the pain increased. Steven fought to control his killing urge. He peered up at the young man whose tongue hung out while he worked.

"Hey, Ryan. There's some kind of computer chip or something in here."

Ryan crept closer, obviously more confident since neither of them were dead yet.

Jeremy muttered, "Wait a minute ... I think ... yeah ... I'm getting it."

The knife felt like a hot poker being crammed into Steven's flesh. Unable to hold still, he turned his head away, but the hot poker pain stayed with him.

Jeremy whispered, "Almost there ... Got it." He held up a bloody object the size of a quarter between his thumb and pointer finger. "It is a chip of some kind."

Steven retreated back against the Dumpster and howled. Something felt instantly different. He staggered and crashed shoulder-first into a pile of broken pallets. Jeremy reached for him, but Steven roared and sent both young men out of the Dumpster enclosure. They stood stunned and watched from outside.

Steven's body cried out in pain as every muscle and bone shifted and cracked. He fell to his side, clawing at the empty boxes and pallets as his bones twisted before his eyes. He tilted his head back and tried to roar, but a human scream filled the darkness instead. He curled into a ball. His legs and arms snapped and deformed with disgusting din. The hair seemed to retract into his follicles. He wailed again as his chest seized and his ribs collapsed.

"Hoooooly shiii …," Jeremy's said, his voice trailing off.

And just as quickly as the pain had started, it ended, replaced by a chill running the length of his body. Steven opened his eyes. The color had returned to the world. He looked at Jeremy and Ryan and they stared back in stunned silence.

Steven tried to remember what had happened but couldn't. The last thing he remembered was some guys in a van. While focusing on his human hands, he whispered, "What am I?"

"I have no idea," Jeremy answered. He removed his jacket and tossed it to Steven, leery of getting too close.

Steven wrapped it around his shoulders. "I'm freezing."

Ryan answered, "Yeah, you're naked, man."

"What happened to me?" Steven asked.

"I don't know," Jeremy said. "One minute you were one of those werepets, and then I cut out a microchip from your neck, and then you were … well, you."

Steven shivered and pulled the coat tight.

Ryan stuttered, "I-I-I thought those werepets were only animals."

"Yeah," Steven said, somewhat baffled himself. "So did I." He groaned and struggled to his feet. The coat hung to his mid-thigh. "Can I borrow this coat?"

Jeremy answered, "It's yours, man."

"You don't have any extra pants, do ya?" Steven asked.

Jeremy shook his head, but Ryan's eyes brightened. "I have some workout shorts in my car."

"Could I borrow them?"

Ryan bobbed his head and raced to his car.

Steven looked around. "Where am I, anyways?"

Jeremy answered, "Brice Street."

"No. I mean what city?"

"Chicago."

Chicago?

Ryan returned with shorts, socks, and tennis shoes. "Here, man. Take 'em."

"Thanks." Steven put them on. He was still cold, but it was better than nothing. "Either of you guys got any cash you could spot me?"

Jeremy and Ryan dug through their wallets and front pockets and handed him a total of seventeen dollars and twenty-eight cents.

"Thanks, guys." Steven grinned and extended his hand. "My name's Steven." They shook hands.

The factory door swung open, and a portly man stepped out. "What the hell are you two doing?" he shouted.

Ryan shouted back, "We'll be right there, Mr. Sullivan." He turned back. "See ya, Steven. Good luck." He and Jeremy hurried to the factory. A pair of wolves howled from the woods.

Steven looked around. *Now how the hell am I getting back to Columbus?*

18

Aiden wasn't accustomed to meeting with Bernard Henderson at the boss's residence, and to be summoned there now told him the gravity of the situation. Mr. Henderson shooed his wife and son into another room before inviting Aiden into his home office.

Aiden broke the silence. "Nice to see you, sir."

"I don't have time for bullshit pleasantries, Aiden. I have pressing matters to attend to that my incompetent staff can't seem to get under control."

"What do you need me to do?"

"What do I need you to do? I need you to kill werewolves. Why else do you think I called you here? Come on, Aiden. Think."

"You're right, sir. I'm sorry."

Mr. Henderson nodded and took a calming breath. "I'm sorry, too, Aiden. I'm just a bit stressed. Have a seat." Aiden sat in a leather recliner. His boss continued, "First, I get word my staff delivered a werg that wasn't fully tamed, which cost us a sale, not to mention a major public relations headache. Then the goddamn beast runs off and disappears. Who the hell knows where he went."

"I'll find him, sir."

"Wait. That's not the problem I called you for. That werg was sold in Chicago. I've got hunters headed there now. I have another pressing issue that is going to require my most loyal soldier. We're getting reports of our products in one area south of the city having some glitches.

"Glitches?"

"Yeah. Tiny bursts of aggression. We don't know why exactly, but we have a couple theories."

"Oh?"

"One theory is they simply need to be recalled for a few days of reeducation."

"You don't sound like you buy that, sir."

"You know me too well. I don't buy it. One, maybe. But several all at once? I don't think so. I think it's more than that—something we've never dealt with before." Mr. Henderson produced a whiskey bottle from behind his desk and offered Aiden a swig. Aiden shook his head. He took one himself and said, "Don't tell the missus I have this in here."

"Of course not, sir."

"Anyway, I read all the reports of abnormal behavior, and though it's very sporadic, it is troubling."

"Are they biting people?"

Mr. Henderson brushed off the question with a wave. "No, no. Nothing like that. What I tell you now, Aiden, goes no farther than this room."

"As always." Aiden leaned forward.

"I think someone has released a female werg into the population."

Aiden almost choked on his own surprise. "What? I mean, how? I didn't realize there were females."

"Well, how the hell do you think they reproduce in the wild?"

"No. Of course I know there *are* female wergs somewhere, I've just never heard of one in the States. You don't sell them, do you?"

"No, we don't sell them. They're too difficult to tame. They are extremely stubborn, and their training doesn't stick without constant work and reeducation. Plus, if I'm correct in my theory, look at what just a female's scent is doing to the males. That would explain why we're having these patches of problem areas."

"If there is a female loose, where'd she come from?"

"I have no idea. It's possible a rival company has found the island and managed to sneak one out from under our noses."

"Do you have any females stateside that may have escaped?"

"No. We keep them on the island to avoid these very problems. We knew they drive the males crazy."

"What do you want me to do?"

"Find her."

"And if I do? I'm not a catcher, you know."

"I know exactly what you are. I want you to kill her on sight."

Aiden nodded.

Mr. Henderson moved closer; Aiden smelled the whiskey heavy on his breath, suggesting that the one swig was far from his boss's first drink of the day.

"I'm serious, Aiden. Kill her on sight. You may only get one chance to find her, and she may be dangerously ferocious."

"I got it. Don't worry. I'll kill her."

"I know you will. You are my best hunter. Take this file and study it. It will tell you all you need to know about female wergs. Their wild temperaments and all the rest."

Aiden looked past him to the whiskey bottle. "I think I'll take one of those drinks now, if it's okay."

Mr. Henderson smirked and passed him the folder and the bottle.

Aiden downed the last of the whiskey.

Aiden, Greg, and Jeffrey considered themselves the "A" team when it came to rogue hunters. Mr. Henderson likely agreed since he called them for every out-of-hand, down and dirty situation he came across.

Since taking Aiden in as a young boy, Mr. Henderson had taught him everything there was to know about killing wergs, and he knew wergs as well as he knew people. Better, actually.

The company GPS had shown a collective spike in the excitement levels of the werepets of Chancellor Drive at the outer edge of the city limits. Aiden and his team were headed there now. As they neared the upscale neighborhood, the anxious howls of werepets told him they were still agitated. If his monitor and his hunches were correct, he might find the female troublemaker before daybreak. Or not. This was his third solid hunch of the evening.

When they turned into the cul-de-sac of Chancellor Drive, Aiden felt increasingly confident his hunch was right this time. There weren't any residents outside in spite of the racket the werepets were making. He found it odd, figuring someone would come out if for no other reason than to tell the creatures to shut the hell up, but no one seemed overly concerned.

Aiden pulled the slide of his 9mm back with a jolt. He hated when rogues stayed near populated areas. "Remember, guys, small arms only. There are too many houses around for the big guns. And watch your crossfire."

Greg shut off the headlights and inched the truck forward into the cul-de-sac. He called headquarters on his cell phone, asked if they were still a go, and then nodded to Aiden.

Aiden opened the passenger door. "All right, boys. Look for anything out of the ordinary. As you can tell by the noise, the neighborhood wergs are keyed up tonight. If she's still here, she'll be nearby."

Jeffrey and Greg started down the sidewalk while Aiden paralleled them on the opposite side.

The door of a three-story mansion on Aiden's right opened. An older man wearing a robe shouted, "Somebody shut those damn mutts up." Apparently, not all the neighbors were as easygoing as Aiden initially believed.

Aiden tucked his weapon under his coat and waved. "We're looking into it, sir."

The older man waved back and slammed his door shut.

Six houses from the truck, the team found what they were looking for—a shattered picture window in the front of a darkened house with no cars in the driveway. It wasn't necessarily the female, but it was a good sign. Aiden waved his team over.

"I'll go in first. Greg, go get the truck and be ready if she runs. Jeffrey, you wait here in the front. If I don't get her, I'll bottleneck her out through that broken window."

Greg nodded and jogged back to the truck.

Aiden glanced at Jeffrey. "This is gonna be delicate. We need to get her fast and then get outta Dodge before some private security rent-a-cop shows up."

Jeffrey stopped at the end of the long driveway while Aiden continued to the porch. Aiden stood beside the door and jiggled the knob. As he expected, it was locked. He stepped back and kicked the door just below the handle. The wooden frame splintered but the lock held. He kicked again, this time smashing the door from the frame. He dove into the entryway and rolled into a squat with his gun trained on the living room.

He couldn't believe his eyes. The first female werg he'd ever seen crouched in the center of the room, seemingly as surprised to see Aiden as he was to see her. The papers in Mr. Henderson's file left little doubt that it was indeed a female werg. She was slightly smaller than the males, but that wasn't what gave her away. It was her narrower snout, smaller forehead, and thinner mane. He supposed she could have been a runt male, but he had never seen one before. Runts weren't good for sales, according to Mr. Henderson.

She glowered at him as she hovered over a freshly killed deer. She slowly rose to her feet, a hunk of deer flesh hanging from her jaws. She tilted her head.

Aiden wondered why she didn't run ... Or attack. Years of training helped him squeeze the trigger without thought. The bullet clipped her shoulder. She yelped and recoiled. How had he missed his mark? He had her dead to rights. He must have flinched. But that was impossible.

She pinned her ears back and her eyes darted to the broken window. Aiden had one more shot before the chase would be on. He aimed again. But before he pulled the trigger, he noticed something strange in her eyes, unlike anything he'd ever seen in his prey before. It was innocence and fear.

She launched herself at the window, faster than any of the other werepets he had hunted. Though he tracked her with his weapon, he didn't pull the trigger. She landed on the front lawn in a full gallop.

Five rapid-fire shots echoed through the neighborhood. Then Jeffrey grunted and cried out in pain. It was a godawful sound. Aiden jumped through the window. She bolted down the road, already past Greg and the truck. Jeffrey was face down on the sidewalk, moaning.

Greg squealed the truck to a stop at the end of the driveway. He shouted, "Come on, Talik. She's getting away."

Aiden stopped long enough to check Jeffrey. Jeffrey rolled to his back and assured Aiden he'd be all right. He coughed and clutched his bleeding chest. "She's a fast one," he said.

Aiden threw Jeffrey's arm over his shoulder and helped him to the truck, never taking his eyes off his prey. She stopped under a streetlight and looked back curiously. There was something very different about this one, indeed. Once Jeffrey was in the cab, Aiden climbed into the bed and pounded on the roof.

Greg stomped on the gas. The female werg tilted her head back and howled as loud as any siren. The neighborhood werepets joined in. Aiden held the roll bar as Greg cranked the steering wheel and rounded the cul-de-sac to face her. She dropped to all fours and sprinted between the houses.

The truck's rear-end fishtailed as black streaks painted the pavement. Aiden held tight while the tires fought for traction.

Once Greg straightened the truck, Jeffrey handed Aiden an AK-47 through the rear sliding window. "No need for stealth now," he shouted. He was right.

The werg knifed from the street, through a front yard, and into a back yard, heading toward a parallel road. Greg slid the truck around the next corner. "I see her," he shouted over the engine's roar.

She was fast, but Aiden and his team gained on her as she ran along the side of the street toward Germain Village south of the sleeping downtown area. Aiden lifted his weapon and rested it on the cab's roof. "Steady," he yelled as he aimed.

He tightened his finger around the trigger and waited for the best shot. She was within fifty feet when she darted from the road and crashed through the window of a three-story textile shop.

Damn. Aiden pounded on the roof again. Greg slammed on the brakes. Aiden hopped to the pavement and rolled before the truck had completely stopped.

He shouted, "Greg, go around back. Jeff, wait here. I'll push her out." He raced to the broken window and dove inside, rolling to a stop with his AK against his shoulder. On the opposite side of the lobby was an open stairwell door with blood smeared near the top.

Aiden sprinted to it, cautious and quick as he burst into the stairwell. A door at the top slammed closed. He barreled up the stairs to the third floor where a ladder led to a closed hatch in the roof and more blood smears. She was smarter than the other wergs he had chased. He climbed the ladder with one hand on the rail and one keeping his weapon up in case she was waiting for him. He pushed the hatch open and poked his head through along with his weapon.

Frantic, the female werg scurried along the edge of the roof, searching for somewhere to hide or somewhere to go. Aiden had her now. He climbed the rest of the way through the hatch. He was close enough to smell the deer on her breath when she spun toward him and snarled.

He whispered, "Don't move." His finger found the trigger. He took aim. He wouldn't miss again.

She crouched and his weapon followed. "That's right. Submission. One quick pain in your chest and it'll all be over."

She tilted her head like she understood. And then suddenly, she lunged forward with speed he'd never seen in a werg before.

He fired off one shot through her side just below her ribs before she was upon him. He dove from her path, but she clipped his side with her nails. The blow spun him toward the edge of the roof. He reached out for something—anything—to stop his momentum, but grabbed only air. His next step met nothingness and he tumbled over the edge.

She dove from the roof as he hurtled toward the street and grabbed him. She hugged him around his waist, twisted in the air, and landed on her feet with a grunt. The impact jarred Aiden's AK free. It smacked the street and slid out of reach.

Headlights blasted them as an SUV's horn blared and tires squealed. The female werg shoved Aiden away and braced for the impact. The SUV slammed into her, smashing the front end and knocking her hard to the ground. She didn't move.

Jeff rushed over. "Aiden."

"Go get Greg," Aiden commanded.

Jeffrey tore off toward the front of the building. Aiden stood up with a groan. His back hurt and he might have bruised a rib. He hobbled to his AK and picked it up. As he passed the SUV's passenger window, he glanced inside. The driver was unconscious and bleeding from a laceration on her forehead. The deflated airbag hung to her lap.

Aiden went to the female werg still lying in the road and pressed his AK against her head. She rolled to her back and moaned. She was still out of it. Before he killed her, he needed to know one thing. "Why did you save me?" he whispered.

It was that hesitation that changed his life forever. As she lay helpless in the street, her snout wobbled and sank into her face. The coarse fur on her cheeks retracted into her skin. He stood in awe and watched. His AK fell to the street.

Aiden staggered against the SUV. The werg's ribs snapped and collapsed inward. Her ears shrank and took on a human shape.

Oh my God. He covered his mouth. "How could this be?" he whispered.

His mind wouldn't accept what his eyes were showing him. This creature—this beast he was sent to kill—wasn't a beast at all. She was human. The horrible realization of what he had done for his entire life struck him like a ballistic missile to his chest. *This isn't possible.* All his training, everything Mr.

Henderson had taught him, argued against what he now saw. Yet here she was, naked and fragile and alone. And human.

Nausea washed through him. None of the other beasts he had killed had done this, and he had killed a lot of them. How could this be? His knees weakened. If not for the SUV's support, they would have given out completely.

Distant sirens told him he and his team needed to do something fast or risk a shoot-out with the cops. He looked toward the front of the building. Where were Jeffrey and Greg? They weren't gonna believe what he had discovered. While he waited, he took off his coat and covered her.

Greg rounded the corner first. "Talik, is that her?" he shouted, which seemed like an absurd reaction to seeing a human instead of a werg.

Jeffrey was right behind him. "What are you waiting for, Talik? Finish her off. The cops are coming."

"What?" Aiden cried. "She's a person, guys. We gotta get her help."

They stopped about thirty feet short. Greg drew his pistol. "Easy now, Talik. We have a job to do. Remember?"

A job to do? "What are you talking about? She's. A. Person."

Greg shook his head as if disappointed. "Mr. Henderson told us you wouldn't go along if you knew the truth about them. Just finish her off and we'll explain everything after we get the hell outta here." He nervously looked toward the approaching sirens. Emergency lights flickered across the buildings in the distance.

"What? Wait a minute. You guys knew?"

Jeffrey pulled out his Glock and stepped from the curb.

Aiden eyed his assault rifle sitting on the pavement a few feet away. It didn't go unnoticed.

Greg held out his hand. "Wait a minute, Aiden. What are you doing? Just come back with us and everything will be fine. I'll take care of her."

Aiden slowly knelt, shoved his arms beneath the woman's knees and shoulders, and lifted. Their truck waited near the front of the building.

"Put her down, Aiden." Jeff said.

"We can't kill her, Jeff."

Jeff stepped away from Greg to flank Aiden. "Just go wait in the truck."

This was insane. Aiden had no other choice. "Okay, Greg. You two stop right there. I'll set her down." He lowered the woman gently to the pavement. "You can have her. I'm just not going to be a part of it. Just let me leave before you do it, all right?" With his back to the others, he subtly removed his 9mm from his belt and stood up, shielding it with his thigh.

Jeffrey said, "That's good, Aiden. Now back away."

Aiden took a step backward. But as he did, Jeffrey noticed his weapon.

"Put down the goddamn gun, Aiden. What the hell's wrong with you?" As he shouted it, he glanced toward the approaching sirens.

That was all Aiden needed. He dropped to his knees and squeezed off a shot. Greg hit the ground with a grunt. Jeffrey returned fire, shattering the one working headlight of the SUV next to Aiden's head.

Aiden fired two more shots, striking Jeffrey in the knee with one and missing with the other. He shoved his gun into his belt and cradled the woman again.

Greg moaned and writhed on the ground.

Since Aiden had taken an errant shot to the chest while wearing a vest once before, he knew Greg would quickly shake it off. He also knew he would be very sore and very pissed.

Jeffrey held his knee as he dragged himself to the curb where his weapon had fallen.

Aiden quickly carried the woman to the truck, sat her in the passenger seat, and started around the front. Two bullets plowed through the front fender, narrowly missing him. He jumped into the driver's seat as the passenger window shattered. He yanked the gearshift into Drive and floored it.

The last he saw in his rearview mirror was a police cruiser sliding to a stop next to the SUV and Jeff and Greg putting their hands in the air. The police would only slow them for a few minutes. He and his team had dealt with the cops plenty of times before, and they knew how to talk their way out of it. The WereHouse had people in high places and the police department was no different.

Aiden didn't slow until he reached a Walmart miles away. He parked near the back of the lot next to a box van that would hide the truck from the road.

The half-naked woman in the passenger seat started to stir. Her eyes blasted wide and then she grabbed her shoulder with a wince.

"You shot me?" She slipped the coat from her shoulder for a look. To Aiden's shock, the wound had already sealed itself and appeared to be mending before his eyes.

"I'm sorry," Aiden said.

She lunged for the door handle.

Aiden shouted, "Wait, wait, wait." But he didn't try to stop her.

She flung the door open and climbed halfway out before pausing. She looked back.

Aiden held up his hands in surrender.

Half in and half out, she said, "You tried to kill me."

He nodded. "I know. But I'm not trying anymore. It was a mistake. Please. Just sit back down and give me two minutes."

She hesitated, looked around the parking lot, and then got back in the seat. She left the door open.

"I'm not going to hurt you," he said.

"You mean besides shooting me?"

"Yes. Besides that."

"What do you want?"

"I want to help you."

"Now you want to help me?"

"Yes."

"Who are you?"

"My name's Aiden Talik. I was sent to kill you. But that was before I learned what you really are."

"I don't understand. What I am?"

"There's a lot to unpack here. I'll explain everything if you give me a chance. How 'bout you let me go in the store and get you some clothes and something to eat? That will give you time to gather yourself."

Her eyes narrowed. "I don't know."

"I'm not stopping you from leaving. I just wanna get you some clothes."

She shrugged.

"Will you tell me your name?"

"Christine."

"All right, Christine. I'll be right back. If you're still here when I get back, I'll tell you everything." He climbed out, leaving the engine running so she could keep warm. He knew she might just as likely steal the truck and never be seen again, but he needed to earn some favor. He leaned in again and gave her a slight grin. "You *are* going to wait for me, right?"

She turned away. "We'll see."

"If you do leave, just know there are others like me, and they'll be looking for you. Okay?"

She made a sour face and flicked her hand at him.

He hurried to the store and gathered a pair of women's sweatpants, socks, undergarments, and a grey sweatshirt with a block "O" for Ohio State on the front. He guessed an approximate shoe size and got three pairs around that size.

After grabbing a case of bottled water, he stopped at the snack bar and ordered a hotdog and soft pretzel. Then he hurried back to the truck. To his relief, she was still there.

He lightly knocked on the driver's side window before opening the door to keep from startling her. He passed her the food and bag of clothes and then waited outside to give her privacy. After a couple minutes, she called his name.

He climbed in. "I promise you, Christine. Despite what you think, I do want to help you."

"Do you shoot everyone you want to help?"

He didn't mean to chuckle, but her smart-ass tone took him by surprise. "Let's get somewhere safe and I'll explain everything. Will you trust me?"

She thought for a minute and then answered, "No … But I'll hear you out. Where are we going?"

"I have a safe house nearby that even my team doesn't know about."

Aiden drove Christine to an apartment building in the middle of a government subsidized brickyard. He ensured they hadn't been followed by circling the block a few times and then led her into one of the apartments. She stood in the doorway while he cleared each room with his 9mm at his side. Once confident they were alone, he set his weapon on the island and went to the fridge. He popped the cap off a beer and took a gulp.

"You want anything?" he asked.

She shook her head, still standing in the open doorway.

"You can come in, you know."

She hesitated and then stepped in and pushed the door closed.

Aiden motioned toward the couch. "Have a seat?"

"I'm fine standing."

He nodded.

"So. Who are you?" she asked.

"I'm what's called a rogue hunter," he answered.

"What the hell does that mean?"

"I work for …," he paused and shook his head. "Well, I worked for the WereHouse. As you can imagine, wild, roving wergs aren't very good for business. I hunt wild werepets."

"When you say hunt, you mean …"

Aiden nodded.

"That's terrible."

"It was my job the same as when a vet needs to put down a rabid dog. My job was just a bit more unconventional."

She sat quietly for a minute and then asked, "How do you even know when one has gone wild?"

"Several ways. Sometimes their owners report them. But mostly, we use a chip implanted in their necks to know if one is acting up." He pointed to the back of his own neck to show her where the chips were located.

She rubbed her neck. "I don't feel anything."

He took another swig. "You haven't gone through the WereHouse procedure yet."

"What's the chip do?" she asked.

"I don't know what *all* it does, but measuring adrenaline spikes is one thing. Since werepets are trained to be completely docile, certain levels of adrenaline can be indicative of one going rogue. When that happens, I investigate."

"So, you kill *people*?"

He sat in a recliner with a sigh. "I've never knowingly killed a person."

"You tried to kill *me*."

"But I didn't know you were a person. I was raised to see those creatures—"

She interrupted, "You mean people."

He looked away and nodded. His hand trembled. His voice was no longer strong when he said, "You're right. I've done horrible things. If I knew…" He trailed off.

"So, what exactly am I?"

"A werg … You know, a werewolf?"

"That's impossible."

"I wish that was true. Though you are the first female I've ever seen."

"And why's that?"

"I've been told female wergs are nearly untamable and that they make the male wergs more aggressive. In fact, that's how we found you."

"Really?"

"Your scent was driving the males crazy whenever you were near them. We followed their adrenaline spikes. You've been creating quite the headache for the company, which is why they sent me. Though I must admit, you were much harder to find than the typical rogue. If you hadn't stayed where you were to finish that deer, we still might not have found you."

"So, you were just going to kill me?"

He couldn't look at her. He nodded. "But that was before I knew. Trust me, my rogue hunting days are way over."

"Yeah, well, that's not really enough, is it?"

He shook his head. "No. Probably not." He'd never been so sick with such guilt.

Christine sat on the edge of the couch closest to the door. "I've never been shot before. Does it always burn like that?"

"To some degree. Most of that burning you felt was from the silver."

"Silver? Like in the movies?"

"Kinda."

"What do you mean?"

He chewed his lower lip while figuring out how to best explain. "Wergs are allergic to silver. It sends them into anaphylaxis if it gets in their bloodstream."

"So, you have to use silver to kill one?"

He shook his head. "You don't have to, but it helps. Hell, I once used an axe when things got a bit dicey."

"And you're proud of that?"

He wasn't. He bowed his head. "A werg's bones are denser than a human's. That's how you were able to survive jumping from that roof. A werg's sternum is especially thick, making it hard to hit its heart with a bullet."

Christine leaned back against the cushion.

Aiden turned away. It was difficult to accept what he'd done. He whispered, "I can't believe I've actually killed people." He rubbed his eyes. "You know, I'll never forgive myself. I'm a monster." He swallowed hard and looked at Christine again. "I can never make up for what I've done. I'm so sorry for hurting you."

Christine returned his gaze. "I'll take that beer now, if you don't mind."

He smiled. "Of course." He grabbed a glass and poured a fresh beer. "Did you know what was happening when you were … you know?"

"It's weird. I did for the most part, but I couldn't control some of my strange urges. Like that deer. I knew I was hunting it, and I don't even like meat that much, but I literally could not stop myself. It was like my body was on autopilot." She leaned forward and looked into his eyes. "Why did you do it? What made you become a hunter in the first place?"

He took a deep breath. It was a tough story to tell.

ANOTHER TIME

21

Aiden struggled to talk about his past, but he knew that's what he needed to do to gain Christine's trust. He drank the final swig of his beer and set the empty bottle beside his chair.

He took a deep breath. "I didn't … I didn't know they were people, I swear. I hunted them in the same way someone would hunt a man-eating grizzly bear. I thought I was protecting people. But I was lied to.

"I wasn't always like this. There was a time when I wouldn't have hurt any living creatures."

"So, what happened?"

"I've never told anyone this before."

She nodded. "It's okay. Take your time."

He took another deep breath. His eyes were glossy. "My dad bought me a werepet when I was twelve. I named him Rufus and he became my best friend. He was the perfect pet … Until he killed my parents." He stopped and looked to the ceiling, the memories too painful. He had spent his entire adult life trying to forget that awful night.

Christine sat quietly.

Aiden closed his eyes. The memories were as fresh and raw as if they had happened last night. As he told his story, he relived every agonizing moment in his mind.

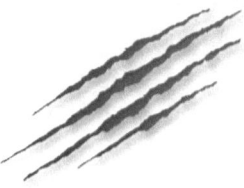

As far as his mother knew, he was in his bedroom doing homework, but he was actually reading a new Wolverine comic book that a friend at school had lent him.

He was just finishing the issue when the front door slammed shut downstairs. He set down his book and listened. His father shouted in a way Aiden had never heard him shout before.

"Rufus," his father screamed.

Aiden opened his door and stood in the doorway. Rufus waited at the other end of the hall near the stairs, his ears pinned back and his head lowered like he'd done something wrong.

Aiden's father stormed up the stairs, shouting for Rufus to come to him, but Rufus cowered away. Aiden wanted to hide his best friend in his room, but he had never heard his father so angry and he was afraid of making him angrier.

When his dad appeared beside Rufus at the top of the stairs, he glanced at Aiden with terror painted across his face. He screamed, "Get in your room and shut your door. Do not come out until I come and get you."

"Dad, what's going on? Why are you mad at Rufus?"

"Just get in your room. I'll explain everything in a bit."

Aiden didn't move. His father grabbed Rufus's collar, dragged him into the bathroom, and slammed the door shut. Aiden heard his dad digging through the medicine chest like a madman.

His mother ran up the stairs, white-faced with panic. "Howard, tell me what's happening," she cried through the bathroom door. Seeing Aiden, she shouted, "Go to your room," but Aiden ignored her too. She pounded on the bathroom door with her open hand. Aiden wanted to get to Rufus and protect him, but fear paralyzed him.

There was a scuffle in the bathroom. And then Rufus yelped. It was the second most devastating sound Aiden had ever heard. The first most devastating sound immediately followed when Rufus wailed in pain.

Aiden found his courage and ran down the hall to the bathroom door. He screamed, "Dad, leave him alone."

"Go to your room," Howard screamed back.

"No," he answered. He had never defied his father before. His mom put her arm around him. He looked up with tears streaming down his face. "Why, Mom? Why is Dad hurting Rufus?"

"I don't know," she answered, and pulled him close. "Can you kick in the door?"

He didn't know if he could, but he would sure try. He stepped back and kicked the door as hard as he could. It barely budged.

"Stop it," Howard shouted.

Aiden kicked it again and again as Rufus continued to wail in pain on the other side. Finally, the doorframe splintered and the door crashed open. His mother pushed past him into the bathroom. She gasped and turned away.

Aiden peered past her. "Dad, why?"

Howard stood over Rufus, who lay submissive on the tile floor surrounded by blood. Jerry stood in a daze, holding a pair of bloody scissors. Rufus whimpered.

"What did you do?" Aiden cried.

Instead of answering, his father turned to the counter and dropped the scissors and something about the size of a quarter into the sink.

Aiden knelt by Rufus and caressed his head. "It's okay, boy." Blood matted the hair on the back of the werg's neck. "Rufus, I'm sorry," he whispered.

"Aiden," his father snapped. "Don't touch him. Don't get his blood on you."

"Dad, what did you do?" he cried again. Howard stared off to the side. "The microchips ... We've done something awful."

Aiden's mother sobbed and backed against the wall. "What do you mean?" she asked.

Howard didn't answer. He collapsed onto the toilet. As he gazed at the wall with dead eyes, he said, "They'll be coming for us."

Aiden's mom gasped. "Who?"

Just then, Rufus perked his ears and growled. He rose to all fours and snarled at the doorway. Aiden had never seen him show his teeth like that and it scared him. "What is it, boy?"

Rufus tore out of the room and down the stairs.

Howard stood up and grabbed Aiden's shoulders. "They're here. Stay in here and don't come out, no matter what. Do you understand?"

"But—" Aiden started to argue.

Howard snapped, "If you come out, they'll kill you. Do you understand?"

Like a coward, Aiden bobbed his head. Howard charged down the stairs.

Aiden's mom cried, "Do as he says, Aiden."

Aiden tried to hold her hand, but she ripped it free, pulled the door partially shut in the shattered frame, and ran down the stairs. Aiden peered through the gap and listened. He wanted to go down but he was too afraid. Instead, he listened.

Rufus's claws scrapped the hardwood floors in the living room. Then he yelped. Aiden started crying and put his hands over his ears. He didn't want to hear any more. But no matter how hard he pressed his hands against his ears, he couldn't escape Rufus's deathly cries or his mother's panicked screams.

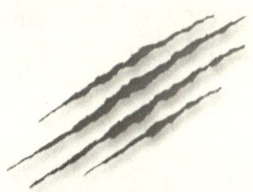

Aiden looked at Christine with wet eyes. He said, "That was the night I promised myself to never give in to fear again. To never be a coward."

"I don't think you were a coward."

"Yes, I was. I ran to my room and grabbed a baseball bat, but that's as far as I got. As hard as I tried, I couldn't run down the stairs. I stood helpless in my doorway." He nervously chuckled. "Can you imagine? All of the weapons I use today to stop werepets, and I thought a baseball bat would help."

"How old were you?"

"Fourteen."

"You were just a kid still."

He bowed his head. "I guess."

"What happened next?"

"That's when I heard the gunfire. It was strange, but that's what snapped me out of my paralysis and gave me strength to save my family. Suddenly, I no longer cared if I was going to die, and I haven't much cared since."

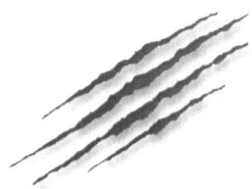

Aiden squeezed the bat as he charged down the stairs. He slowed before he reached the bottom. After all the horrifying sounds of the struggle in the living room, it was the abrupt silence that followed that gave Aiden the most pause. "Mom? Dad?" he loudly whispered.

They didn't answer.

The front door in the foyer at the bottom of the stairs was open. The bolt was still extended and the doorframe was shattered with pieces of wood jutting outward. Aiden considered continuing through the doorway and running to the neighbors for help, but he couldn't leave without knowing what had happened to his family. From the bottom stair, he peeked around the banister down the hall to the living room. The one wall that he could see was covered in blood and claw marks. Panic and fear grabbed his gut. He dropped to his knees, unable to will himself any farther. He wanted to hide, but he needed to know what had happened.

Behind him, the front door creaked open. He slowly turned.

A man with an assault rifle stood in the doorway, his weapon trained on Aiden. Aiden dropped his bat and lifted his hands in surrender. The man marched past him and down the hall toward the living room. Aiden waited, still on his knees, as a second man entered. This man was wearing a dark suit and there was something familiar about him.

"Aiden?" the man asked.

This man didn't have a gun. Aiden picked up his baseball bat again. "How do you know my name?" he asked.

The man said, "I met you at the WereHouse when your dad purchased your pet."

Aiden studied his face for a moment and then said, "Mr. Henderson?"

Bernard nodded. "Stand up, son. Don't be afraid. We aren't here to hurt you. You should probably see what happened." He held out his hand.

Aiden ignored it as he stood up.

Before leading Aiden down the hall, Bernard shouted, "Is the product secure?"

A man's voice answered, "Affirmative."

As they entered the blood-soaked living room, Aiden's heart fell to the floor. In the center of the room were three men with rifles surrounding Aiden's mom and dad. They were both dead with wide, claw-like gouges covering their bodies. Aiden ran to his mom, dropped to his knees, and lifted her head to his lap. "No, no, no," he cried.

Mr. Henderson let him have a moment and then placed a hand on Aiden's shoulder. "Sorry you had to see this, son. Unfortunately, Rufus went bad. Your dad knew it and called us. Before we got here, Rufus had killed your parents."

Aiden shook his head. "No, no. Not Rufus. He would never do something like that."

"I'm sorry, kid."

"It's not possible. Where's Rufus now? I want to see him."

"Don't do that to yourself, kid. We've already removed him and he's on his way to the WereHouse for a proper and respectful burial."

There was an open window on the other side of the room that faced the turnaround driveway where a dark van was pulling away. Aiden watched the taillights until they disappeared.

"You need to be strong now, kid. Take as much time as you need." Bernard stepped back and stood quietly with his hands clasped in front of him.

Aiden stayed on his knees and held his mom's hand. He wanted to die, too. He had never cried so hard. He couldn't believe Rufus would do such a thing, but he couldn't argue with his eyes either. His parents had been ripped to shreds. He dry-heaved until his stomach ached. He leaned in and kissed his mother's cheek.

Eventually, Bernard gently took Aiden's upper arm. "Come on, son. Stand up. You've been through enough."

Aiden reluctantly got to his feet, his eyes still trained on his mom. He walked over to his dad, reached down, and touched his chest. "I love you, Dad."

Bernard nodded to one of his armed men and the soldier dragged a sheet over Howard's body. They did the same with his mom. Aiden turned away.

Bernard smiled sadly. "Remember what you see here, kid. This is going to help you in the next stage of your life. You've got a calling; you just don't know it yet." He put his arm around Aiden's shoulder and led him to the door. He turned back and said, "Clean it up." One of the guards struck a flare as Bernard led Aiden to a running car. The driver opened the door.

"Shouldn't we wait for the police?" Aiden asked.

Bernard guided him into the backseat. "My men will take care of all that. I'm going to help you through this. I'm going to take care of you now."

Aiden knew he probably shouldn't go with Mr. Henderson, but he no longer cared what happened anymore. Bernard climbed in on the other side.

"Have you ever heard of rogue werepets?" he asked.

Aiden shook his head.

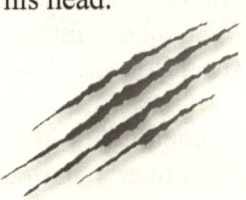

Christine held her hand over her mouth. "You mean he kidnapped you?"

Aiden nodded. "In a way, I guess. Though I didn't see it that way at the time. To me, the world had ended, and I had nowhere else to go."

"Didn't anyone look for you? Family?"

"Probably. But I wasn't looking for them. I was sad and angry and confused. Bernard Henderson seemed to always have the right answers. I didn't care about the world anymore and he fed that feeling."

"What did he do with you?"

"He taught me how to kill wergs. He told me how they sometimes snapped and needed to be put down. Because of my anger and feeling so betrayed by Rufus, I bought into his words with tremendous zeal. It became my sole focus in life."

Aiden stopped talking and turned away. He was sickened just thinking about what had happened to him and how everything he believed was wrong. He wiped his eyes and took a stuttered breath.

Christine said, "I think you've said enough for today. I don't need to hear any more."

He shook his head. "I need to get it all out. I was seventeen when that bastard put me in a pen with a rogue werg for the first time. He told me to take any weapons I felt I would need. I chose a single knife because I wanted to prove myself to him.

"Before I killed that animal … that person … I thought about my mom and dad. When that werg attacked, I shoved that blade into its heart without remorse. After he was dead, Mr. Henderson left me in there with that filthy carcass for the rest of the night. I think it was at that moment that I lost any compassion I had left for those creatures. I started seeing them as ravenous monsters in need of killing, and I couldn't wait for my first mission."

He swallowed hard and looked up from the floor. "But now I've found you. Seeing you as one of those creatures and seeing you now … it's more than I can explain. I'm sickened by my own hatred and brutality.

"Finding you has made me realize something else, something besides the horrors I have inflicted. The chip that my dad removed from Rufus's neck didn't keep him tame like Mr. Henderson told me. The company's sick torture did that. No, the chip kept him from transforming back into a human."

"If Rufus didn't kill your parents, how were they so torn up?"

"Knowing what I know now, I think they used the Savages."

"Savages?"

"They are special wergs trained to hunt for the WereHouse. I've used them in especially difficult cases. They are vicious and highly dangerous." He looked to the floor. He had told her enough for one day. "Thank you for listening, Christine. It's been a long time since I've had anyone to talk to like this."

"Of course, Aiden. I'm sorry you went through what you did."

"I still can't believe I've been killing people this whole time. I'm nothing more than a murderer."

Christine shook her head. "I don't think you're a murderer. You didn't know. Now that you do know, you don't have to kill anyone else ever again."

Aiden gritted his teeth. "No. You're wrong. Mr. Henderson groomed me and manipulated me into a cold-blooded killer. I now know he's the one who slaughtered my parents. It wasn't Rufus. It wasn't the chip in his neck. It was Mr. Henderson and his men. He needs to see first-hand what he turned me into. We need to bring down the WereHouse and free everyone in the world of this vicious curse."

"And how can we do that?"

"I think I know someone who might be able to help."

"Really?"

"Have you ever heard of Senator Wooten?"

"Of course."

"I've met him a few times. He might be the only man powerful enough to go against Mr. Henderson."

"Then we should go see him."

Aiden shook his head. "Not we. This will be too dangerous. I'm going alone."

Christine stood up. "That's not fair. I'm as much a part of this as you are. They sent you to kill me. They're not gonna stop now. I'm going with you, and that's that."

"I don't think it's a good i—"

"I don't care what you think. I'm a big girl. I can help."

Aiden looked into her serious eyes and saw there would be no denying her. He quietly nodded.

"Great. Where do we find him?"

"I believe he'd be at his getaway house this weekend."

"And how do you know that?"

The WereHouse makes it their business to keep tabs on their greatest threat."

"Can we call him or something?"

Aiden shook his head. "The phones won't be secure. We need to go there."

"All right. When?"

"Tonight. We'll sneak in."

Christine glanced to the hall and then back to Aiden. "Is your bathroom down there?"

He nodded.

"Would you mind if I got a shower?"

"Be my guest. There're clean towels on a shelf in there."

She smiled and headed down the hall. While Christine showered, Aiden dozed off in the chair. When he woke, she was sound asleep on the couch. He hated to wake her but it was time to go.

It was 2:30 in the morning by the time they reached Senator Wooten's private property. A long lane led into a wooded area that Aiden said ran parallel to the senator's lane.

Aiden flipped off the headlights and stopped on the side of the road. "We won't be able to get there with a vehicle. We'll have to go on foot from here."

"Do you think he'll even listen to us?"

"I think so."

"Why?"

Aiden paused in thought. Then he answered, "He wants to bring down the WereHouse as much as we do."

She hoped he was right.

"We just need to convince him that, despite breaking into his home, we aren't there to hurt him." He grabbed a flashlight from the glove box and removed an army-green duffle bag from the back seat.

"What's in the bag?" she asked.

"Weapons. If they arrest us, we're done. I can't allow that to happen."

"But he won't help if we go in guns blazing. We're hoping to get him on our side, right?"

Aiden shrugged. "I'm not going to take them in. I'm just going to leave them where I can get to them in a hurry if shit goes south."

She nodded reluctantly. They started into the woods. They walked for nearly ten minutes before she asked, "How do you know where you're going so well?"

He winked. "I've been to the senator's house a few times in the past."

She side-eyed him.

"Let's just say, the WereHouse had reasons for keeping a close eye on the good senator. He is their biggest threat, after all."

"So, you watched him?

"Yep."

"And then what?"

"What do you mean?"

"Would you have killed him if they told you to?" she asked, afraid of the answer.

He appeared surprised by her question. He shook his head. "I've told you that I've never knowingly killed a person, and I didn't have any plans to start. I was ordered to watch him for a while in case he had some unethical hobbies. You know drugs, underage girls, stuff like that. Blackmail."

"Did you ever find anything?"

"Eh. Not really. He does a little coke here and there. But nothing earth-shattering." Then he held up his hand and stopped. "We're getting close." He set his duffel bag next to a tree. "We won't be able to get much farther without being detected. Are you good with the plan?"

She nodded.

"Stick with it no matter what. Walk toward the front door and get security's attention. He should have three guards walking around in the front. Keep them busy for as long as you can. If all goes well, they will escort you to the senator. I'll already be in there waiting. If they send you away, go out of sight and then duck in the woods." He removed a small package that looked like a cell phone strapped to a dark green tube similar to a road flare and set it next to a different tree. He flipped a toggle switch which turned on a dime-sized red LED. "If things go bad, make your way back to here."

"How will I find it?"

"Trust me, you won't be able to miss it."

He led her to the road and then turned back for the woods. She grabbed his arm. She didn't say anything.

"Relax," he said with a sincere smile. "We'll be fine."

She released his arm. Then he turned and disappeared back into the woods. She started down the lane.

It didn't take long before a flashlight beam bounced toward her.

"Who are you?" the guard behind the beam shouted. "Stop where you are."

Christine lifted her hands in surrender. A second guard joined the first. He said, "Don't move a muscle. What are you doing out here?"

She answered, "I need to meet with Senator Wooten. It's urgent."

The guard with the flashlight chuckled and looked to his partner. His partner shrugged. "Go away. The senator doesn't meet with crazy people walking down the road in the middle of the night." He started to turn away.

"Wait," she said and took a cautious step forward.

The other guard lifted his weapon slightly. "Don't take another step."

She froze. "I'm not here for trouble. I have important information for the senator which I believe will help his cause."

"And which cause is that?" The guard paused and then added, "Scratch that question. I don't care. Now turn around and go back the way you came, or you'll be arrested for trespass—"

She interrupted, "I can help him bring down the WereHouse."

The guard's shoulders slouched. "Is that so?" He waved her forward. "Come 'ere."

She walked to him. "I'm only telling what I know to the senator. Not some two-bit lackey."

He grinned. "Two-bit lackey, huh? Turn around. You got any weapons on you?"

She shook her head and turned to face the opposite way. He patted her down. "All right. Let's go see the senator."

The other guard walked about five feet behind her with his weapon trained on her back.

While they walked, the guard beside her asked, "How'd you get all the way out here without a car?"

"It broke down a couple miles back. When we're finished, maybe you could give me a ride back to town."

"Heh. Don't count on it."

FRIEND OR FOE

23

With Christine safely on the road, Aiden returned to his duffel bag, removed a six-shooter revolver, and continued through the forest toward Senator Wooten's home. His previous surveillance of Wooten's place had revealed plenty of access points to sneak into the house without notice. Having the security code helped too, as long as it hadn't been changed. It wasn't a very original password. Matilda. The name of the baby daughter he had lost to SIDS. He picked up the pace, knowing Christine wouldn't be able to keep the guards occupied for long.

Two guards patrolled the back of the house, and their complacent pattern hadn't changed much over the years. Aiden ducked into a weeded area and waited for the closest one to pass. This was his best chance. Careful to stay out of view of the motion-sensor security lights, he hurried to the side of the house. With his back against the stucco siding, he shimmied around to the rear and ducked beneath a two-story deck.

Steam lifted from the top where a hot tub sat. After another guard passed, Aiden quietly climbed the stairs to the first landing and waited.

That he heard a woman's voice from the hot tub told him the security system probably wasn't armed yet. She said, "I'm going to bed, love. Are you coming?"

Aiden had heard Senator Wooten's voice enough times to recognize it when he answered, "I'll be in after I finish this cigar."

"Okay. Don't be long."

Water splashed over the side of the hot tub and through the gaps in the deck flooring. Aiden knelt in the shadow of the upper deck. From his angle, he could see the double sliding-glass doors. A naked, red-haired beauty pulled a towel from a hook beside the door, wrapped herself in it, and disappeared into the house.

Aiden took another step up but froze when a handheld radio chirped.

"Hey, boss?" a man's voice said, followed by a burst of static.

Senator Wooten answered, "What is it?"

"We've got some crazy chick down here who wants to talk to you about something she says is important."

"Tell her to come by the office in the morning and then call the paddy wagon to take her to a padded cell."

It was time. Aiden covered the last flight of stairs in a flash with his revolver in hand. Seeing him, the senator froze with his thumb still on the walkie-talkie's button. Aiden held a finger to his lips and the senator slowly eased his thumb off the button.

The voice on the other end of the radio continued, "She says she has information that will help you bring down the WereHouse, whatever the hell that means."

Aiden nodded and whispered, "Send her in."

"If you say so." Wooten keyed the mic again. "Send her on up. This should be interesting."

Aiden pointed his gun toward an empty spot on the deck. "Now toss the walkie over there." After Wooten complied, Aiden added, "Very good. Now, let's go inside."

Wooten looked around as if contemplating a way out. Like a good politician, he stalled. "Can I have some privacy to put something on? I'm naked here."

Aiden became increasingly annoyed. "I'm sure you've been in locker rooms before, as have I."

"Very well." Senator Wooten climbed out of the hot tub in all his naked glory. Aiden tossed him a towel which he wrapped around his waist.

The sliding doors opened to a large game room with a pool table in its center and a bar to the left. A Ms. Pacman arcade machine was against one wall next to a popcorn machine. Across the room were a loft, a door, and a flight of stairs that led down to the foyer.

The senator reached for a robe draped over the back of a leather chair. "Do you mind?" he asked.

"Go ahead," Aiden answered.

The senator pressed his luck. "Do you mind if I put on my slippers as well?"

"Whatever. Just quit stalling. When my friend gets in here, we need to talk. I know it's hard for you to believe right now, but we're not here to hurt you."

Wooten rolled his eyes. "Would you like a cigar?" he offered, and stepped into a pair of slippers.

Aiden brushed off his offer with a wave.

"Do you mind if I have one?"

Aiden was a tad stunned at how relaxed the senator seemed and he got an uneasy feeling about the whole situation. Wooten casually lit his cigar with a lighter that was sitting on the bar.

The door in the foyer opened. Aiden ducked out of sight behind the loft's half-wall. Hidden from the guards, he aimed his revolver at Wooten and hissed, "Send her up alone and then dismiss them."

Senator Wooten went to the top of the stairs and stopped two feet short of where Aiden crouched. Aiden prayed he wouldn't call his bluff and bolt down the steps. The last thing he wanted to do was kill a senator or get into a gunfight with only six rounds.

The guard escorting Christine shouted, "Should we come up with her, sir?"

"Did you frisk her?" Wooten asked.

"Yes, sir."

"Then that won't be necessary. Come on up, my dear." He backed away as Christine's footsteps approached the top of the landing.

When she reached the last step and saw Aiden out of the corner of her eye, it startled her. But she was a good actor and hid her surprise from the guards.

"Send them away," Aiden whispered.

Wooten did as ordered. Once the front door closed, Aiden glanced over the half-wall and then stood up.

Wooten took a toke from his cigar and mumbled, "I gotta get new guards." He turned to Christine. "Well, you've got me. What do you want?"

"Sir, my name's Christine Alt. This is Aiden Talik."

He eyed Aiden. "Yeah, I think I've met him before. Is that right, Aiden?"

Aiden nodded.

"At the WereHouse?"

Aiden nodded again.

"So, what can I do for you two?"

Christine answered, "We have information I think will shock you concerning the WereHouse and its practices."

"Oh?" Wooten motioned for them to have a seat on the leather couch while he went to the bar. "Drink?"

Aiden waved off his offer, gun still raised.

Wooten poured whiskey into a shot glass and then tossed the empty bottle into a waste bin.

Christine continued, "Sir, what would you say if I told you that the WereHouse isn't dealing in animals as we all have been led to believe?"

"I'd listen."

"We have proof that the werewolves aren't creatures at all, but ..." She paused and took in a breath. "Senator, there's no easy way to say this."

Wooten's eyes widened. Aiden couldn't tell if his expression was surprise or condescension.

"They're people," Aiden blurted. He wanted to shock the senator and see his reaction.

"Really?" Wooten answered, which wasn't at all the reaction Aiden had expected.

"Did you hear what I said?" Aiden asked.

Senator Wooten held the shot glass to his lips and jerked his head back, swallowing with a distorted whiskey grimace. "I heard you. But you aren't the first to tell me this. Excuse my skepticism, but to date these claims have never been proven. Yet another conspiracy theory is what it sounds like to me."

"We can prove it," Christine insisted.

Wooten set his glass down and walked toward a doorway behind the bar. "Will you excuse me for a moment?"

"Uh … no," Aiden answered, and shoved his weapon out farther.

"I'm afraid you have no choice," Senator Wooten said as he reached for the door handle. "I'm through with your games. Fire your peashooter if you'd like, but I'm getting another bottle of whiskey whether you like it or not."

Aiden crossed the room, knowing he wouldn't get to the senator in time to stop him. Wooten disappeared through the doorway.

"Damn it," Aiden whispered. The senator had called his bluff.

He felt Christine's eyes on him and glanced back with a shrug.

She whispered, "What's he doing?"

"I have no idea." Aiden turned to the stairs and then to the sliding doors. "Something's wrong here. We need to go. Right now."

He grabbed her hand and tugged her toward the stairwell, but the two armed guards burst through the front door into the foyer.

One of them shouted, "Senator? Where are you?"

Aiden pointed his revolver down the stairs. "Don't come up here," he yelled. "I'll kill Wooten." Maybe his bluff would work better with them.

Both guards lowered their weapons. One of them smirked. "If you say so. You have no idea what you've gotten yourselves into, do you?"

The door behind the bar opened again and Wooten emerged with a politician's smile and another bottle of whiskey. His robe was half open, exposing his hairy chest.

Aiden nudged Christine to the floor next to the loft wall. He aimed his revolver at Wooten with his right arm outstretched and steadied it with his left. He moved to the side and away from the stairwell to avoid exposing his back to the guards. "Tell them not to come up here," he shouted.

Wooten answered, "You heard the man. I've got things quite under control up here." He seemed unconcerned that a gun was pointing at him as he strolled across the room to the pool table. "There's no need to be so nervous, Aiden. As you can see, I am unarmed."

"Senator? Christine said. "I'm sorry for this. If you just let us leave—"

Before she finished, Wooten shook his head. He said, "Nonsense. Come on over here and have a seat. We can discuss this werewolf situation."

Aiden tightened his jaw but didn't move. Christine stepped beside him. He surveyed the room in search of an alternate escape. There was a door beside the stairway, but if the door led to a bathroom or a closet, they would be trapped.

Two more guards stepped into view through the sliding doors beside the hot tub.

Aiden whispered, "This isn't going to end well."

24

The senator poured another shot of whiskey and downed it. Then he smiled and dropped his robe, exposing himself. Christine looked away.

Aiden whispered, "When I move, stay behind me. Got it?"

She nodded, keeping her eyes on the guards at the sliding doors. "What's he doing?" she asked.

Aiden didn't answer.

Wooten rubbed his chest and made a pained, twisted face. His head jerked and then snapped backward with a violent crack.

Aiden cursed under his breath. "How could I have been so blind?" he whispered.

Senator Wooten's ribs jutted outward, and his body flopped in jerky, seizure-like movements. His already hairy chest sprouted an even thicker coat of grayish hair until his flesh was completely hidden beneath.

Aiden whispered, "Can you change, Christine?"

She shook her head. "I don't know how."

"You either figure it out, like, right now, or we're fucked."

The sliding door slid open and the guards stepped into the room. Aiden turned to the stairs. "Christine, now."

Senator Wooten's nose and mouth stretched away from his face and black ink filled his eyes. Aiden grabbed her arm, breaking her trance. Wooten roared, and Aiden heard laughter in it.

Just then, the door next to the stairs squeaked and started to open. Aiden rushed to it and kicked it the rest of the way open as the two guards from the sliding doors started to advance. The redhead from earlier shrieked. She still wore a towel around her body. Aiden grabbed her by her wet hair and yanked her out of the bathroom.

The two guards froze beside the pool table. The two from the foyer stopped midway up the stairs. Aiden pulled the redhead against his chest and pressed his gun against her cheek. "I'll kill her," he lied.

The guard closest shouted, "He's got Helena. Everyone be cool." His tone softened when he addressed Aiden. "Relax, mister. No one needs to get hurt here."

Aiden moved closer to Christine with his hostage in tow. "Come on," he whispered. As he led her down the stairs with Helena tight to his chest, the two guards backed away. From the loft, Senator Wooten roared again, now fully transformed and in a rage.

Aiden didn't like his chances against such an obviously seasoned werg and prayed his hostage would be enough of a deterrent for their escape.

As Aiden, Christine, and Helena reached the bottom of the stairs, Senator Wooten soared over the loft wall and landed in the foyer near the front door.

Aiden screamed, "Back away, Wooten, or I'll blow her head off." He tried desperately to sell his bluff. He pointed the gun at the guards. "And you. Leave your weapons on the floor and get on your knees against that wall."

Wooten tilted his head and watched curiously. He snorted.

The guards shuffled to the wall.

Christine retrieved their rifles. And then Senator Wooten pounced. Aiden spun Helena away and fired all six shots at Wooten's chest. The senator yelped but barely slowed. Aiden dove out of the way as Wooten crashed against the staircase.

Aiden dropped his empty revolver and Christine tossed him a rifle. "Do you know how to use one?" he shouted.

She shook her head.

Senator Wooten bounced to his feet and pounced again. Christine fled through the open front door. Aiden unloaded his rifle, riddling Wooten with bullets. If only they were silver. Then the weapon clicked. Aiden's eyes went wide. Wooten turned back, blood pouring from the many bullet holes. His chest rose and fell in angry breaths. Aiden drew the rifle over his shoulder like a baseball bat. Wooten moved like lightning, swatting Aiden in a flash.

Aiden slammed into the wall, an awful gash across his chest. He recovered quickly—he had no choice. His chest burned like lava. Before Wooten could attack again, another barrage of bullets strafed him, this time from the door. It was Christine. She looked as surprised at her use of the weapon as he was. Wooten dove behind a sofa.

Aiden chased Christine through the door. She handed him the rifle and he sprayed the room as he fled. Once on the porch, he shoved the door closed and continued firing through it until this weapon clicked as well. He tossed the gun aside. He shouted, "Get to the woods."

A dark WereHouse van sped down the lane and Aiden's heart sank. Wooten and Henderson were in it together. Christine ran for the tree line. Aiden followed. He caught up to her at the trees as Wooten's front door exploded from its hinges.

Senator Wooten burst through the opening, panting angrily and clutching his chest. He stumbled against a porch post, leaving a red stain behind.

The van stopped near the fountain at the end of the drive and the side door slid open. WereHouse employees poured out, Bernard Henderson's private army, assault weapons at the ready.

"Go, go, go," Aiden shouted. A hail of gunfire erupted. The rounds whizzed past Aiden's and Christine's heads, tearing the trees apart around them.

Christine shouted, "Which way?"

Aiden yanked out a small device that resembled a keyless entry remote from his pocket and pressed the button. There was a distant popping sound, followed by a bright green glow deeper in the woods.

He pointed. "That way."

"I see it," she answered.

"Keep running. I'm right behind you."

Aiden kept one eye on her and one eye on their trail as they ran toward the green glow. He grabbed the green flare at the tree's base and plunged it into the dirt to snuff it out. He snatched his duffel bag with one hand and Christine's arm with the other. "Are you all right? Have you been hit?"

She shook her head.

"Can you go on?"

She nodded. She appeared hardly winded, and he was nearly sucking the bark from the trees. He heard sticks snapping behind them. "Get down," he whispered, and knelt beside her. He removed two pistols from his bag.

He saw the first soldier step between two trees ahead, cautious but still unaware of how close he was to his prize. Aiden aimed his pistol. He didn't want to shoot the man, but he wasn't going to let those bastards kill Christine, either. And make no mistake, kill her was what they would do.

As the soldier's flashlight beam bounced from tree to tree, landing on the one next to Christine, a distant voice shouted, "Franklin." The soldier spun toward the voice. "Get the hell outta there. They're sending in the Savages."

Aiden's heart sank. Pistols would do little against Savages.

The guard turned and fled.

Christine's face filled with dread. "The same Savages you talked about earlier?"

Aiden shoved his guns in his waistband. He nodded. He removed a harness from the bag and slung it over his neck and wrapped it under one arm.

A howl from the road paralyzed him. He whispered, "They're here already." A second howl joined the first.

Christine's eyes widened. "Should we hide?"

"They've already found us. That's the howl they give when they lock on to a scent."

She gasped. "My God. How many are there?"

"I don't know. It depends on how many teams the Senator keeps nearby. I didn't know he kept any." He reached into his duffel bag and retrieved his last surprises—his trusted AK-47 and a flash grenade.

"We're going to die," she whispered.

He didn't argue.

"What are we gonna to do?"

Aiden nudged her behind him. Without looking back, he said, "You need to change into a werg. It's your only chance to escape."

"I don't know how."

"Are you scared?"

"Yes."

"Are you pissed off?"

"Yes."

"Then use that. Accept it and allow yourself to give in to the anger."

"How do you know that'll work?"

"I don't. But you've gotta try something."

Christine closed her eyes.

Aiden whispered in her ear, "If you change, don't look at the flash from my grenade. Wergs hate them. It disorients 'em. After the explosion, make a run for it. You'll only have a few seconds. Don't stop until you're safe."

"What about you?"

He forced a sad grin and said, "I'll be fine. I do this for a living, remember?" Then he winked.

The Savages grunted as they ran. They were getting close.

"Christine, they're going to kill us both. They're the ones who turned you into a monster. They're the ones who sent me to kill you." Though he'd never hit a woman in normal circumstances, he felt he had no choice now. He slapped her.

She stared back in horror.

"I'm so sorry, Christine, but you've gotta let it out."

She winced like she needed to sneeze.

"Come on," he shouted. "They're going to kill you."

Her nose began to contort and bleed.

"That's it. They're going to kill your family. Do it …" And then, although he hated to do it, he added a cold-hearted, "Bitch." It was as painful to say as it was to see in her face how hard it landed on her ears.

She didn't have time to react as she snorted and her head twitched violently to the side. Her eyes bulged and she roared like a blood-thirsty tigress. Her blue irises turned black. Her pupils went red like blood. The bones in her spine snapped and crackled. Her mouth and nose pushed outward to form a snout. Fur sprouted from her forehead and cheeks. She moaned and writhed in pain. Her neck jerked to one side and then the other.

Aiden stepped back. If Christine had any chance of surviving, this was it. And even that chance was slim. The sounds of shattering tree limbs echoed from all directions, coming closer with each passing second. There were too many of them. This was his final stand. His adult life had been only about death, yet now he had a chance to save someone, and it became his sole purpose. Maybe, in some way, dying to help her escape could redeem him of his horrible crimes. Her moaning ceased behind him. He smiled. She had a chance now. He felt her hot breath on his back.

He pulled the pin from his grenade and glanced over his shoulder. She lifted her elongated finger and caressed his cheek with her knuckle. It was a gentleness he hadn't felt from a werg since Rufus.

Everything went quiet. The Savages now knew there was another wild one in their midst and they were hesitating. It was time.

He whispered, "Run, Christine."

The first Savage shot from between the trees in a blur as another landed within a few feet of him.

Aiden screamed, "Now." He heaved his grenade toward the rushing beasts. With his arm shielding his eyes, he turned his head. "Look away, Christine," he shouted.

She cowered from the blast. His ears popped. The Savages yelped, letting him know he had hit his mark. They stumbled around, blind and confused. Having seen them hunt plenty of times in the past, he knew they had already surrounded their prey. "Run between those two," he cried, and shoved Christine toward where the flash grenade had exploded.

Christine dropped to all fours, snorted, and sprang for the gap between the disoriented beasts. Still blinded but no less deadly, they caught her scent and lunged at her as she passed. She ducked and dodged their attacks.

Aiden spun in slow circles as tree branches snapped all around him. He cried, "Come on, Savages. Do your worst." His excited breathing reminded him of his earliest days as a werg hunter. At first, he silently urged himself to calm down, but then decided the adrenaline rush would help him stay sharp. One more glance toward where Christine had fled revealed she had gotten a good start. He only needed to stay alive long enough for her to put distance between them. That was her only chance.

The Savages stalked him in slow, cautious steps, as if aware they weren't the only predators in the woods that night. He counted a half-dozen surrounding him and smiled. "Bring it," he muttered, ready for battle. He squeezed his trigger. Their howls were replaced by the beautiful *rat-tat-tat* of his assault rifle. He spun in a circle as bullet after wonderful bullet tore into his enemies' flesh.

Blood splattered. Tree bark blasted from trees.

The creatures roared as chunks of flesh ripped from their bodies. The air filled with the sound of sizzling meat as the silver met their skin. Two wergs dropped when the bullets found their hearts.

The flashes of light and bursts of thunder from Aiden's weapon ended, yet he continued squeezing his trigger until his knuckles turned white. A werg leaped from six feet away. Aiden heaved his empty AK at the pouncing beast before diving for his duffel bag. The werg swatted the rifle away and landed beside him. Aiden retrieved the last flash grenade from his bag.

Another werg pounced. Aiden pulled the pin and dropped the grenade. The werg swung his deadly claws. Aiden rolled to his side with his wrists pressed against his ears. This was going to hurt. White-hot pain exploded from his left thigh as the beast's claws tore his flesh. He didn't have time to suck up the pain as his eardrums popped from the concussion of the grenade. Heat from the blast seared his back through his clothing and threw him violently across the ground.

He opened his eyes. The world slowed and blurred around him. The disoriented wergs staggered and stumbled, trying to regain his scent.

Aiden accepted his impending death; he just wasn't going to make it easy. He drew a silver-bladed knife from its sheath.

His back throbbed. His leg ached with each pulsating pump of arterial blood from his femoral artery. He pressed his left hand against the wound, but the blood continued flowing through the cracks between his fingers. A sudden rush of weakness washed over him. It was a fatal blow—there was no doubt. It wouldn't be long now.

One of the Savages caught his scent and staggered toward him, still partially blinded from the grenade. Aiden heaved his blade upward into the beast's gut, piercing its heart. The creature wailed. Aiden withdrew his blade. The werg retreated before collapsing.

Another werg snorted behind him. They had gotten too close, too quickly. Aiden tried to turn, but the creature's claws raked down his back. He bit his lower lip so the monsters wouldn't have the satisfaction of hearing his cries.

Though his ears rang incessantly, he still heard his attackers' excited grunts. They were regaining their senses; he was losing his. A third Savage rose up for a killing blow in front of him. Aiden spun his knife in his hand so the blade was directed downward and drew it back over his shoulder. Yet another werg stalked closer from behind. They were brilliant hunters. Aiden took a deep, final breath, white-knuckled the hilt of his knife, and forced a crazy grin. *Goodbye, world.*

But the creature didn't attack. Instead, his ears perked, and he sniffed the air. The others mimicked him. Aiden grabbed his duffle bag and scooted his back against a tree as the Savages refocused away from him. He stretched one of the shoulder straps taut and cut it with his knife. He wrapped his thigh just below his groin as the blood poured from his leg. He looped the strap over the hilt and twisted until the strap pulled tight and dug into his flesh. Then he twisted some more. The spurting blood slowed. He realized he might have been too late. His sight faded. He held the blade against his leg while he waited for the Savages to turn their attention back to him.

But they didn't. Instead, a smaller werg burst from the trees and slammed into one of them.

Christine, no. You should have run.

The two creatures rolled along the ground, ripping and clawing at each other in a screeching fury of blood and hate. They squealed and yelped and snapped their teeth until one of the beasts, the bigger one, lay with his throat opened.

Christine rose to her hind legs and roared in victory. Blood dripped from her snout and claws. The other wergs hesitated, unsure of how to attack and not accustomed to another werg fighting back so effectively. Christine wasn't some rogue werg who had been previously tamed. She was raw and wild and fast as lightning. The Savages' confusion helped her.

She darted toward Aiden, dug her claws into his coat—and some of his flesh—and yanked him from the ground. The Savages pounced, spit and snot spraying from their snouts.

As Christine dragged Aiden through the brush, he caught a glimpse of his blood-drenched leg and wondered how much blood a person could lose before they reached the point of no return. He concluded he was about there.

Christine yanked him over her shoulder like a sack of potatoes. Aiden gripped her fur as tightly as he was able and watched the Savages giving chase. Christine was faster than they were, and she slowly pulled away.

Stay awake, Aiden told himself as she weaved through the trees. She carried him to his truck and ripped the door open, almost tearing it from its hinges. She slung him into the driver's seat, and then hopped into the bed.

The Savages exploded from the forest.

Aiden found the strength to turn the key. A Savage slammed against the tailgate, rocking the truck's ass end sideways.

With all his strength, Aiden pulled the gear-shift into Drive and mashed his foot down on the gas pedal. He watched the rearview mirror.

Aiden's truck was built for power, not acceleration. Christine crouched as the Savages gained on them. Aiden realized what Christine was about to do.

"No," he cried.

But she was enraged and sprang from the bed. She slammed against the nearest Savage. Aiden dropped his foot off the gas and looked to the side mirror as she tumbled with her foe along the road. The other Savages continued the chase.

He saw Christine in the side mirror as she rose up victoriously and then fled back into the woods. Two of the Savages broke off their pursuit of Aiden and gave chase. Aiden smashed the gas pedal again and slowly pulled away. Unable to hold the tourniquet any longer, he felt it loosen slightly and blood started filling the footwell.

A glance at himself in the rearview mirror revealed how pale his face had become. He approached a bridge and his foot fell off the gas pedal again. He wanted to sleep. He shivered until he feared his teeth would shatter. *I'm so sorry, Christine.*

He could no longer see the road. His head lolled against the side window and his hands slipped from the steering wheel.

He heard an explosion of tearing metal and shattering glass. He felt weightless for the briefest of seconds before his chest slammed against the steering wheel with enough force to break bones. His neck snapped forward and then back again before he collapsed to the bloody footwell between the seat and the steering wheel.

And then, as if to antagonize him, the driver's side airbag exploded into the nothingness above his head. Even as his chest ached from the impact, he couldn't help but chuckle at the faulty airbag. It was just his luck.

His vision blurred. It wouldn't be long now.

Silence replaced the carnage.

A CURSE FOR LIFE

25

Christine heard the crash and knew it had to be Aiden. He had looked pretty bad when she'd jumped from the truck bed. With the two Savages chasing her, she circled around while putting distance between them. She was much faster.

She burst from the tree line onto the road between a bridge and the Savages. Aiden's car was wrapped around a pillar and dangling over the edge of a drop-off. Christine raced to it. The two Savages that were chasing her joined the others and they all stopped suddenly as if called off.

Christine reached Aiden's truck. He was slouched half on the seat and half in the pooling blood in the footwell. She didn't need vital signs or blood tests or doctors to recognize the look of death growing on his pale face. Despite her difficulty in concentrating, she still understood no amount of paramedic work could save him. She ripped the door free with ease. The rise and fall of his chest slowed from panting breaths to sporadic, dying gasps. He had minutes, maybe seconds, left to live.

Aiden's increasingly distant eyes lifted to hers and his lips moved slightly. She leaned closer.

"Change me," he whispered.

What? She shook her head.

"It's … only … way."

She would never give someone such a cruel curse.

"Please," he moaned.

She had no reason to believe changing him would save his life, but she remembered how quickly she had healed before.

She dreaded doing what she knew needed to be done. She leaned in toward his shoulder. The smell of his blood gave her an almost insatiable urge. She opened her mouth and leaned in closer. It was impossible to resist. What she was about to do tore at her conscience. She let go of her restraint and sank her teeth into his flesh. His blood was thick and salty, and a distant part of her was horrified at how much she enjoyed the taste. She gulped it down with euphoria, even as her brain screamed through the static to pull away. She continued to feast on his blood with guilty delight, unable to resist.

She had wanted to help him, but she was more likely to send him over the edge if she didn't find the strength to pull back. She focused on who she was as a person and forced herself to remember what it meant to be in control. As Aiden's body increasingly lost its fight, something clicked in Christine's brain. With every ounce of restraint she could muster, she ripped her mouth away and bellowed to the sky.

The sudden rumble of an approaching engine snapped her back. She grabbed Aiden and pulled, but his leg was pinned between contorted metal and the dash. Headlights brightened the truck cab. Christine ripped the already broken seat from the floor and wedged it between Aiden and the coming vehicle, hoping to cushion the impact somewhat. She dove out of the way as a black van crashed into the truck. The truck twisted around the bridge's concrete pillar and slid farther over the edge, teetering above the cold, rushing water.

The van backed away, its grill and headlights shattered, and its front end a gnarled, crumpled mess. Steam spit from its cracked radiator. The doors flew open. Two men climbed out with flashlights and guns raised.

Christine looked helplessly to Aiden as the truck scooted closer to the edge. She couldn't stop it unless she could stop gravity. And then the truck fell. She lunged for the bumper but missed. The truck hit the water and started sinking fast.

The men from the van started laughing.

Christine scrambled to the edge and prepared to dive in after Aiden. But before she could take the leap, a stinging pain struck her neck. She brushed her hand at it and a yellow dart fell to the street. Another dart punctured her left shoulder and sent her to her knees. The world faded fast. She dropped to her rear.

One of the men stood over her with a disturbing smile. "Well, that couldn't have worked out any better," he said.

His partner laughed again.

"Go help Rex gather the Savages. We need to beat feet." He cocked his head as he looked at her. "Mr. Henderson has plans for you." He said something else, but Christine could no longer understand him.

She fought to stay awake but her arms were made of lead. Her head became too heavy to hold up and drooped forward.

She fell to her side.

Christine woke up outside lying on the ground with nothing on but a pair of men's boxer shorts and an oversized T-shirt. She sat up and pulled her knees to her chest, shivering. Something was around her neck. She gingerly touched metal with sharp edges and realized she wore a collar of some kind. A chain fastened to it led to a hinge on a wall.

She tried to slip her finger between the metal and her neck, but it was too snug. The sharp edge cut her finger and the wound sizzled like when Aiden had shot her with silver.

She looked around, careful not to turn her head too quickly. She was inside a small fenced-in area like a horse stall. It reminded her of her grandpa's horse ranch in Texas. The combined stench of an old litter box and rotten meat burned her nostrils.

As she rubbed her arms, her paramedic training told her hypothermia was a real possibility. The moon plodded across the sky. She curled into a ball in the corner, hoping to block some of the breeze. Her stomach rumbled. Her fingers and toes were numb. She could see her breath. It was the longest night of her life. What did they want with her?

Eventually, a sliver of early morning sun peeked into her enclosure. She stretched her feet into the warm ray. As the sun rose and reached her hands, she heard someone approach the gate. Christine scooted back against the opposite wall as the gate was flung open. Two men stepped inside. One of them carried a pail of water and dumped it into a trough. The other man set a bucket of what smelled like scrambled eggs on the ground.

"What am I doing here?" Christine asked.

They ignored her, finished their business, and left. They didn't shut the gate. Christine's stall opened into a larger corral. She cautiously crawled to the bucket. Though the eggs could have been drugged, she was too hungry to care. She devoured them. Then she went to the trough for a drink.

While cupping her hands in the lukewarm water, she heard another gate open nearby. Then she heard an animal grunt. Somewhere else, a creature howled.

She listened as the two men moved from gate to gate, opening each of them. It wasn't long before a werg appeared at her gate. She tensed up at the sight of him, hoping he didn't notice her. *Don't move,* she told herself.

The creature sniffed the ground and then the gate. He nudged the gate open with his snout and rose to his back legs. He sniffed the air. Christine sat motionless. The werg's eyes searched the stall until they landed on Christine. Then he dropped back to all fours. His fur had a silverish tint. He crawled toward her.

"Eeeaasy," she whispered.

He stopped short and sniffed her foot and then tilted his head curiously. She yanked her foot back and he flinched. The dirt cloud from her quick movement puffed around his snout and he recoiled. His mouth twitched and crinkled, exposing his teeth. He ducked his head to the side as his snout quivered. And then he let loose a violent sneeze. He shook his head, as if trying to rid himself of a tickle still in his nose. His face contorted and he sneezed again … and again … and again. Christine counted seven before he finished. Then he looked up and she saw something familiar in his eyes.

She covered her mouth. Could it be?

He brought his head to within a couple of inches from her face. Something moved beyond the gate. She leaned to look past him. He followed her with his own head, blocking her view. She leaned the other way and he followed her again. She half snorted and half cried.

"You know I hate when you do that, Billy." She couldn't believe her own words as they left her lips.

He looked away for a second and then turned back. Did he understand her? He scooted within reach and lowered his head submissively. She touched the side of his snout and he leaned into her hand. Tears filled her eyes.

"I can't believe it, Billy. It's you."

She thought she saw him smile as he backed away.

"I'm so sorry, Billy," she whispered.

Behind him, the gate was yanked the rest of the way open and he whipped his head around. His ears spiked and the fur on his back lifted.

Another werg stood in the opening, drool dripping from his jowls. He sniffed the air and released a menacing growl. Billy stood up straight, revealing that the other werg was bigger than him. The werg dropped his head back and roared. His breaths quickened and his eyes turned evil.

Billy dropped to all fours again and squared off. The werg pounced, meeting Billy in the center of the stall. The impact was like a meteor hitting the earth. Billy was slammed to his back with the other beast on top. Christine dove out of the way.

Other wergs in other stalls howled in excitement.

Billy lunged for the beast's throat but missed. The werg slashed Billy's face with his nails, clamped his teeth around Billy's shoulder, and effortlessly hurled him across the stall against the gate. Billy lay motionless on the ground.

The beast turned to Christine. She backed against the wall. He stalked closer on all fours, sniffing the air, and shoved his snout against her leg like a nosey dog. She kicked him. He flinched but moved in again. Using his snout, he tried to lift her shirt. His nose was cold and wet. She pushed him away. He grunted as if annoyed and shoved his nose up her shirt again.

"What do you want?" she cried.

He snorted and stepped back. He showed his teeth and dug at the dirt like a bull preparing to charge. But before he attacked, he hesitated and his ears perked.

Billy slammed into his side, knocking them both against the wall beside Christine. They roared and thrashed, each going for the other's throat. Again, Billy ended up on the bottom. He was just too small.

Christine needed to do something. She grabbed her chain between both hands and gave it some slack. As Billy thrashed beneath his foe, she leaped onto the beast's back and looped the chain over his head. The edge of her collar cut the side of her neck. She wrapped the chain around her fists and pulled with both hands. She was barely strong enough to pull the beast away from Billy enough for him to wriggle an arm free. He slashed at the bigger one's gut, splattering blood across the wall. The beast bucked violently, throwing Christine back to the ground with a thud. She lost her wind. In her anger, an animalistic roar escaped her.

"No," she cried, remembering the sharp collar. She scurried to her rear and scooted against the wall. *Don't change. Don't change. Happy thoughts.*

With the larger beast momentarily distracted, Billy sank his teeth into his neck. Blood spurted from between his teeth. The beast wailed. Billy ripped his mouth free, tearing a gash in the other werg's throat. The creature recoiled across the stall. He tried to flee, but he was losing blood fast. Within a few steps outside of the stall, he collapsed to his face. His body quivered and he held his throat until he was too weak and his hands dropped to the ground.

Billy stalked him, ready and thirsty for more.

Christine called to him. "Billy, come back. Leave him." But Billy was incensed and paced before his dying prey.

After the bigger werg breathed his final breath, Billy howled in victory to tell all the others a new king had emerged. Then he paced in front of the gate as if guarding Christine. She wanted to go to him, but the chain wouldn't reach. She pleaded with him to come back into the stall. Once he was finally confident there were no other threats, he crawled to Christine's feet and lay down.

She touched his neck. "Thank you for saving me," she whispered.

He began licking a fresh wound on his forearm. She sat with him for hours. He fell asleep. His battle, though short, had been exhausting. She held him as she dozed off as well.

Suddenly, Billy bounced up with an angry snarl, startling Christine awake. "What is it?" she cried. "Is there another one?"

Billy stood on his rear legs, his complete focus on the gate where the two men from earlier had arrived to drag the carcass of the fallen werg away. Once they were gone again, Billy turned to Christine with sad eyes.

"What is it?" she asked.

He lowered his head as if to show her something on his back. She touched between his ears, but he maneuvered his head under her hand until she brushed across a rough lump on the back of his neck. He winced. She leaned in for a closer look, parting his fur with her fingers. There were eight medical staples covering a scabbed-over knot.

"I know about the chips, Billy," she whispered.

He nudged his head against her hand.

"What? I don't understand."

He took her hand and dragged her finger over the tender spot.

"I don't know what you want me to do."

He pulled his hand back and picked at the ground with a pointy nail.

Christine cocked her head. He nudged his head against her hand and picked at the ground again.

Then it hit her. She shook her head. "No, Billy. I can't do that. I can't take it out here. You need a doctor."

Billy growled and pushed his neck against her hand again.

"I can't, Billy. I'm sorry."

Just then, the two men returned. They wore army fatigues. One of them carried a cattle prod, the other a rifle. They charged into the stall. Billy pinned his ears back and tucked his head. The soldier with the prod gave Billy a nasty jolt. Billy yelped and immediately lowered his chest to the dirt.

Christine screamed, "Leave him alone." She lunged at them, but the chain stopped her short, nearly cutting her throat.

The soldier kicked Billy in the side and snapped, "Get back, you filthy mutt." Sparks popped from the end of his cattle prod, and he shoved it against Billy's shoulder. Billy yelped again and scrambled to the corner.

Christine was enraged. The bones in her face popped and shifted.

The prick with the cattle prod grinned. "I wouldn't do that if I were you," he said, pointing at his own neck.

Christine turned away, the sight of him too provoking. She searched her mind for something that would bring her joy and settled on the guys at the firehouse. The thought of Alex making jokes in the kitchen gave her a warm rush.

The guard motioned to his partner, "Go get her, Trent."

Trent was the one with the rifle. He was a younger man with dark features and a soft, almost prepubescent face. "Put your hands behind your back," he said. His voice had a soft tone.

She scowled at him.

"You don't listen very well, do you?" the other guard shouted, and kicked Billy again.

"Okay," she answered. "I'll do what you say, just don't hurt him anymore."

Trent said, "I'll say it one more time. Hands behind your back."

She slowly did as ordered. "What are you going to do to me?"

"Just relax," he answered. He zip-tied her wrists and then reached for her neck with a brass key from his pocket. "When I take that off, you'd better behave. If you try to change or escape or anything, we'll kill your friend. Understand?"

She glared back coldly.

Trent winked and said, "It'll be warmer inside, won't it, Jim?"

Jim grunted.

Trent ran his finger between the zip tie and her wrist. "Not too tight?" he asked.

She shook her head. She glanced at Billy as he cowered against the wall. Jim shoved a black hood over her head and the two guards grabbed her arms and led her away.

I'll be back for you, Billy, she silently vowed.

As they walked, Trent said, "Hey, Jim. Did you know that werg the other one killed used to work for the WereHouse?"

"What do you mean?"

"He was a guard like us. I heard he allowed a werepet to be delivered without being completely tamed."

"No shit?"

"They said his name was Ray or something. I guess they never found the werepet he lost, so his punishment was to take his place."

"Damn. That seems kind of harsh."

"No kiddin'."

Jim and Trent escorted Christine from the corral, through a door at the rear of a large building, and into a long hallway. The tile was like ice beneath her bare feet, but at least the hall was heated. They led her up several flights of equally cold stairs and into another long hallway. This hallway was carpeted.

Jim pounded on the door. A muffled voice from the other side invited them in. Trent removed Christine's hood as Jim opened the door.

The brightness from three large picture windows along the farthest wall momentarily blinded her. She blinked away the blur. A magnificent grand piano was on one side of the room and a bar was on the other. A white leather couch sat on a fluffy, white shag rug in the center.

Jim nudged her into the room.

An older man sat on a barstool next to one of the windows, gazing outside. He glanced at her, and then back out the window. He said, "Beautiful day outside today, wouldn't you agree, Ms. Alt?"

She didn't answer.

He took a deep breath and sighed. "Thank you for joining me."

Christine wanted to shout, "I didn't have a choice," but thought better of smarting off, at least until she found out what he wanted.

Trent remained at her side.

The older man stood up. He was wearing a tuxedo with an emerald-green handkerchief stuffed in the breast pocket. He moved across the room toward her as he spoke. "My name is Bernard Henderson."

Mr. Henderson? She thought back to Aiden's story and found the courage to say what she was thinking. "I've heard your name before. You're a monster."

He snorted. "Oh? And where did you hear my name? From your new friend, Aiden?"

She didn't answer.

"Let me tell you a little about Aiden. He was my best hunter. He killed more werewolves than I could keep track of. And he did it with a smile."

"He didn't know they were people," she snapped.

"Oh, I bet he knew on some level. He either knew or he didn't want to know. His team knew." He scratched his head. "Although, he has always been a bit of a … how can I put this? Let's just say Aiden never wanted to know the down and dirty parts of the job. Maybe it was his way of telling himself he was better than the other hunters. I mean, shit, some of those guys are just flat-out evil."

"I think you're evil."

Bernard chuckled and then shrugged. "Perhaps."

"Will you just tell me what I'm doing here?"

"Well, Ms. Alt, it just so happens that I am in need of a date for a very special occasion tonight, and you happen to be available."

Christine glared at him. "You realize there are people for that. You obviously have plenty of money, so why don't you buy a date? Maybe whoever you paid would at least pretend to like your company."

Bernard smirked and turned back toward the windows. "Why would I buy a date when I have you just lying around?"

"Have me? Are you crazy? You've kidnapped me. I'm not going anywhere with you but the police station."

Bernard whirled around and grabbed her face with one hand, squeezing her mouth into a pucker and digging her teeth into the insides of her cheeks. His eyes darkened. "You listen to me, mouth."

Christine jerked her head away. He glared at her with cold, calculating eyes. She glared back defiantly.

"Maybe you don't quite grasp who I am. I have plans for you. If you don't go along with those plans, I will gut you where you stand."

Jim cleared his throat. "Sir?"

Without taking his eyes from Christine, Bernard snapped, "What?"

"Just so you know, her friend is werg number seven-three-two-eight down in the stables."

"Oh yeah? Which one is that again? I mean, what was his name before he joined us?"

"Billy, I think."

"Ah, yes. Billy. He was your friend on the fire department, wasn't he?"

Christine's heart broke. It must have shown on her face because Bernard grinned.

"Yeah, he's a paramedic. What a great guy he must have been. You know what? Hey, Jim. Why don't you go down there and kill our good friend Billy? We won't be needing him."

Christine gasped as Jim reached for the door handle.

She believed he would do it.

"Wait," she said.

Jim looked to Bernard for direction, and Bernard nodded. "Yeees, Ms. Alt? Is there something you'd like to say?"

Christine lowered her head.

"Well?"

She mumbled, "What do you want me to do?" It killed her to say it.

Bernard smiled again. "Now, that's more like it." He looked to Jim and Trent and said, "Take her to the bathroom so she can get cleaned up. She looks like hell."

Jim grabbed one of her arms and Trent grabbed the other.

Before they took her to Bernard's private bathroom, Bernard added, "There should be plenty of girly things in there, but if you need something else, just ask. My wife uses that bathroom to prepare for nights on the town, and I don't figure you think you're any better than my wife. Do you?"

Christine didn't answer.

"Do you?" he asked again, his voice a little harder.

Jim squeezed her arm. She shook her head.

The bathroom was nearly as big as her condo. The sweet smell of vanilla wafted from a candle burning next to a Jacuzzi tub. The marble floor was heated.

Jim drew a small pocketknife from a pouch on his belt and sliced the restraints from her wrists. He motioned toward the shower. "What are you waiting for? Get cleaned up."

She stepped into the shower, pulled the frosted glass door closed, and tossed her clothes over the top.

She sighed in the warm spray of water. It was soothing to her sore muscles.

There was a shelf that held every type of soap and conditioner she could ever need. She scrubbed her body raw, as if trying to wash the ugliness of Bernard from her very pores.

After a bit, Jim loudly cleared his throat to hurry her along. She'd have stayed in there all day if she had a choice. She asked for a couple of towels, and Jim draped them over the shower door. She wrapped a towel around her body and another around her hair and stepped out.

Jim handed her a long garment bag. "Wear this," he said.

She unzipped the front and found an emerald-green strapless dress that matched the green handkerchief in Bernard's breast pocket. At the bottom of the garment bag was a pair of black, high-heeled shoes.

She hesitated.

"Well?" Jim asked.

"A little privacy?" she answered.

"I don't think so."

Sitting on the vanity was a matching bra and panties. It disgusted her that Bernard had taken the time to pick them out like a boyfriend might. He even had the right sizes, which creeped her out even more. She pulled on the panties under the towel and then turned away to put on the bra. She slipped the dress over her head as fast as she could. She felt Jim's prying eyes searing her back the whole time.

As she dressed, he backed up to a chair in the corner of the bathroom and sat down. She put on makeup and did her hair all while he ogled her from behind.

Eventually, she finished and said, "I suppose I'm ready."

Jim looked at his watch and groaned. "It's about time. Come on." He led her back to where Bernard was talking to Trent by the piano. They were having a drink.

Bernard looked her up and down and said, "You look stunning, Ms. Alt."

She scoffed.

He flicked his wrist at Jim and Trent. "You two can leave now."

They nodded and left. Bernard walked to the bar. "Thirsty?" he asked.

"I'll take some water." She wondered why he wasn't worried about her shifting and ripping out his throat.

He poured a shot of bourbon into one glass and filled another with water from a pitcher sitting in a pail of ice. He asked, "Have you ever heard of the Expeditioner's Club?"

She shook her head.

"I don't suppose you have. Most people haven't." He handed her the glass.

As she reached for it, she looked into his eyes. There was no warmth behind them, and she immediately understood what Aiden had said about working for the devil.

Bernard stepped back and looked her up and down as he sipped his bourbon. "Well," he said. "Spin around and let me see the whole dress." Before she had a chance to comply, he added, "Slowly."

She felt like a piece of meat as she twirled. When she had her back to him, he touched her bare shoulder. His fingers felt like ice and she cringed. She suddenly wanted another shower.

He stopped her mid-turn and said, "Just a second. You forgot to remove the tag. Here, let me get it."

She closed her eyes, inwardly pleading for him not to touch her again. He opened a pocketknife. But instead of cutting the tag, he leaned in and blew lightly on the back of her neck. She flinched and turned, bumping his hand.

He grunted. His pocketknife fell to the carpet. He held his left hand with his right. "You stupid bitch. You made me cut myself."

Blood dripped onto the hardwood. He wrapped the handkerchief from his breast pocket around his hand and the rich, silky material instantly changed from emerald-green to a darker, wetter green.

Christine fought back a smile.

He walked to the bar and pulled out a blue and white box that she recognized as a first aid kit. "Sit down," he said, and pointed at the piano seat.

She sat and watched him tend to his wound. In any normal situation she'd be the first to help someone who was injured, but this bastard could bleed to death for all she cared. He wrapped his hand in gauze and tossed his handkerchief onto a white, padded barstool, staining it as well.

"You might need stitches," she said, hardly able to hold back a chuckle.

"Shut up."

"I'm just saying. As a medic, I'd recommend stitches, or you'll have a nasty scar."

"Do you think I care about scars? We ain't going to no hospitals. Now, shut up." He glanced in the mirror beside the bar and then froze briefly. His shoulders drooped and his upper lip crinkled. "You gotta be kidding me," he mumbled, and gave her a backward glare. "You made me get blood on my shirt. If I didn't need you looking your best, I'd knock the piss outta you." He made his way across the room to a walk-in closet and stripped out of his jacket, his shirt, and his undershirt, which also bore a faint red stain.

Though his muscles had the sagginess that men inevitably gained later in life, his physique was strong and fit. He dressed in a new shirt and retied his tie.

Once his jacket was on again, he said, "Let's go." Then he swigged another shot of whiskey and led her from the room.

A stretched Hummer limousine waited for Christine and Bernard at the entrance of the compound. The chauffer held the door open. Bernard stepped aside and gestured for her to get in first like the gentleman he wasn't. She climbed in and he followed.

As they headed to God-only-knew-where, Mr. Henderson laid out a few rules for the evening. "Make sure you call me Bernard. Not Bernie, Bernard. Is that clear? No one calls me Bernie."

She looked out the window.

He grabbed her chin and turned her head toward him. "I said, is that clear?"

"Yes," she snapped, and pulled away. "I got it, Bernard."

"Next, I think it's important you understand the pain that I will give you if this night doesn't go exactly how I planned. I hope you believe me when I tell you that I will kill you, your family, and your friend Billy, if you ask anyone for help or even hint that you are anything but my newest squeeze."

From what she already knew about him, she had little doubt he was telling the truth.

He looked through the window for a second and then said with a smirk, "Hey, do you think someone might recognize you tonight? I mean, your picture has probably been in the Dispatch and all over the news channels."

Christine sat up a little straighter. She hadn't thought of that possibility.

Bernard burst out laughing. "Oh, Christine, you must think I'm stupid." He slapped her thigh as he laughed even harder. "These people aren't going to recognize you. And do you know what? Who cares if they do? They aren't going to say a word. The ones who know me know better, and the ones who don't, let's just say the dirt I have on them will keep their lips shut. No one's going to recognize you, and even if they do, no one's going to care. Hell, as you've already seen, I have the future President of the United States, Senator Wooten himself, under my thumb. I guess you could say I'm not terribly worried about it. And, to be honest, half these guys probably have women of their own chained in their basements. We're not going to a Boy Scout meeting, after all."

Hoping to somehow sway him into abandoning the night altogether, she said almost under her breath, "Still a risk, if you ask me."

"Well, I didn't ask you. In fact, I hope somebody does recognize you. You know why? Because I've had more important men than these people taken care of, and I rather enjoy the game of it. So, I wouldn't worry my pretty little head if I were you."

"What if I just shifted and ripped out your throat right here?"

"You could. But I have contingencies in place to ensure you won't." He held out his cellphone out for Christine to see what was on the screen. It was a photo of her fire house. "If you screw this up tonight, every one of your firefighter friends will pay the price. Understand?"

She nodded and sank deeper into her seat. He drank another glass of whiskey. She hoped he got so drunk he passed out. At least then she wouldn't have to listen to him anymore, and maybe they'd miss whatever event they were attending.

It was quiet for most of the drive until Christine blurted, "What do the chips do?"

"Excuse me?"

"The chips in their necks. Aiden said they measure adrenaline spikes. But that doesn't seem worth the effort of designing them. So, what else do they do?"

Bernard looked stone-faced at her. "I like you, Christine. You're quite curious. What do you think they do?"

Christine thought for a moment. "Well, I don't have one in my neck. And I can shift back and forth." She tried to read his face but he didn't falter. Then she answered, "They keep 'em wergs, don't they?"

Bernard gave her a sly smile. That was all she needed. She didn't say anything else, and neither did he, until they arrived.

As they drove up to the valet stand at the front of the Penrose Lodge, he reminded her, "Remember, I don't go by Bernie. It's Bernard. Or honey if you must."

The valet opened the back door. A crowd of equally well-dressed attendees walked a red carpet through the front doors. Bernard took Christine's hand and led her into the lobby.

They were met by an older man and his stunningly gorgeous trophy girlfriend. He introduced his lady-friend to "my old tight-ass buddy, Bernard," as he put it.

Bernard leaned toward the woman and kissed her cheek. He pulled back and said, "This is my best girl, Christine."

The older man said, "Nice to meet you. How long have you two been a couple?"

Bernard gave her hand a slight squeeze. She answered, "Three months. But it seems like forever, huh, Bernie?" She tugged her hand away before he could give it a harder squeeze.

Bernard smirked.

The older man said, "Young love, huh? Bernard, you old devil, you never disappoint. She might be your best-looking date ever. And here I thought you didn't like to be called Bernie."

"Well, you know. She's quite special." He tensed his jaw and spoke through his teeth. It was subtle, but Christine noticed.

A waiter interrupted their conversation with a platter of hors d'oeuvres.

Bernard asked, "So, what do we start with this fine evening?"

The waiter answered, "Madagascar hissing cockroaches stuffed with blue cheese."

Christine quietly gagged.

Bernard picked out a stick with a vile, half-dollar-sized insect speared on the end. "Mmmm," he moaned at the mere sight of it. His old friend and the geezer's gold-digging girlfriend grabbed one for themselves. All eyes were on Christine.

There was no way in hell she was eating one of those creatures. She looked to Bernard with pleading eyes. He nodded. She shook her head. He reached into his inside coat pocket. "If you all will excuse me for a moment, I need to make a call. Honey, what's Billy's number again?"

She reached for his hand and pulled it gently from his pocket. As she reached for one of the cockroaches-on-a-stick, she said, "Can't it wait, honey?" Then she looked at the couple and said, "Business. He can't stop thinking about work for even one night."

With three sets of eyes on her, she held the giant cockroach kabob up to her mouth. Bernard was the first to take a crunchy bite of his. The other two psychos followed suit.

Her stomach turned. After Bernard stared her down with cold eyes, she touched the cockroach to her lips. *Think about something else. Think about something else.*

She poked part of the dead insect into her mouth, closed her eyes, and chomped down. Chilled blood, cheese, and what she was pretty sure were bug guts squirted into the back of her throat. The audible crunch seemed louder in her head. She gagged and hid her mouth behind her cocktail napkin.

"Not for you, honey?" Bernard asked.

"Not really, Bernie," she answered, the inflection of her voice on the name "Bernie" giving away her disdain to anyone who cared to listen closely enough.

Bernard brushed her cheek with his knuckle. "Oh well. You were a good sport. Maybe you'll like the next treat better." He finished his cockroach, and then ate hers as well.

"I have to pee," she blurted, hoping to miss the next "treat."

Bernard's eyes widened as though he was slightly surprised and even more excited. He clapped his hands together. "Well, by all means, let's go then." He turned to his friends. "If you'll excuse us, we have to hit the ladies' room."

His friend smiled and winked like a perverted old man. He said, "You're a devil, Bernie. Don't be in there all night." Then he made a cheesy growl, just like every generic pervert did in the movies.

Bernard grabbed her arm in a painful grip and led her to the bathroom. He nodded pleasantly at a couple of women as they exited, and then he followed Christine through the door. Once alone in the bathroom, his fake smile turned angry.

"Any more of that Bernie shit and we may have to leave early. And let me tell you ahead of time, if we leave early, I'll be going home alone, if you know what I mean. Now, go pee if you gotta pee."

"A little privacy?"

"I don't think so. Hurry up."

Christine entered a stall and pushed the door closed behind her. Bernard slammed his hand against it, forcing it back open. "Maybe you don't get the seriousness of this."

Two giggling women opened the bathroom door. Bernard didn't break his glare into Christine's eyes and said, "Occupied. Go do your coke somewhere else, girls." They huffed and went on their way.

When Christine finished, she pushed past him to the sink. She said, "You still haven't told me why you haven't killed me yet."

He grabbed both of her shoulders and spun her toward him. Her wet hands dripped soapy water on his tuxedo, but he didn't appear to care. "You are here as my guest. You will not embarrass me tonight. Very few people are privileged enough to eat some of the most exotic foods in the world, and you are about to be one of them. I needed a date, and you are it. I will tell you what I have planned for you in due time. For now, you will go out there and put on a happy face and eat whatever garbage they put in front of you."

"What if I gag?"

"You can gag. A lot of people gag. That's the fun of it. But what you will not do is be rude or refuse the food. You got it?"

Christine nodded.

"Now, let's go out there and have us some grilled maggots."

Oh God.

Christine was a champ. She chewed on deep fried tarantulas, bit into pickled cow eyes, and drank chilled grizzly bear blood with the best of them. She mingled and made jokes with every despicable person, all while pretending to be in a budding love affair with a man she couldn't despise more.

Bernard noticed a man standing near a window at the other side of the room and his eyes lit up. "Come on, Chris. I want you to meet someone." He practically dragged her across the room. One would have thought Jesus Christ was standing there by the way Bernard had turned giddy.

When the man saw Bernard coming, his eyes lit up as well. It was like an actual love affair. Bernard grabbed his hand and shook it. He was a handsome, dark-skinned man with a thousand-dollar haircut. He lifted Christine's hand and kissed it.

"Madam," he said. He had a thick Italian accent.

Christine nodded politely.

He bowed. "I am Pietro Salvatore at your service. And you are?"

"Christine."

"Ahhh, Christine. Such a lovely name."

Bernard interrupted, "Pietro, how's life on the island?"

Pietro grinned. He looked to Christine and said, "If you would excuse us for un minuto?"

Christine nodded.

Pietro took Bernard's arm like a prom date, and they stepped away. Their secret conversation lasted about five minutes before Bernard returned alone. Pietro nodded politely to Christine and then joined the conversation of another group. She wondered what kind of monster he must be to genuinely like Bernard as much as he seemed to.

While mingling with the crazies, there was one sight that seemed to haunt Christine for most of the evening, one that promised to put the rest of the horrible night to shame. Each time a waiter passed through the double doors with their trays of sickening delicacies, she could see the elaborately decorated dinner table in the next room, complete with place settings and a promise of something likely much worse. Christine couldn't imagine anything that would top what she had already eaten, but she figured, like the main event in a three-ring circus, the spotlight would be on the main course.

Right on cue, a bell jingled, and a waiter announced, "Dinner is ready." She looked to Bernard, and he looked back with a disgusting grin. This was why he had brought her.

He took her hand and led her to an exquisite dining room, complete with two piano-sized crystal chandeliers and a table that stretched farther than she cared to walk.

Each gold-rimmed china plate held an elegant, diamond-encrusted place setting with a card bearing the name of a guest. The silverware sparkled. Bernard led her along the table until he found a card that read "Bernard Henderson + guest."

He pulled her chair out. Christine nodded a phony thank-you as he slid her chair to the table. He took his seat at her side.

She couldn't believe how many of the women had the same excited faces as the men. It was absurd to see these heavily made-up women in their expensive gowns and shining accessories, clearly society's upper crust, merrily awaiting the next horror to put in their mouths. Some of them giggled with their escorts, while others engaged in nervous chit-chat with the couples next to them.

Christine wanted to shout, "What is wrong with you people?" but that wouldn't bode well for her continued good health. Hers or Billy's.

Pietro sat dateless farther down. With his obvious swagger and suavity, Christine surmised his coming alone was intentional.

The kitchen door swung open, and the room fell quiet. Tuxedoed waiters filed into the dining hall, carrying bottles of wine, pitchers of blood-red liquid, and more of their "delectable" appetizers.

Christine waved off the red liquid, which she imagined was probably blood, instead accepting a glass of what she hoped was truly wine.

A very proper, middle-aged man made his way from the kitchen to the head of the table. He, too, wore a tuxedo, only his coat had tails. His cummerbund and tie were a dark maroon, unlike the black ones worn by the serving staff. As he cleared his throat to speak, the guests began tapping their silverware against their wine glasses. After a nudge from Bernard, Christine joined in on the ovation.

The man waited, soaking in the welcome with a regal stance and smile like he was the King of England. After what felt like forever, the crowd settled and allowed him to speak.

"My fellow Expeditioners, I welcome you to this momentous event. This dinner has taken me two years to prepare, and I trust everyone has been pleased thus far."

The crowd nodded in unison.

"This year is a bit different than the previous years. I am proud of each and every exotic meal our club has served over the years, but tonight I have outdone myself, I must say."

Christine chugged the rest of her wine in anticipation of his "wonderful" announcement and held up her glass to be refilled posthaste.

He continued, "I am about to serve you a feast so exotic, so tasty, that no one in this room shall ever forget it. Tonight's meal will prove to be the most expensive meal I have ever delivered. In fact, this feast is more expensive than our last seven dinners combined." He paused and smiled. "We have a single man to thank for such a generous donation. We should all hold up our glasses and toast the head of WereHouse Enterprises. If not for him, such a meal would not be possible. Mr. Bernard Henderson, on behalf of the Expeditioner's Club, I thank you."

The crowd began tapping their glasses again. The old-timer from the lobby shouted, "Way to go, Bernie."

Bernard glared at Christine before nodding his gratitude to the rest of the members.

Christine whispered in his ear, "My God, how much did you donate?"

Bernard winked and whispered back, "Just enjoy the next hour. This, after all, is why we're here."

The kitchen doors opened again. Two dozen waiters passed through with covered dishes on fancy silver trays and stood behind each of the guests. The final three waiters in the line carried large, round covered platters and placed them at six-foot intervals in the center of the table.

The host spoke up again, "Fellow Expeditioners, I present you ..."

At that moment, the three waiters lifted the centerpiece lids. Christine pulled back in horror. The rest of the crowd gasped in delight. Sitting on the platter, not two feet away, was the severed head of a werewolf. Two more heads rested on the other two platters. All at once, she felt like crying, puking, and shoving her fork through the side of Bernard's head.

"You animal," she whispered to her "date."

Bernard leaned over like he had dropped his napkin. She felt his cold hand slide under her dress up to her thigh. She flinched. An older woman sitting across the table guessed where his hand had gone and gave him an offended shake of her head. Bernard winked and she turned away.

Smiling, he squeezed Christine's leg and whispered, "I'm not the one on the table."

She forced a fake smile for anyone who was watching. "One day, you may be," she whispered back.

Bernard let out a phony laugh.

The host sat at the head of the table and began eating. With a mouthful of meat, he had another tidbit of information to pass on. "Oh, yes. I almost forgot to tell you of the legend of werewolf meat. It has been said that consuming it will give you longer life and stronger bones."

Christine whispered to Bernard, "Where did he hear that bullshit?"

Bernard chuckled. "Well, I told him, of course."

"Something I don't understand. I changed because I got a werg's blood in my mouth. Won't your friends change into wergs after they eat the meat?"

"Maybe they will."

Her eyes widened.

Then he laughed. "Seriously, though. The werewolf trait is like a virus. That's why the meat is so well done." He held up a chunk of blackened meat with his fork and waited for her to fill in the blanks. "We cook it out of them," he finally said. "Same as E. coli in hamburger."

The host went on to explain the "benefits" of eating such an "exquisite" meal, but Christine didn't listen. While he spoke, she whispered, "Are you going to tell me why I'm here?"

Bernard feigned a cough and held his closed fist in front of his mouth. "I wanted you to see what will happen to you if you don't do exactly what I ask from here on out. Our host has been begging me for female werepet meat for years. As rare as werewolf meat is, female meat is even rarer."

"And what is it you want *me* to do?"

"What if I told you that we at the WereHouse believe breeding wergs could quite possibly be more efficient and lucrative than how we have been procuring our pets thus far?"

Christine soaked in his words. She opened her eyes wide and whispered, "You. Are. Disgusting."

He laughed out loud, which brought on a real cough.

"Just kill me," she moaned. Their closest neighbors looked up from their meals.

Bernard gave them a politician smile and then turned back and hissed, "Shhh."

Christine lowered her voice and added, "I'll die before I'd let you do that to me."

"Calm down, Christine. Just sit back and enjoy your meal. We'll talk about this later."

She covered her mouth with her napkin. "There's nothing to talk about."

"We'll see."

She could no longer force a smile for the other guests. She leaned closer. "Oh, and I'm not eating another person no matter what you threaten me with."

He nodded with another grin to the guests who were paying closer attention to their growing rift. He leaned closer to her ear, "You've been a good sport. I think you can skip this meal. Politely decline and we'll leave it at that."

He sat up tall and straightened his coat with a dark look to the nosier guests. She could tell he was getting annoyed. His eyes narrowed when one lady continued to stare.

"Mind your business," he snarled, and she refocused on her plate.

Christine fought the incredible urge to scream out the true nature of their meal. All that held her back was the thought of Billy and the fact that no one in the room would probably care. They were all monsters.

While the psychos feasted on what could literally be their own neighbors, employees, or even relatives, Christine sat and stared into the dead eyes of the mutilated head that sat in front of her.

I am so sorry for what's happened to you.

Her chest started aching.

29

Christine scanned the roomful of old, rich, fat men and their trophy wives or girlfriends as each of the Expeditioners dragged their last bites of human flesh through their leftover gravy and crammed them into their bloated faces. Some of the women exchanged inane laughs, while others leaned back in their chairs with the wide-eyed look of discomfort that comes from gorging. The waiters gathered the empty plates.

"Not agreeable to you tonight, miss?" one of the waiters asked as he removed her untouched plate.

She ignored him. Bernard chuckled.

She leaned closer to him and whispered, "I hate you," which made him laugh even louder.

The host stood up again. "Ladies and gentlemen, I would like to thank you all for coming this evening. I think we can all agree that this meal was truly one in a million. Please join us, once again, in thanking Mr. Hen—"

A woman screamed on the other side of the dining room doors, cutting him off. Bernard turned his head from the host to the double doors, still chewing his last chunk of charred meat.

At the head of the table, the host stood confused. The other guests turned in their seats to see the dining room doors, curious but not as fearful as maybe they should have been.

The dining hall fell silent, but only for a few seconds. Then the dining room doors burst open. To Christine's shock, Aiden stood in the doorway. His face was bloody, deformed, and covered in patches of hair. She barely recognized him. He held a pistol in his half-human, half-werg hand. He stumbled against the doorframe and roared. His forehead jutted unnaturally outward.

He shouted, "Let her go, Bernard," but his voice was deep and grizzled, more animalistic snarl than human.

The women shrieked. The cowardly men overturned their chairs in their haste to escape. Only Pietro charged straight toward the threat. Aiden violently swatted him aside and he crashed against a glass case full of vases. Some of the party-goers stampeded past Aiden as the half-man, half-beast fought his transformation. The others cowered to the four corners of the room.

Bernard rose from his seat with his left hand tight around Christine's arm.

Aiden pointed his weapon at Bernard, and Bernard maneuvered Christine between them. Aiden's leg popped and deformed at the precise second he was ready to fire, throwing his shot wide to the right.

He pulled the trigger again as Bernard ducked below the table. Aiden's jaw protruded outward and his skin stretched. The gun fell to the floor.

Bernard pulled Christine under the table. "Tell him to stop or I'll kill you," he shouted, terror written across his face. He fumbled with his pocket and pulled out his cell phone. This was her chance. She swatted his hand, sending the phone sliding across the parquet floor.

Aiden dropped to all fours.

Bernard reached for his phone, but Christine shoved him off balance and he fell to his face. She kicked the phone away. He dove for her, but she scurried away from his outstretched arm.

Aiden leaped over the table, landing behind Bernard. Bernard reached blindly above his head and grabbed a fork. Aiden lunged with snapping teeth and then recoiled with a yelp. Bernard scrambled to his feet and fled through the kitchen door as Aiden fell to his back, Bernard's fork protruding from the side of his neck. Christine ran to him. It was silver. She ripped the fork free.

"Aiden. You have to change back," she screamed.

The remaining party-goers fled from the room. Aiden writhed on the ground.

Christine searched the room for something— anything—to help, but there was nothing useful. And then she remembered Bernard's phone. She grabbed it and dialed the number to Fire Station 22. Each unanswered ring was a stab to her heart.

Willie finally answered, "Y'ello."

"Willie, it's Christine."

"Christine, where the hell have you b—"

"No time. I need your help. Bring the medic to the Penrose Lodge."

"What's up, Chris?"

"Just hurry. You know where it is, right?"

"Yeah, I know. We'll be right there."

She tossed the cell phone and hurried back to Aiden. He dug at his wound until it was raw and bleeding worse than before. His mouth filled with thick, frothy phlegm that oozed past his teeth.

"Hold on, Aiden. Please."

She cradled his head while waiting for the sirens. She pleaded with him to hold on, rocking nervously back and forth.

Finally, Willie shouted from the entryway, "Christine?"

She cried, "In here, Willie. Oh God, in here."

Willie and Mick rushed through the door. Mick carried a large square medic case while Willie held an equally bulky airway kit. They froze when they entered the dining room.

Mick cocked his head. "Christine? What's going on?"

She gently lowered Aiden's head to the floor and ran to Mick. "No time to explain. You have to help me save him."

"But he's a werepet. We don't work on animals. He needs a vet."

"No," she snapped. "You don't understand." She pulled the orange kit from his hand and yanked it open, spilling unopened medication boxes all over the floor. "He's got silver in his blood," she said, as if that would mean anything to them. She handed Mick an IV bag and tubing. "Set this up," she shouted.

"What are we doi—?" he started to ask, but she interrupted him.

"He's having a reaction to the silver."

"What kind of reaction?"

"Like anaphylaxis. This is his only chance." She tied a tourniquet around Aiden's furry arm. Mick began to come around, or at least he knelt down to help.

"What do you want me to do, Chris?" Willie asked.

"Draw up Benadryl and Epinephrine. If it's like anaphylaxis, maybe our allergic reaction protocol will help."

"But he's not a person. He's a ... a ... a dog."

She glared at him; he got the message. He dug through the kit for the requested drugs.

Aiden jerked and thrashed, the wheezing in his lungs growing loud enough to hear from across the room.

She caressed the soft skin at the inside bend of his elbow until she felt the spongy lump of a vein. With the IV needle crammed into his flesh, dark red blood filled the IV chamber. She removed the needle and fastened the tubing to the IV catheter.

"Hold on, Aiden," she said, and caught a curious glance from Willie. Aiden convulsed briefly before going limp. He gasped a last breath, exhaled, and the life faded from his soulless black eyes.

"No, no, no," she cried. "Give me the Benadryl, Willie." He did. She pushed the meds into Aiden's veins.

Mick touched her shoulder. "Chris, it's over. The Benadryl won't work if his heart isn't pumping."

"Well, start compressions, then," she screamed.

Mick hesitated a second before rolling Aiden to his back and pressing on his sternum. "Chris, it isn't doing any good. His chest is too hard. There's no give."

"Give him the Epi shot," she shouted.

Willie shoved the syringe needle into Aiden's shoulder. "It still won't circulate without his heart beating, Chris."

"Then push harder on his chest, damn it."

Mick grunted as he pushed.

"Any give?" she cried.

"A little. Not enough."

"Use your foot, then."

Mick stood up and stepped on Aiden's chest.

"Better?"

"I think." He continued stomping rhythmically on Aiden's chest until, miraculously, a clump of thick hair fell from his neck.

"Keep going, Mick. I think it's working."

Red welts and hives replaced the hair. Aiden's snout distorted and shrank back into his face.

Christine grabbed Mick's leg. "Stop, stop, stop."

Mick and Willie backed against the dining room wall. They silently watched as Aiden finished shifting back into his human form.

Christine put her ear to his chest. "His heart's still not beating." She pressed on his sternum in rhythmic thrusts. "Help me, guys."

They stood, stunned, like statues against the wall. Mick whispered, "He's a … man?"

She shouted, "Guys, help me."

Mick shook away his shock and rushed to the airway kit for a bag-valve-mask. He pressed it over Aiden's mouth and nose and squeezed.

"Breathe," Christine cried, the tears streaking down her cheeks. "I can't fight him without you."

Willie took over the compressions and Mick continued pushing air into Aiden's lungs. Christine collapsed to her rear. She knew it was over.

Willie looked to Mick for direction, and Mick nodded sadly. They knew it too. Mick stopped squeezing the bag.

Willie slowed his compressions until he stopped altogether. "I'm sorry, Chris."

Mick whispered, "What the hell did we just see, Chris?"

She lifted her eyes and then lowered them back to Aiden. She whispered, "The werepets are people. They always have been."

Willie's jaw dropped.

Mick nodded toward Aiden. "And who's he?"

"A man who was going to help me make things right."

Mick touched her shoulder.

She took a deep breath and stood up. "I can't stay here and wait for the police."

"What do you mean? Why not?"

"They can't help me … They can't help Billy."

"Billy?" Mick gasped. "You know where Billy is?"

"I've seen him. I've gotta help him."

"Where is he? We'll help you."

The anger and sadness of seeing Aiden lying on the floor brought the crushing pain back to her chest. She needed to fight the change.

Mick tried to grab her arm but she yanked it away. "No," she roared.

"Chris, what's happening?" he asked.

She felt her calves cramp and her face go numb. And then something touched her ankle. She looked down through colorless sight.

Aiden looked up at her. He blinked and tried to focus.

Her hands shot to her mouth. She couldn't believe what she was seeing.

The welts and red patches on Aiden's skin faded before her eyes. Mick rushed to him and helped him sit up.

"What happened?" he asked.

Christine dropped to her knees and hugged him. "I can't believe you're alive."

He rubbed his head. "Where's Bernard?"

"He got away."

He looked at Mick and Willie. "Who are they?"

"Friends. They saved you."

He nodded. "Many thanks, guys." He rubbed his chest. "Man, my chest hurts."

Willie said, "Your heart stopped. We had to do compressions."

He groaned and pushed to his feet. He wobbled, and Mick helped steady him.

Christine asked, "How'd you find me?"

"That bastard never misses an Expeditioner's party. I knew there was one tonight because he'd been talking about it for weeks. I figured if I found him, I would find you."

Willie handed Aiden his fire department coat to cover up.

Aiden wrapped the coat around his waist. "He'll either send the Savages or my team of hunters for us. We need to get out of here." The approaching police sirens emphasized his words.

"What if we wait for the police?" she asked. "The WereHouse won't send hunters with the police here … Will they?"

"With what we now know about them, they'll kill anyone in their way to get to us. Including the cops." He looked into her eyes.

She dragged her hand along his cheek and smiled. "Okay, I trust you." She turned to her friends. "Willie, Mick, stall CPD for us."

"Where are you going?" Mick asked.

Aiden answered for her. "This ends tonight. We have to expose the WereHouse, and we have to help their victims. If we don't make it, remember what you saw here tonight."

Willie stepped forward. "I don't know *what* I saw."

Aiden smiled grimly. "Everything you think you saw, you did."

Christine started to leave with Aiden and then turned back to Willie and Mick. She mouthed, "Thank you."

Three police cruisers cleared a distant hill as they approached the Penrose Lodge. Aiden scanned a field that butted against the back of the building. He said, "If we shift, we can run." He started to remove Willie's coat.

Christine grabbed his arm. "Wait. I have a better idea. Come with me." She led him to Medic 22.

"We're stealing a medic?" he asked.

"Borrowing," she answered.

"We'll never get past the cops."

"Just trust me. Get in the back and lay down on the cot like you're a patient."

He climbed in and did as she said. She fetched a bullet-proof Kevlar vest with the fire department emblem on it from one of the outside compartments and threw it on. She climbed behind the steering wheel and headed toward the street as the first police cruiser pulled into the drive.

She slowed and lowered her window, hoping that the officer would be someone she knew and that the vest would help disguise the fact that she was out of uniform.

The cruiser slowed. It was an officer named Brian whom she knew. He shouted, "Hey, Christine. Where the hell have you been? Everyone's been searching for you."

"I know, Brian. I got back last night. I'll explain everything later."

"You're going to have to talk to my supervisor. We thought someone kidnapped you."

"I will. I just can't right now."

"What's going on at the lodge?"

"Someone's werepet was acting up and scared everyone. Willie and Mick are still inside."

"Where are you going, then?"

"When the werepet jumped on the table, some old geezer fell and hit his head. We're taking him to the ER."

Brian popped his gearshift into park and opened his door. "Mind if I talk with him for a second before you go?"

Christine's heart sank. She emphatically shook her head and said, "He's unconscious and we need to get him to the ER. You know the deal. You'll have to talk to him at the hospital. We can't wait. I've already waited too long."

She slipped her foot from the brake and pulled forward, praying Brian wouldn't push the issue.

Instead, he answered, "Yeah, yeah, I know. I'll see you at the hospital. You've got a lot of explaining to do."

"I'll wait for you there," she lied. She waved and smiled to the other two officers that were pulling in. They didn't stop her. She shouted back, "We're in the clear."

Aiden climbed through the opening between the front seats and sat in the passenger seat.

BETRAYED

30

Twelve-year-old Max Henderson was sound asleep in his upstairs bedroom when the front door slammed shut downstairs, jolting him awake. He slid from his bed and crept into the hall.

In the kitchen downstairs, his father was screaming at his mother. Max froze. He'd never heard his father so angry before.

"Don't ask me where I've been," Bernard shouted.

His mother answered, "But it's midnight. The phone has been ringing off the hook for the last couple hours. What's going on, Bernard?"

"Did you answer it, LeAnna?"

She didn't say anything.

"Did you?" Bernard screamed.

"Yes," she finally said, a nervous quiver in her voice. "I thought it might be you calling."

"What did they say?"

"I didn't understand. One of them asked if it was true."

"If what was true, LeAnna?"

"If one of the wergs had attacked people tonight."

"Goddamnit. What did you say?"

She started crying. "I told them I didn't know what they were talking about. What did you want me to say?"

"You shouldn't have answered the phone. Did they say anything else?"

"They said they were sending a camera crew over to speak with you. They asked me when you'd be home."

"And?"

"I said I didn't know."

Bernard took a deep breath. His voice calmed. "Okay," he finally said. "You did good, honey. I'm sorry for scaring you. Come here."

Max started down the stairs but stopped short of the foyer when he heard Bernard say, "You're too good for me, LeAnna. You may hear some ugly things about me and the company in the next few days that will be painful. You don't deserve any of this."

"I don't understand," she said.

Max wanted to hug his dad because he was scared. When he reached for the kitchen door, a new disturbing sound came from the other side. He paused and listened.

LeAnna grunted as the kitchen table overturned. Max was paralyzed with fear. It sounded like they were fighting, but they had never physically fought before. And then the grunting and struggling stopped. Max built up the courage to nudge the kitchen door open enough to see what was happening.

His father sat winded on the floor beside his mom. Her head rested in his lap. She wasn't moving. Max looked closer. A toaster lay on the floor beside her with its cord digging into her neck.

"Dad?" Max whispered.

Bernard jerked his head around. His eyes were wet.

"What did you do to Mom?" Max asked.

Bernard gently lowered her head to the floor. "Max, come 'ere. We need to talk." There was something strange in his eyes.

Instead of doing as Bernard said, Max backed away. Bernard grunted as he struggled to get off the floor. His voice turned angry when he said, "Come 'ere, Max."

Max shook his head. He had never disobeyed his father before, but something told him he needed to now. Max scrambled to the front door as his father hobbled through the kitchen on his old, worn-out knees.

"Wait, Max. I'm too old to chase you."

Max yanked open the front door and raced outside. He didn't look back as he sprinted toward the road. Bernard's chauffeur climbed from the stretched Hummer and called Max's name, but Max didn't stop.

Bernard shouted from the front door, "Max. Wait."

Max ran as fast and as far as he could, not stopping until he reached the Ghiloni's back yard and ran out of breath. He put his hands over his eyes, sat in the grass, and cried.

31

After killing his wife, Bernard had his driver take him to the WereHouse compound. He needed to get rid of the servers before the FBI started snooping around, which they were likely to do in the very near future. Bernard ordered his driver to drop him off at the gate.

"I don't want you here," he said. Then he paused and added, "But stay close."

"What's going on tonight, boss?"

Bernard shrugged. "Nothing I can't handle." He climbed out and leaned into the driver's window. "Things are changing, my friend. Tomorrow will be a new chapter for the WereHouse. You with me?"

"To the death, sir."

"I'll explain everything soon. For now, just get away from here and wait for my call. I'm taking the burner phone, so watch for that number." He stepped back and his driver pulled away.

Bernard waved to the two guards at the gate.

"Late night, sir?"

Bernard ignored them.

Once inside, he hurried to his private quarters and grabbed a flashlight and a trash bag from behind the bar. He gathered the clothes Christine had worn from the bathroom and stuffed them in the bag. Then he headed to the basement of the WereHouse's main building.

A guard at the desk at the bottom of the steps looked surprised to see Bernard so late. "Everything all right, boss?"

"Fine," Bernard answered. He held out his hand. "Keys."

"You're visiting The First?"

Bernard snapped his fingers.

The guard fished out a key and passed it to him. "Want me to come?"

Bernard nodded. "What's your name?"

"Perry, sir." Perry reached for the tranquilizer gun, but Bernard stopped him.

"You won't need that." Bernard led the way. He hadn't set foot in The First's dungeon since before the werg had been brought there to live. After going through two steel doors, he was in The First's cell. His flashlight did little to illuminate the darkness. His hands shook, bouncing the flashlight beam along the floor and causing the garbage bag to rustle.

"Are you sure we should be in here, sir?" Perry asked.

Bernard ignored him. He stopped behind a single chair in the center of the room. For the first time, he felt what his many pets might have felt before their change.

A chain rattled in the darkness followed by a nasty and terrifying grunt. He lifted the beam to two soulless eyes. Perry backed up to the door.

Bernard smiled. "Good evening, my boy."

The beast lunged forward suddenly and roared inches from Bernard's face where the chain stopped him short. Bernard cringed but stood his ground. He had watched enough soldiers meet The First through the cameras from the safety of the control room to know his boundaries.

The werg grunted and took a step back. He sniffed the air; he knew the routine. Bernard wondered if the creature remembered his scent from so many years before.

When Bernard spoke, his voice lacked its usual dominating strength. "Easy, boy. I don't know if you can understand me, but if you can, I want you to know that I'm the one freeing you."

Perry blurted, "What?"

The First breathed in and let out a slow, staccato growl.

"I have a treat for you." He opened the garbage bag. The werg's breathing quickened. Bernard reached in and removed Christine's balled-up clothes.

The First grunted and tilted his head.

Bernard whispered, "This is yours if you want it."

The creature dropped to all fours and slowly dug at the ground with his front claws. Bernard tossed the clothes to the stone floor and backed up.

Perry stood behind him. "What's going on, sir?"

"I just needed to slow him down a bit."

"I don't understand."

Bernard spun, his fist connecting with Perry's jaw. It was a good punch. Perry dropped like a weight, unconscious. Bernard left the dungeon door open and climbed the stairs from the basement, up past the first floor, and into the hallway of the second floor. At the end of the hall was the control room, jammed full of computers and monitors that were stacked from floor to ceiling. The room was protected by a steel vault door which he closed and locked behind him. At the far end of the computer room was another vault door leading into an impenetrable panic room full of more computer monitors.

He went straight to the panic room and flipped on the breaker, slowly bringing the lights, computers, and monitors to life. He locked the door behind him.

Monitor one showed the stables were quiet as the inventory of wergs slept away the boredom of their confinement. On monitor two, the only movement at the front gate was from his two complacent guards. Monitor three showed nothing but darkness until he switched on the spotlight in the basement cell.

The First looked up from his gift to glare at the light and camera before shoving his snout back into the fabric. Perry still lay unconscious. The other monitors focused on views of the property and the perimeter. There were a few guards.

Bernard grabbed a walkie talkie. "Attention, WereHouse staff. Everyone except those guarding the front gate is to vacate the premises immediately. You will be contacted in the near future with further orders. This is a direct order. Is everyone clear?"

The order was necessary. He didn't want his number one pet to be bogged down killing his own men when he should be hunting Christine. Perry was just a treat to get the creature's juices flowing.

Bernard set the walkie on the desk as countless answers of "Copy, sir," flowed from the speaker. A glance at the monitors revealed they were obeying.

"Forgive me for what I'm about to do," Bernard whispered as he watched the basement cell on monitor three. He pressed a button on the console. The First's chains dropped to the floor. The beast looked around, leery of a trap, and then roared. Perry lifted his head and shook it.

The First crouched briefly, and then pounced. Perry only had time to realize he was about to die. The First slaughtered him with one swipe of his claws. Then he shot through the open doorway, his chains dragging behind him.

Bernard watched in horror as the beast headed straight for the control room as if he had known where it was all along. Within seconds, he was at the top of the stairs outside the control room door. He clawed at it in a rage.

Despite Bernard being safe behind several feet of steel, a fearful part of him wasn't completely convinced the doors would withstand the werg's fury. He stood frozen in place, sick to his stomach at the thought of being mauled. For ten more terrifying minutes, the clawing and banging against the door continued, each dull thump sending jolts up Bernard's spine.

But eventually, The First gave up. Finally able to relax for a second, Bernard plopped into an office chair with a relieved sigh. He desperately needed a drink. If he were ever to create another panic room, he would stock it full of bourbon. After collecting himself, he swiveled to the desk and flipped switch after switch until all the stable gates swung open.

None of the wergs left their stalls at first. But then, after a few minutes, one of the docile creatures gathered enough courage and curiosity to creep into the open corral. Another werg followed from his stall, and then another. Within a few minutes, all the wergs had ventured out into the open.

There was no turning back now. "If nothing else," Bernard said to himself, "I've unleashed a new human experiment into the world." He smirked at his own attempt at humor. "I wonder if the authorities will see it the same way." He found himself laughing out loud at the absurdity of his rationale.

Bernard sent out a group text to the cell phones of each WereHouse board member, informing them they should turn on their computers and link to the WereHouse live feed. Then he fired up another computer with a built-in webcam. He set the video feed to broadcast to the WereHouse network and to several major news outlets as well. He knew from past experience that his word would spread within seconds. With his webcam software activated, he began an impromptu address.

"Good evening. I am Bernard Henderson, founder and CEO of the WereHouse. I have an important statement to make. Since our inception, we have prided ourselves on our safety record as an organization, which is why it pains me to give you this information now.

"First and foremost, I need to make it clear that there is no need to panic. If you have a werepet, he should not be affected in the near term, but he will need to be recalled within the next six months. It seems another company has attempted to duplicate our success and has released an untamed, unhealthy werg into the population. We believe this werg carries a rare and dangerous strain of rabies and has infected some of our werepets. We can no longer guarantee your safety if you come into contact with one of the infected creatures. We as a company feel terrible remorse over what has happened, and we will make things right in the future."

As he spoke, a light on a red company phone along the back wall flashed and vibrated. He had no doubt it was the first of many board member calls, but now was the time for every man and woman to take care of themselves.

He continued his address, ignoring the constant flashing. "We are asking you all to keep your werepets inside your homes for now. Do not approach any strays that you may find wandering the streets. Do not try to return your werepets at this time. We will notify you of the recall instructions in the future. Again, we are sorry for the inconvenience and want to assure you that our company will always take care of our loyal customers. Thank you for your patience and understanding."

He shut off the webcam and sat back in his chair with another sigh. A glance at the monitors showed the corral was now packed with confused wergs, some tamed, some not so much. As he watched the monitors, unsure of how to proceed, a familiar werg appeared in the corral.

It was The First.

He leaned closer to the monitor. This was going to be interesting. The First tore into the nearest werg with murderous rage. Before he finished ripping out that creature's throat, the others panicked and scrambled. The First lifted its bloody snout toward the front gates.

Bernard turned to monitor two, hoping The First would leave the compound so he could flee. The two guards stood next to the entrance, trying to see what the commotion was. Their movements were slow and confused. Warning them via the intercom system would be the right thing to do, but Bernard rather enjoyed the show.

The guards' suddenly terrified faces indicated they saw The First before the camera did. They fumbled with their weapons.

The First leaped into view and slaughtered them both before they got off a single shot. And just like that, Bernard's most violent werg was in the wild, as they said. While the guards lay choking on their own blood in the drive, Bernard rose to his feet, proud and confident. He looked around the room one last time.

"Well," he whispered to himself. "It was a damn good run."

He pressed the monitor power button and backed up to the panic room door. With a one-finger salute to his crumbling life's work, he turned his back and opened the door. On some level, he had always known this day would come.

Bernard passed through the next room into the hall. An old metal locker with a rusty combination lock stood against the wall. He spun the lock to his son's birthday and opened the locker. At the bottom sat a red gas can and a box of flares he had kept just in case. The flares were old but should still work. He carried the gas can and two of the flares back into the control room.

With the computers drenched in gasoline, he lit the flare. As the room burst into flames, he stood and watched without emotion until the heat became too much. He made his way through the hallway and down the stairs to the front entrance of the building. A sense of closure washed over him.

Bernard thought about his son and wished he could have handled things a bit differently. He remembered a Harlem Globetrotters game that he had taken Max to a few weeks ago and found himself whistling "Sweet Georgia Brown" as he descended the stairs.

He passed into the cool night air where he could once again see the entrance gates and freedom. He reached for his burner phone. *Just call for my car and everyth—*

And then something moved in the shadows next to the slaughtered guards. Bernard's whistled song faded from his lips. His heart skipped as he looked closer. Crouching next to the front gate, apparently waiting for him, was the one thing in the world he feared most.

"No," he whispered in disbelief. "Why did you turn back? Why didn't you go for her? I gave you the scent."

The First crawled from the shadows. Nearly twenty years of fury filled his face. He was a better hunter than Bernard could have ever imagined. The bastard had tricked him.

Bernard glanced over his shoulder at the smoke pouring into the stairwell, essentially cutting off the panic room as an escape. Fighting The First without a weapon would be equally futile. The terror he'd felt all those years ago when he had cowered beneath this very creature in the Sandalio jungle came rushing back.

The First stalked toward him, seemingly savoring the moment. Though there was distance between them, Bernard knew how quickly the creature would close that distance if he tried to run.

Bernard slowly lifted his arms. "Eeeaasy, boy. Remember, I'm the one who freed you."

The First tilted his head, blood still painting his fangs and claws. One of the guards who were face down on the ground moaned. As The First crept past, he reached down and ripped out the guard's spine and tossed it aside.

Bernard staggered backward a step.

The First might have smiled. He pounced, covering the distance between them in a flash. Bernard dove to the side as the creature struck, but not fast enough to escape a swipe of the beast's nails. Pain exploded in Bernard's left shoulder. Beneath his shredded shirt were three jagged rips in his flesh. Blood welled up in the deep gashes and then spilled out.

The First righted himself and lunged again. Bernard rolled to his back with his eyes closed. His left leg erupted in flesh-tearing agony. The pain forced him to open his eyes and see what the creature had done, even as he begged himself not to look. The First rose, meat and blood from Bernard's thigh dangling from his nails.

As horrible as the torture was, it was the realization of what the beast had just done that fueled Bernard's fears more than anything. The leg wound wasn't intended to be fatal. It was to lessen his chances of a quick escape. Years of imprisonment hadn't dulled The First's instincts. This creature was skilled. And Bernard had just become his play toy.

Bernard pressed his hands to the gaping wound on his thigh. His stomach turned and he rolled to his side on the chance he might vomit.

The First crawled over him, straddling him just like in his memories and nightmares of Sandalio. Blood and hot spittle dripped onto Bernard's cheek and forehead. Bernard scrambled beneath the killer, but the beast pinned him, sinking razor sharp claws into his wounded shoulder. Bernard cried out. It was as if The First wanted him to relive every terrifying moment of their first encounter.

The beast roared inches from his face, just as it had so many years before. His breath smelled like rotten meat and death. *Just do it,* Bernard silently prayed. *Enough with the torture.*

But as The First prepared to deal his death blow, he hesitated. Had he remembered the tranquilizer darts from the last time? Instead of simply reenacting that first day, was he actually reliving it, expecting another threat stalking him from behind?

The First sniffed the air and then leaped from Bernard's chest as if another threat had indeed arisen. Bernard scrambled against the wall as The First charged into the shadows again.

The fire on the second floor crackled and popped. Bernard pressed a hand against his leg wound and struggled to stand on his good leg. An upstairs window exploded and glass rained down on him. With his hand still on his shredded thigh, he searched the darkness for his enemy. Instead of seeing the beast, he heard a car engine and saw a pair of headlights illuminate the front gates. It was an ambulance, of all things. Now he knew why he had been momentarily spared.

Despite his pain, he smiled.

TRAPPED

32

Thick smoke poured from the second floor of the WereHouse main office as Aiden and Christine got out of the medic and approached the main gate. They'd left the headlights on and Aiden had a flashlight.

Christine asked, "What do you think's going on here?"

"I don't know. But we don't have much time to find out. The fire will bring everyone." He slipped past her and cautiously stepped through the open gate. She followed.

He froze. "Oh, shit."

"What is it?"

He pointed his flashlight beam at two slaughtered security guards, one with his entire spine ripped out. Aiden lifted the beam toward the burning building where Bernard Henderson stood staring back. He was hunched over and holding his leg. Aiden tapped Christine's shoulder and nodded toward him.

He moved toward Bernard. "Don't try to run," he shouted over the crackling fire. "It's over."

Bernard glared back with disdain. He shouted, "Nothing's over, Aiden. I just need to disappear for a bit while I get things straightened out."

"We're exposing you and your God-forsaken company," Aiden screamed, picking up his stride. "You're going to prison … or a grave. It's your choice."

Bernard scoffed. "Oh, I don't think so." He smiled. "You're not the only predator out here tonight."

Aiden slowed, a sick feeling washing over him.

Christine stopped beside him. "What is it?"

The sound of a chain dragging across the pavement behind them threatened something much worse than a murderous CEO. Aiden slowly looked over his shoulder. He couldn't see what hid in the shadow of the perimeter wall. "Another one of your Savages?" he shouted.

He could almost hear Bernard's smile when the bastard answered, "You wish."

A werg stepped into the medic's headlights. His fur was matted with blood.

Bernard shouted, "I call him The First, Aiden. He is quite exquisite. You should get to know him. If it's any consolation, you always were my best hunter."

Aiden nudged Christine behind him. "I'll take care of this one. You go get Bernard. Don't give him any mercy. He won't give you any."

"But let me help y—"

"No. I've got this."

The First pounced, covering the ground between them in a flash.

Aiden shoved Christine away and swung his flashlight. The beast swatted his arm aside and slammed against him. The two struck the ground. Aiden's flashlight skidded across the pavement. He screamed, "Christine. Run."

She froze.

"Damn it, Christine. You have to run. Go after Bernard. End this."

The First attacked again. Aiden dove out of the way, but he wasn't quick enough. The werg's claws raked his back, sending brief numbness down his left arm.

Christine turned and ran after Bernard as he hobbled along beside the burning building. The First turned away from Aiden and sniffed the air. He licked his teeth. Aiden followed his line of sight to Christine.

"Oh no you don't, you bastard." Aiden retrieved his flashlight and struck the distracted beast's thick skull. The First hardly budged. "Change, Christine," Aiden shouted.

As she ran toward the corner of the building where Bernard had gone, her leg jerked awkwardly and she stumbled, falling on her face. She lifted her head and howled.

Aiden smiled, knowing Bernard wouldn't get away this time. Now it was his turn. The First charged. Aiden let the anger take root in his chest. The First was on him in a flash, swatting him against the guard booth with an effortless swing. Aiden's snout grew from his face. The bones of his legs snapped and reconfigured. His transformation was quicker and less painful this time, but it wasn't instant. He was on his feet, half-wolf and half-man, when The First pounced again.

Aiden still didn't have the strength for a head-on assault and he knew it, so he needed to fight smart.

He retreated toward the gate, using the momentum of The First's next attack to deflect the beast into the wall of the guard booth. While The First shook off the effects of his collision with the wall, Aiden completed his change. He was ready and full of rage. He could think of nothing but murder.

The First dove at him. Aiden met the creature in mid-air and together they crashed to the ground. Aiden lunged for the beast's throat. Tearing pain shot up his arm. He pulled away, but more pain ripped through his chest. He collapsed to his back, momentarily free of The First's clutches but in a world of hurt. He roared, and The First roared back.

Aiden bounced to his feet. His claws met The First's flesh, but the enemy werg was unfazed and clamped his teeth down on Aiden's shoulder. Aiden howled in pain. With all his strength, he yanked The First's snout from his flesh, tearing meat and muscle away. The First was relentless and dragged his claws across Aiden's face.

Blood burned Aiden's eyes, momentarily blinding him. He fell to his back again before pain exploded in his abdomen.

Aiden swung his claws in a blind fury. By sheer luck he struck the beast's chest, sending his enemy crashing against the wrought-iron gate, the impact knocking it from its hinges. The First yelped. Aiden rubbed the bloody blurriness from his eyes. The First writhed in pain, impaled on one of the decorative iron spikes of the fence. The pointed end protruded from the right side of The First's chest. He squirmed to free himself.

Aiden wanted to pounce—every primal urge screamed for him to finish it—but some hint of conscious thought held him back. Perhaps it was self-preservation or even fear. Perhaps some part of him knew he was too wounded to stand a chance. Or perhaps it was the faint sound of a truck speeding toward the compound.

The First pushed against the fence and slowly pried himself free of the bloody spike. He was furious and released a hate-filled howl to show it.

Instead of engaging, Aiden backed away. The sound of the approaching truck grew louder. More headlight beams joined those from the medic, but from a slightly different direction. The First hesitated and looked to the approaching vehicle. He scrambled like a startled rabbit as the truck burst through the gate and crashed into him in an explosion of metal and plastic and blood. The First hurtled through the air and thudded on the ground near Aiden.

The truck's front doors slung open. Greg jumped out. Jeffrey followed, one of his legs in a brace. "There's one," he shouted. He aimed his assault rifle.

Aiden spun away, dropped to all fours, and retreated as gunfire erupted from behind. He zigged and zagged and then leaped over a wooden fence into the corral. A barrage of bullets ripped through the fence above his head as he pressed himself flat to the ground. The gunfire ceased.

Desperately outgunned, Aiden's only chance was to shift back. He needed to convince his former friends that the battle was over and the WereHouse was finished. He concentrated, and the color slowly returned to the world. He was surrounded by docile werepets wandering aimlessly. The gunfire had scattered some of them but not all.

Aiden peered through a gap in the corral's wooden fencing. Greg and Jeffrey approached, guns at the ready. Aiden stood up with his hands raised.

Greg and Jeff stopped. "Talik?" Greg shouted. He lowered his gun slightly. "Is that you? What the hell's going on?"

"Cut the bullshit, Greg. I know why you're here."

"Well, I'd say it's rather obvious." Greg waved Jeffrey off. "Go check on The First and make sure he's dead. I'll deal with Aiden." Greg turned back and smirked. "How do you plan to get away this time? I see you're not hiding any weapons. Or if you are, I don't wanna know where."

Aiden shrugged. "No weapons. I have no way out. I'm asking you as your long-time friend to give up this assignment. The WereHouse is finished. You're not going to get paid for killing me. We were friends once. Try to remember that."

"You're one of those filthy creatures now, Talik. We aren't friends anymore. Besides, you attacked us for one of those creatures. Not to mention, you know what we've done, and you now know we did it willingly. We kill people. That's our job. You did it, too."

"I didn't know they were people, Greg."

"Details." Greg lifted his gun to his shoulder and trained his sights on Aiden. "Turn around, Aiden. I don't wanna see your face when I do this."

Aiden shook his head. "You're going to look me in the eyes when you pull that trigger, Greg."

Greg shrugged. "Suit yourself." He rolled his shoulder and repositioned the butt of his gun against it. He cracked his neck and then took aim again.

Aiden took a deep breath. His chest throbbed. He had done all he could to spare his former friends and he needed to shift again to have any shot at survival. He tried one last time.

"Don't do it, Greg," he whispered.

And then Jeffrey hobbled up and shouted, "Hey, Greg. The First is gone. He's—"

Jeffrey's chest exploded as a clawed fist burst through it. He gurgled and went instantly limp. The First stepped from the shadows and lifted Jeffrey's body above his head. Then he slammed him to the ground. Before he finished, he leaned in and tore out Jeffrey's throat with his teeth.

Greg spun and unleashed a barrage of bullets at the murdering beast until his magazine was empty. The First charged, undaunted by the hail of gunfire.

Greg tossed his empty weapon and drew a pistol as The First closed in. He fired a single shot before the beast knocked him down and landed on his chest. Aiden sprinted past them toward Greg's truck. He knew there'd be weapons in there.

Greg squeezed off two more shots before his screams and gurgling cries replaced the gunfire.

Aiden climbed into the truck and lifted the back seat. He pulled out a duffel bag. A yank of the zipper revealed a beautiful arsenal—a loaded AK-47, several pistols, a flash grenade, and a custom-made silver-bladed knife. He cocked the AK-47 and threw the bag over his shoulder.

The truck suddenly rocked sideways. Aiden spun toward the front as The First ripped the driver's door from its hinges and tossed it aside like it was weightless.

Aiden squeezed off three rounds. The First retreated and ducked behind the front of the truck. Aiden considered turning back into a werg, but his painful failure the first time they fought proved he was no match for the older, more experienced creature. Instead, he decided his only chance was to face The First as the rogue hunter he had always been. He dove from the passenger door, twisted in the air, and landed on his back.

The First sailed over the hood. Aiden aimed and fired three shots from the AK, one of which sizzled through The First's chest, narrowly missing his heart. The First didn't flinch and swatted the gun with a roar.

Aiden ripped the pistol from the bag and fired two more shots into the beast before the creature's flesh-tearing claws laid open his forearm and knocked the pistol to the ground. He had seen very few wergs in such a rage that they withstood the effects of silver for more than a few seconds, but this beast was no ordinary werg.

The First threw his head back and howled.

Aiden pulled the pin from the flash grenade, counted to three, and tossed it straight up in the air. He pressed his arms over his ears and rolled to his side. The First lunged forward, his teeth snapping at Aiden's throat.

The flash grenade exploded near the beast's face. The concussion rattled Aiden's bones. His ears rang. He moved his arms, surprised he was still able, and the pain that came with his movements let him know he wasn't dead. The First staggered backward, his arm across his eyes.

Aiden scrambled to his feet, pushing away the throbbing pain that enveloped him. He dropped the bag and pulled out the knife.

"Don't change," he begged the crushing ache in his chest. "Not yet." He leaped onto the beast's back.

The First spun and tried to buck him off, but he held on tight and drove the silver blade between the beast's shoulder blades. The creature howled in pain, his flesh sizzling. Aiden ripped the knife free and sank it into the werg's flesh again and again until The First dropped to his knees. In his rage, Aiden lost count of how many times he plunged the blade into the beast's back, but he didn't stop until the creature ceased to move.

Aiden fell from The First's back and then stood up behind him. He fought his change with every ounce of restraint, even as he let out a howl that matched The First in ferocity. The muscles in his face twitched and his bones snapped and cracked, but he continued fighting the inevitable. With his foot, he rolled the gasping beast to his back before straddling him.

Aiden couldn't slow his breathing. He heard animal snorts and realized they came from his own mouth. His leg jolted and twisted, throwing him off balance, but he steadied himself. *Just a few more seconds.* Without remorse, he drove his blade into the beast's heart again and again and again, the silver penetrating the sternum. His own skull deformed as he finished his bloody work.

The First released a final cry before his eyes clouded over and he died. Aiden used every ounce of humanity he could muster just to stop plunging his knife into the creature's gaping chest cavity. He raised his blade above his head and released a primal scream.

Then he roared like a beast.

Like the king of beasts.

Then he looked around. Where was Christine?

33

Christine followed Bernard's scent along the side of the burning WereHouse building until the heat forced her to pull away. His trail led to a walkway between the stables that continued to a long, one-story building lined with overhead doors like a storage facility.

Bernard was four overhead doors away when he slowed and doubled over with his hands on his knees. Still holding his injured leg, he turned to face her. She smelled fear, and he had a good reason to feel it. She was going to kill him. She stopped in her tracks, cautious like a hunter.

He held his hands up in surrender and backed up against one of the overhead doors. "Wait, wait, wait," he said between gasps for air. "Before you kill me, I have …," he panted and gestured at the door behind him, "… something for you."

She tilted her head, curious. Bernard fished through his pockets and removed a key fob.

Christine stalked closer.

He shouted, "Wait. It's your friend, Billy. He's behind this door. I'll free him if you let me live."

No deal. There was no reason she couldn't just kill him, take the fob, and free Billy on her own.

He pressed the button before she could get to him. All the doors lifted. She knew instantly she had been too slow, even before she saw him smile. She pounced.

Two wergs exploded from their stalls, intercepting her. She froze.

Bernard shouted, "I believe you've already met my Savages. Get 'er, boys." He backed away while the wergs squared off with her.

Christine braced for their attack. It came quickly and recklessly. The closest Savage came at her side. She shifted her weight and hurled him against the wooden corral fence, tearing open a gap between two posts. The other Savage struck her back, knocking out her breath.

She spun in his grip as they hit the ground together. His throat flashed past her eyes, and she lunged for it with her teeth. Blood sprayed her face. He recoiled, pawing helplessly at his torn throat and gurgling with wet wheezes. She had gotten him good, but not good enough to be fatal. He'd be back in the fight soon.

The other Savage sprang from the broken corral fence in a rage. Christine bounced to her feet and spun to face him. He lunged for her throat before she could reset. She grabbed his snout, stopping his teeth inches away. They both went to the ground. He tore at her flesh with razor-like claws. She ignored the pain, concentrating instead on keeping his teeth from her jugular.

He ripped her belly open, and she feared he had gutted her. She immediately released his snout to hold in her guts just in case. He took the opening and lunged for her throat again. She winced.

But instead of pain, he grunted, and she opened her eyes. The beast tumbled off her, another werg ripping at his flesh. Teeth and claws sprayed snot and blood. It was Billy.

The Savage she had wounded was on her again. He swiped at her injured stomach with his toenails. She pulled away just enough that he missed.

She stumbled backward against the fence as he attacked again. She lost her footing and fell beside a broken board that had been splintered into a point. She grabbed it and wedged the blunt end against the ground next to her. The Savage yelped as the splintered end punctured his gut and his weight and momentum drove it up through his heart. His eyes went wide. Christine didn't hesitate. She ripped out the rest of his throat. Then she shoved him aside and looked toward the other two.

Billy stood victorious above his motionless foe. She staggered to his side and gently touched his cheek with the back of her finger. He leaned into her hand. Sirens approached, telling her they needed to flee. Her only escape was the forest where Bernard had fled. *Come on, Billy,* she silently urged, and gave his hand a tug.

But Billy resisted. She tugged again but he didn't budge. She pleaded with her eyes. Why wouldn't he follow?

He pulled at her hand and then lowered his head under it. Frantic, Christine scanned the corral for the next threat. Billy turned his head and brushed the back of his neck against her hand.

No, Billy. Not now.

But he wouldn't let it go. He desperately wanted that chip gone. He brushed his neck against her hand again and leaned into her claws.

She shook her head. Just the thought of how she would have to do it was sickening. He nudged against her hand again and then looked back with sad, begging eyes.

There was no way she could hurt him like that. Even if she tried, she could just as easily paralyze him as free him from his curse. Though it broke her heart, she withdrew her hand.

Gunshots erupted somewhere in the compound near the front gate, and she feared more of Bernard's Rogue Hunters had arrived. Sirens were getting closer, too. She didn't have much time. She looked to the forest before looking back toward the sporadic bursts of gunfire. She looked to Billy again. They would kill him for sure if he didn't flee.

Then his ears perked and he sniffed the air in the direction she wanted him to go. *Yes, Billy,* she thought. *Go.* He snarled. Then he bolted for the woods on all fours.

She started to give chase, but Aiden shouted her name from behind. He was in human form, wearing camo pants with a horse blanket over his shoulders. His chin and chest were covered in dried blood. He hobbled toward her. She rushed to meet him.

He whispered, "Thank God you're all right." He threw the blanket over her shoulders. "You need to get through the forest to escape. Can you shift back?"

She shook her head—she was faster and more powerful as a werg.

"You must, Christine. The forest is full of traps to keep wergs from escaping. They're marked with orange flags that wergs can't see. You have to avoid them. Do you understand?"

She nodded. A horrible vision of Billy blindly charging through the forest turned her stomach. She had sent him straight into danger.

"You have to hurry, Christine. Get to the forest. There's a path near that gap." He pointed toward where the forest led up a hill. "Follow that path to the top. There's a perimeter fence surrounding the property. Wait for me there. I'll be right behind you." More gunfire rang out, closer this time. He spun toward it. "They're killing innocent wergs. I've gotta stop them."

She shook her head. She wanted him to go with her.

"They're people, Christine. I know that now. I may never be able to live with what I've done, but I can start to try and make amends right here and now." He stepped away.

Pain pierced her skull deep in her brain. Her skin crawled. Aiden looked over his shoulder and winked as her bones popped and shifted and mended back together. He raced toward the buildings. As he ran, he dropped to all fours. Fur sprouted from his back. By the time she completed her change to human, he was fully beast. He disappeared into the dark.

She whispered, "Please be careful, Aiden," and then turned to the forest to face another worry. "I'm coming, Billy." She pulled the horse blanket around her body. With one hand holding it closed and the other against her mending stomach, she hobbled toward the forest and found the cleared path.

Her slow climb brought her to the first orange flag. She gave it a wide berth. She was terrified that Billy wouldn't be so lucky.

SNAKE ESCAPE

34

Bernard's leg throbbed unbearably as he fled up the hill. His only consolation was that he'd left Christine in the fight of her life against his Savages. She may have brought down his company, but she was going to pay dearly for it.

Though mostly docile, the escaped wergs still gave him pause. What if they remembered his scent and what he had done to them? Even one of the yet to be tamed creatures finding him would be fatal. But he had no other way to freedom. As dangerous as it was, he had to get through the forest to the road at the top of the hill. Going back the way he had come meant facing the cops, Savages, and maybe even The First again. No thank you.

He was less than twenty feet into the trees when he came across two wergs. They perked their ears and sniffed the air. One of them twisted around to look at him.

Bernard froze. "Eaaasy, boys," he whispered. What he wouldn't give to have a gun. That they hadn't already ripped out his throat was a positive. Cautiously, he took a step, eyes fixed on them for their reaction. The second creature turned as well. Bernard took another cautious step. He remembered a saying his dad had told him about bears when he'd taken him camping as a boy. He had said, "If it's black, fight back. If it's brown lay down. And if it's white, say good night." He hoped they were more like brown bears and less like polar bears. Since Bernard had no time to lie down, his only option was an unenviable one.

Bernard threw his hands in the air and waved them frantically. "Get outta here," he shouted.

They straightened, more surprised than aggressive.

Bernard lunged forward. "Git," he snapped.

They both flinched. It was working. Bernard hissed and waved his hands frantically above his head. The two wergs dropped to all fours and retreated.

Bernard lowered his arms with a sigh. That's when he remembered his damaged thigh again. It had gone numb, but at least the bleeding had slowed. The trees swayed, telling him how much blood he had lost.

Nauseated, he leaned against a tree to gather his wits. After the wave of nausea passed, he pressed on. The hill was a tough climb. A werg yelped somewhere close but out of sight. Probably found one of the traps, he figured.

He struggled up the hill, repeatedly leaning against trees to rest, until he neared the top. He found his burner phone in his pocket and fumbled with it. There were only three numbers stored in it. Number one was his wife. Number two was Senator Wooten. And number three was his driver. He pressed and held number three.

His driver answered after the first ring. "Where you at, boss? I'm on my way back to the compound. There's smoke everywhere. There are cops and firemen coming from every direct—"

"Shut up for a minute," Bernard interrupted. "I know about the fire. I set it. I'm in the woods west of the compound headed for the fence at the top of the hill. Meet me there."

"I'll be there in a minute, sir. Are you all rig—"

Bernard pressed "end" and shoved his phone back into his pocket. Other wergs howled or yelped or whined in the trees behind him.

He came to another planted orange flag at the top of the hill near the ten-foot-high perimeter fence. All he had to do was follow the fence to one of the locked gates and wait for his car to arrive. As he gave the flag a wide berth, a sinking feeling made him pause. The hairs lifted on the back of his neck. He heard a slight grunt. He silently pleaded, *Please don't be The First.* Slowly, he turned his head.

A beast stood beside a tree not twenty feet away. Its dark eyes burned a hole through his chest. If there was anything good about the creature staring back, it was that it wasn't The First. The werg had a silver streak in its mane.

Bernard sighed, relieved. He turned the rest of the way around. "Get outta here," he shouted, and waved his hands over his head.

But the werg didn't flinch. Instead, it dropped to all fours.

"Hmph." Bernard looked him over. Then he said, "You're Christine's friend, Billy, aren't you?"

Billy's upper lip crinkled.

Bernard bobbed his hands. "Easy, boy."

Billy took a step forward.

Bernard started to step backward but remembered how close he was to the orange flag. With his foot still in the air, he glanced over his shoulder. The flag gave him a nasty idea.

He turned back to Billy. "If you want me, beast, come get me." He lifted his fists as though ready for a fight.

Billy stalked closer, cautious yet bloodthirsty. Bernard shuffled to the side and backed around a small mound of leaves surrounding the flag. Standing with the pile of leaves between him and Billy, he egged him on with a cocky wave. *Come on, you filthy beast.*

Billy crept closer, almost like he knew it was a trap but was unable to resist. *One more step,* Bernard silently begged. But Billy stopped short as if he'd had a revelation.

Oh shit.

Billy tilted his head.

Bernard had to distract him. "Come on, you bastard," he shouted. "Come get me." Searching his pockets for anything he could use as a weapon, he found his phone again. He hurled it at Billy's face. Billy recoiled. The phone smacked his forehead with unbelievable accuracy—or, more likely, unbelievable luck. Billy released a furious roar. Hatred filled his eyes. Then he lunged, already forgetting whatever premonition he'd had seconds before. Bernard stumbled backward against the fence as Billy's front paw struck the leaves.

Billy's eyes widened. A metallic clunk rang out, followed by a deafening howl. He recoiled, pain contorting his werg face. A steel bear trap chained to a stake embedded in the ground in a concrete plug had sprung shut around his wrist. As he reared back, the chain pulled taut. He thrashed and pulled, but the teeth of the trap only dug deeper into his flesh.

Bernard started laughing. "You stupid creature."

Billy lunged at him with snapping teeth, but the chain on the trap stopped him short and made him yelp again.

Bernard looked back to the fence. Headlights approached down the road. He knew there was a gate somewhere nearby because the fence was designed with gates every seventy-five feet. He glanced back at Billy with a grin. "See ya around, Billy."

Billy dug at the concrete with his free hand.

Still laughing, Bernard reconsidered. "Well … I guess I probably won't, huh?" He gave Billy a dickish wave and then made his way to the nearest gate. His driver stopped and got out of the limo. "What the hell's going on, boss?"

Bernard grabbed the lock. "I'll explain everything in the car. You got your keys?"

"Yeah, yeah. Just a second." He ran back to the open driver's door and grabbed a hoop keyring crowded with keys. He quickly found the one for the gate and removed the lock.

Bernard shook his hand and then limped to the limo.

His driver trailed him. "Boss, you're hurt. Do you need the doc?"

Bernard brushed him off with a wave. There wasn't time for the doc. He climbed into the limo and poured himself a whiskey.

His driver climbed behind the wheel. Bernard downed the whiskey with a wince. He tapped on the glass between him and his driver and said, "Let's get the hell outta here."

FREEDOM'S PRICE

35

Christine had reached the edge of the forest at the bottom of the hill. She tried not to picture all the horrible things that could be happening to Billy, but the deafening howls and cries of wergs throughout the forest didn't bode well for him. Before she started up, she caught a familiar scent tracking her from behind. *Aiden.*

She waited beside a tree. He was back in human form and limping. More blood was smeared across his bare chest and face. He carried a bundle of clothes.

Christine met him with a hug. "Thank God you're okay."

He winced in her embrace and pulled away. "Here." He gave her the clothes. "A few of them won't be hunting wergs anymore."

Christine hurriedly got dressed. "We have to find Billy."

Aiden shook his head. "We gotta get outta here. The cops are here, and more are coming. These woods will be crawling with them soon."

"I'm not leaving without Billy."

"Have you got his scent?"

She shook her head. "No. But I've got Bernard's, and Billy was going after him."

"Yeah, I got it too. Let's go."

Aiden led the way up the hill, police swarming the corral below. When he neared the top, he froze and turned back. Worry saturated his eyes. "Stop, Christine."

Christine paused and narrowed her eyes. "What is it?"

"Don't come any farther."

Christine tilted her head. "Why?" Then she caught Billy's scent and the smell of blood. Her eyes widened.

"You don't want to see this, Christine," Aiden said, and stepped into her path.

"What is it?" She nudged him aside and stepped next to a tree. She saw the orange flag first with a bloody chain fastened to a stake. She followed the chain to a bloody steel trap. What she saw beside the trap punched her in the chest. She staggered and covered her mouth. "No, no, no." Lying in a puddle of blood was a mangled half-human, half-werewolf hand with teeth marks gnawed into the wrist bone.

Aiden touched her shoulder.

She dropped to her knees beside the trap. "Oh, Billy. What have you done?"

"It might not be *his* hand," Aiden whispered.

She looked up through wet eyes. "It's his. You know it is …" Unable to completely accept what she knew to be true, she added an unconfident, "Right?"

Aiden turned his head away.

Christine's shoulders collapsed and her head dropped forward.

Aiden knelt and touched the blood around the trap. Then he looked to where it led into some heavy brush. He slowly stood up. "Chris?" he said.

She followed his eyes to the brush. "What is it?" She stood and took a cautious step toward it. She heard a low groan. "Billy?" she quietly called out.

"Hey, Cougar," Billy answered weakly.

Christine's knees nearly gave out. She raced to the brush and ripped it aside. Billy lay naked on his back with his left hand in a fist. His right forearm ended at a stump. A bit of bone poked through the shredded flesh where his right hand should have been. His mouth was smeared with red.

She covered her mouth. "Oh, Billy. How?"

He opened his left hand. A bloody computer chip rested in his palm. "Heh. I dug it out myself. Boy, did it hurt like hell." He dropped it, motioned for Aiden, and held out his hand. "A little help here, pretty boy?"

Aiden grabbed beneath Billy's good arm and lifted him to his feet.

Billy grimaced. He grabbed his stump, winced, and gave Christine a shit-eating Billy grin. "Hey, Chris. Why do *you* look so pale? I'm the one bleeding to death."

Christine wanted to cry and hug him and kill Bernard all at once. But her medic training kicked in and she turned her focus to his bleeding nub. She tore a strip of fabric from the shirt Aiden had stolen for her and tied it around Billy's stump. Aiden tossed Billy's left arm over his shoulder and helped him toward the open gate.

Christine followed until someone shouted, "Don't move," from behind.

A lone police officer stood behind them with a drawn Taser. It trembled in his hand. He was young, probably a rookie. Everything he'd seen to get where he now stood must have been eye-opening at the least.

Aiden slowly ducked away from under Billy's arm and Christine took his place.

"I said don't move," the officer cried. His voice shook.

Aiden smiled and held up his hands. "Chill out, my man. Everything's cool."

The cop brandished the Taser as if that was going to scare Aiden. "Keep your hands to the goddamn sky or I'll Taser your ass."

Aiden shrugged. "I'm sorry, officer, but we're going through that gate. Turn around and go the other way if you know what's good for you." He took another step forward.

The cop panicked and squeezed the trigger. The Taser popped and two needle-like prongs shot toward Aiden's chest. Like lightning, Aiden twisted his upper body out of the prongs' path, snatched the trailing cables in midair, and yanked the Taser from the stunned officer's hand. To the officer's horror, Aiden caught it.

The cop reached for his gun.

Aiden closed the distance between them. He ripped the used cap from the end of the Taser and pressed the exposed prongs against the officer's shoulder. "I'm sorry," he said, and squeezed the trigger. The cop grunted, stiffened for an instant, and dropped.

Aiden grabbed the gun before the cop could recover and tossed it into the weeds. He leaned in and showed the cop the wolf behind his coal-black eyes. "I'm not going to hurt you, but we ARE leaving now." Then he gave a low growl.

The cop nearly pissed himself. He nodded frantically.

Aiden backed away.

Billy looked at Christine with wide eyes and asked, "Is your new friend Superman or something?"

"Sometimes I wonder," Christine answered.

Flashing lights approached. Once Christine and Billy were through the gate, Aiden pulled it closed between him and them. Christine spun toward him.

"Aiden? What are you doing?"

"You're safe now. You can't run from your lives. You need to surrender to the police. Billy needs a hospital. The police can get you help."

"And what will I tell them?" she cried.

"Everything. It's all coming out now. You need to tell them how you were kidnapped by the WereHouse and how evil Bernard is. Tell them how you barely escaped and—"

"And how we're werewolves, Aiden? You want me to tell them that, too?" She shook her head in disbelief.

He grinned. "I'd probably leave that part out."

She interlaced her fingers in the chain link fence. "And what about you?"

He touched her fingers through the fence. "I'll be fine." He looked over his shoulder. "I'm going to help the rest of the wergs."

Christine pleaded, "Stay with us. Don't go. They'll kill you."

"No one knows who I am. Remember, I hunted wergs for a living. I'm good at this shit." He pulled his hand away and took a step back. "I'll see you soon, Christine."

As she watched, the look in her eyes begging him not to leave, he turned and took off. The first of several police cruisers slid to a stop. She surrendered.

Billy sat down at the edge of the road. "I don't feel so good," he said.

The cruiser's door flung open and the officer hurried to her side. "Ma'am, are you okay?" Then he noticed Billy's arm and immediately called for a medic truck on his radio. He helped Billy up and escorted him and Christine to the back seat. "Wait here where it's warm. I've got medics coming."

Christine leaned her head on Billy's shoulder as the officer closed the door. "You'll be okay," she said.

"I'm right-handed, Chris."

"I know." She held his left hand. "I know."

SECRETS

36

Christine sat in an emergency room hospital bed. An IV dripped fluids into her arm and an EKG was attached to her chest. The doctor had already been in and said she was going to be fine. They wanted to monitor her for a bit before sending her home since she had "been through a lot." They had no idea how much.

It was the first time she could relax and reflect on the whirlwind of what had happened since going to Senator Wooten's house. She thought about Aiden. She wondered if Bernard had escaped, and hoped he hadn't.

She had been there for an hour or so when someone approached the curtain. "Christine?"

"Yeah?"

"Are you decent?"

"Yeah."

Senator Wooten poked his head through the curtains.

She groaned.

He wore his famous politician's smile. "May I come in?"

Christine didn't feel she had a choice. She nodded reluctantly. He strolled to the foot of her bed. She didn't take her eyes off him.

"How're you doing?" he asked.

"I was better thirty seconds ago."

He smirked.

She wasn't playing his games. "What're you gonna do to me?" she blurted.

He tilted his head, as if surprised by her question. "I don't know what you mean. I'm not here to do anything to you. We just need to talk before the detectives arrive. They have a helluva mess out at the WereHouse compound, but you already knew that." He motioned to the chair beside the bed. "May I?"

She nodded.

"As you might imagine, you and I share a few secrets now that I'd very much like to keep as such."

Screw you. "I'm telling the cops everything I know about the WereHouse. I don't care who you are. This is all coming out now, and I don't care what you say."

He rolled his eyes. "Just settle down for a minute. I don't give a damn what you tell them about the WereHouse. I'm not as exposed as you may think. That Bernard guy's a psychopath anyways. Always has been. My intentions here are strictly based in self-preservation."

"What do you mean? You're here because you don't want me to tell them what you are … what we are? That's it?"

"Exactly. I'd say it's mutually beneficial that we keep our little shapeshifting secret between us, wouldn't you?"

Christine thought about it for a few seconds. "I suppose," she finally answered. She didn't sound as confident as she'd hoped.

"Wonderful, then. Sounds like we're on the same page." He started to stand up, but sat back down and bit his lower lip. He touched his chin. "But even so. I think I need a little insurance." He winced. "This is the unpleasant part of my visit."

Christine glared at him.

He looked around and then leaned closer. He whispered, "While I would love to simply trust you, I think we both know that's not how this world works. Everyone has an agenda. Now, how can I put this delicately? Let's just say your shapeshifting secret isn't the only thing I'll protect if you keep your end of the bargain. Do you understand what I'm telling you?"

She shook her head. She wanted to hear him say what he meant.

He sighed. "You have a lot of friends and family that don't need to become a part of this entire mess. I'd love nothing more than to keep them out of it. Does that make more sense?"

She got the message loud and clear, but instead of scaring her, it only pissed her off. "You know, I'm so sick of threats, Senator. Just don—"

The Senator calmly cut her off. "Now, now, now. Let's not get angry. Let's just leave it be. I think you understand, and that's all that matters. As much as we might not like it, we have a connection now that we both need to protect. This goes both ways, Christine. In return for you keeping our secret, I'll keep some of the heat from the cops away. Just answer their questions. But if they start digging too deep, clam up and have your lawyer call me."

"I don't have a lawyer."

"You do now." He fished a card from his pocket and set it on the bed beside her leg.

"And what about Aiden?"

"Ah yes. Aiden Talik. Well, looks like this is your lucky day. As part of our new truce, I'll not send anyone looking for him either. We'll just be one little happy family."

"I don't know if I believe you."

He held up his hand like he was taking a Boy Scout oath and said, "You have my word."

The word of a politician was about as good as Xeroxed money, but it was all she had. She didn't see any other option that would help her out of her mess as well as this one. She looked at the wall for a minute and contemplated all the angles. Then she faced the senator and conceded.

"I won't tell anyone."

He clapped his hands together and smiled again. "Perfect. I knew level heads could work things out." He stood up. "Welp. I guess that's it." He reached into his inside coat pocket and set a second business card beside the first. "This is my private number. If you ever need anything, don't hesitate to call. It seems you and I are going to be friends for a looong time."

As he got up to leave, someone else called her name from outside the curtain. With exaggeratedly wide eyes and half a grin, Senator Wooten mouthed, "The fuzz." He slid the curtain open. Two police detectives stood next to the Senator's personal bodyguard. "Good evening, gentlemen," he said.

"Senator?" one of them said, his forehead creased. "Uh … I didn't expect to see someone of your stature here."

"Oh? Christine and I go way back. I had just heard she'd been injured and wanted to check in on her." He nodded toward Christine and waved. "It was good seeing you. I'm glad you're okay." Then he left.

The detectives stood at the foot of her bed. "Ms. Alt, my name's Detective Fritz, and this is my partner, Detective Bird."

Detective Bird nodded.

"Can we ask you some questions?" Detective Fritz asked.

Christine shrugged.

"First, let me ask if you're doing okay."

"I am. Thank you."

He held a notepad and a pen. "We're just starting to figure out what went on at the WereHouse compound this evening and, quite frankly, it sounds crazier by the second."

She couldn't agree more.

Detective Bird didn't say a word the entire time while Detective Fritz questioned her about her relationship with Bernard Henderson and she recounted her kidnapping. Detective Fritz seemed to accept her story. He also asked about Billy, and she started from the beginning with the medical alarm call that started the entire mess. The only parts she left out were her and Billy's transformations, her visit to Senator Wooten's home, and anything having to do with Aiden. She talked with them for at least forty-five minutes before Detective Fritz closed his notebook, advised her he would be in touch if anything else came up, and left with Detective Bird.

Christine could finally breathe again. A glance around the room revealed a TV remote on the bedside tray. A flat TV hung on the wall. Curious how the entire mess was being reported, she flipped it on.

The first channel she tried had a reporter standing outside the burned-out WereHouse headquarters. The chyron at the bottom read "Breaking News." As the reporter spoke about the police search for a "person of interest," the screen went to wobbly footage of an empty field shot from a helicopter.

The reporter said, "This is footage from earlier this evening. Now watch the bottom of the screen closely as the camera zooms in along this creek."

A werg burst into view from the bottom corner of the screen, and then quickly disappeared into a line of trees. Seconds later, a shirtless man appeared, chasing the creature.

Though the picture was dark and grainy, Christine recognized Aiden.

The reporter continued, "The authorities say that the man you just saw chasing that werepet is wanted for questioning."

The picture returned to the reporter.

"Also, the Werewolf Oversight Committee, or WOC, in conjunction with CPD and the FBI, is requesting that anyone who comes in contact with this man or with any unclaimed werepets notify the authorities at once."

A stock photo of Bernard Henderson filled the screen. "The official rabies story Bernard Henderson, CEO and founder of the WereHouse, released earlier cannot be disproved yet. So if you come across a lost werepet, call the authorities and don't approach him. We're going to go to Mindy now outside Bernard Henderson's residence with more on this developing story."

The screen switched to one of the biggest mansions Christine had ever seen. The yard was roped off with yellow crime scene tape.

"Thank you, Angela. As we reported earlier in the broadcast, the CEO of the WereHouse, Bernard Henderson, is wanted in connection with the possible murder of his wife in addition to the possible arson at WereHouse headquarters. A major announcement concerning werepets will be made within the next few days, and we can expect a plethora of new charges will be brought against the WereHouse and its founders at that time. All the board members have been detained as of this morning, except for Mr. Henderson, who has still not been located. You are urged to call the authorities at once if you see him."

Christine had heard enough. She turned off the TV.

Bernard Henderson limped through the revolving doors of the hotel where he had been hiding out for the last two days. He used a cane to take some of the weight off his badly injured leg. If not for the WereHouse's on-call physician, he might have lost his leg entirely. It was still quite sore. His wigs, prostheses, and new facial hair obscured his identity enough that he felt safe to finally flee the country. Pietro's place in Italy was practically a fortress, and all he had to do was get there.

Disguises aside, a smaller stretched limo procured by his driver was as much of a concession as he was willing to make. He was used to his life of luxury and wasn't ready to give it up just yet.

His driver opened the back door and helped him inside.

"Where to, sir?"

"Airport. I have a private jet waiting for us."

"Won't they be looking for us there?"

"No, no, no. We aren't going as ourselves. I've always feared this day might come, so I set up an entirely different identity years ago just in case. No one is looking for international jet-setter, Dick Bachman, after all."

"So, where are we going?"

"My old friend, we are going to Italy where I have a new business venture to look into with my friend who runs our camp on Sandalio."

"Mr. Salvatore?"

"That's him."

"So, it's not over?"

"Not even close. There's a lot of money still to be made, my friend."

The chauffeur nodded like a loyal soldier. Bernard handed him a passport and said, "This will get us out of the country."

As the chauffeur started to shut the door, a man interrupted from the sidewalk. "Excuse me?"

Bernard couldn't see the man past his driver.

The driver turned around. "What do you want?" Before the man could answer, the driver snapped, "Get the hell out of here. We're busy." He turned back to Bernard. "Freaking bums. Always in the way when you're in a hurry." He started to close the door, but Bernard stopped it with his foot and leaned around him.

The stranger on the sidewalk wore a piss-soaked army jacket and baggy cargo pants. He held a can in one hand and a handwritten "Please Help" sign in the other.

"What do you want?" Bernard asked.

"Can you spare a dollar?"

Bernard cocked his head and smiled. "I can do better than that. You wanna take a little plane ride with us?"

The homeless man's forehead wrinkled. "Where to?"

"Italy first, and then a little island off the coast of Costa Rica. I might have a job opportunity for you."

The homeless man glanced side to side before shrugging his shoulders and getting into the limo. As he slid across the seat, Bernard scooted to the opposite door. "You really smell like shit, buddy," he said.

The homeless man nodded and dropped his head as if ashamed.

Bernard held a handkerchief over his nose.

Still looking to the floor, the homeless man asked, "You have anything to drink in here?"

Bernard snorted. "I think we can find something." He grabbed a glass and a bottle of Jack Daniels from a mini fridge and poured a shot for his newest employee.

The homeless man slipped his arms from his baggy jacket and tossed it into a heap on the floor.

Bernard bounced his eyebrows. "Go ahead and make yourself comfy," he said.

The homeless man downed the whiskey in one gulp and then held it out in hopes of another. Bernard handed him the bottle.

The limo pulled away from the curb and into traffic.

Neither man said much while they traveled along the city streets. It wasn't until they reached the freeway that Bernard asked him his name.

The homeless man whispered, "You don't recognize me?" He rubbed his bare chin.

"Have we met before?"

"Once."

"Yeah?" Bernard chuckled. "I'm terrible with faces. Perhaps I could remember you better if I knew your name."

The homeless man grinned. "My name is Steven, and I've been looking for you." His eyes darkened. He grabbed Bernard's arm and Bernard winced from strength of his grip. "Do you even know what you've done to me?"

Bernard wasn't a fool. "Hey, listen, man. It was just business."

"Business? You've turned me into an abomination. Not to mention the torture to get me there."

Bernard glanced at Steven's hand and then into his murderous eyes as they morphed into black orbs. He had witnessed enough transformations to know what was coming. He yanked his arm free from Steven's grasp.

Steven's bones contorted and cracked and popped. Hair sprouted from his flesh. His clothes tore at the seams and he ripped them away with a beastly growl.

Bernard grabbed for the door handle and screamed, "*Stop*," to his driver.

Bernard kicked the door open and dove toward the pavement racing by. Dagger-like claws dug into his back and dragged him back into the car.

Terror filled his gut with the realization of what this man had come for. He rolled to his back, half on the seat and half on the floorboard, and stared up at the enraged werg.

"Please, no. Please don't do this. I'll make things right. I'll—"

Steven roared to the heavens. Thick, frothy drool dripped from his jowls.

The limo screeched to a stop. Bernard scrambled to his belly and clawed at the open door frame, pulling himself toward the pavement again. He touched the road before searing pain screamed between his shoulder blades and shot down his spine. He felt his flesh tear open. Blood poured down his side. Steven's hot breath pounded the back of his neck before ripping pain exploded in his back. He tried to scream but had lost all his strength.

Steven dragged him back into the car, leaving Bernard's bloody fingernails on the street. He yanked the door closed. The driver watched through the glass partition, eyes wide with horror. Bernard screamed at him for help but the man appeared frozen. Apparently, his loyalty had limits.

Bernard stared into the cold eyes of a monster, and for the briefest second thought he saw mercy.

"Please," he begged.

And then Steven attacked.

The terror Bernard felt was only eclipsed by the pain of his flesh pulling away from his throat. His open wound gurgled with each drowning attempt at a breath. Blood poured from the gaping wound. He watched through glassy eyes as Steven settled back into the seat as if preparing for a nice summer drive. Bernard's blood dripped from Steven's snout. The world swayed around him. He felt nauseous and tired. He wanted a breath so badly but couldn't find one.

Steven slung the door open and jumped from the limo.

Unable to move, Bernard could only listen as concerned voices approached the limo. The world faded to white. Everything went numb. A woman screamed.

38

It was Christmas Eve. A few months had passed since Steven had enacted his revenge on Bernard Henderson, and the guilt hadn't subsided. Not even the bottle helped most days. Though Bernard deserved everything he'd gotten, Steven had never killed in cold blood before. It ate at him daily. Had he known how much he'd regret it, he might not have followed through.

He had stopped by a shelter earlier in the day to get cleaned up and sneak a drink before making his way to the porch where he now stood. He was as nervous as he had ever been. He should have brought the bottle along.

Money from panhandling had bought him a new sweater, dress pants, shoes, and a haircut. When he told the barber the occasion, the older man threw in a shave free of charge.

The condo was two stories with a covered porch and lighted candy canes two feet tall lining the walkway. The parking lot was full of cars.

Steven stood on the porch for ten minutes trying to find the courage to press the doorbell. His finger hovered inches from it.

He took a deep breath. With his eyes closed, he pressed the bell. "Jingle Bells" played instead of the typical ding-dong. Steven stepped back to the edge of the porch with his hands clasped together in front. When the handle jiggled, his stomach turned. The door was pulled open.

A young man in his early twenties answered.

Steven held out his hand. "Hello. My name is Steven."

The young man held out his arm, revealing a stump.

Steven felt like a shithead and jammed his own hand into his pocket. "I'm sorry," he said.

The young man snorted and said, "No worries, man. I'm Billy. Whatchu sellin'?"

"No, no, no. I'm not selling anything. I'm looking for someone."

"Oh, yeah? Who would that be?"

Before Steven could answer, a woman's voice called out from inside. "Who is it, Billy?"

"I don't know. Some guy. What'd you say your name was again?"

"Steven."

When the woman joined the young man in the doorway, she froze. Her eyes widened and she lost her breath. She grabbed her chest.

"Dad?" she said.

Steven saw himself in her eyes. Though he hadn't seen her in many years, he felt as though he had been with her just the day before. He nodded.

"I can't believe my eyes. What are you doing here?"

"I missed you, Christine," he said.

She wiped her eyes.

He wanted to hug her but was afraid she wouldn't let him. "I'm so sorry," he said, years of pain and heartache dripping from his words.

She was speechless.

Steven swallowed hard. "Can I hug you?"

With tears streaking her cheeks, she nodded.

Billy backed out of the way.

Steven embraced her and squeezed, never wanting to let go. He held her for an eternity while she sobbed against his shoulder. It took everything he had to not cry himself.

Eventually, she pulled away. "I can't believe you're here."

"I can't believe I wasn't here sooner."

She wiped her eyes again and gathered herself. "Will you come in? I want you to meet my friends."

Steven smiled. "Of course." He followed her inside and wiped his feet on a mat. Billy closed the door and followed them down the hallway into the living room.

Proudly, she announced, "Everyone, I'd like you to meet my father, Steven."

A man who had been sitting on the couch approached with an extended hand. "Aiden," he said.

Steven shook it. "Steven," he said.

"Nice to meet you, sir."

She continued around the room, introducing him to Willie and Mick and their wives. Steven met her lieutenant, Alex, next.

Just then the timer on the stove rang. Christine smiled big. "Will you join us for dinner?" she asked.

"I would love to."

She went to the oven and removed a glazed ham. Aiden joined her in the kitchen. Steven watched as they prepared the food.

"What can I do to help?"

Christine passed him a stack of plates and silverware. "You can set the table, if you don't mind."

"I'd be happy to." This was going to be the best Christmas Eve he'd had in years.

ABOUT THE AUTHOR

Douglas R. Brown is a fantasy and horror writer living in Pataskala, Ohio. He began writing as a cathartic way of dealing with the day-to-day stresses of life as a firefighter/paramedic in Columbus, Ohio. Now he focuses his writing on fantasy and horror, where he can draw from his lifelong love of the genres. He has been married since 1996 and has a son and some dogs.

ALSO FROM EPERTASE

THE LIGHT OF EPERTASE BOOK ONE
LEGENDS REBORN
THE LIGHT OF EPERTASE BOOK
TWO
A KINGDOM'S FALL
THE LIGHT OF EPERTASE BOOK
THREE
THE RISE OF CRIDON

DEATH OF THE GRINDERFISH

A FIREFIGHTER CHRISTMAS CAROL
AND OTHER STORIES

A WICKED LINE

AND COMING IN 2023, THE LONG
AWAITED SEQUEL TO TAMED:
UNTAMED